The Showdown in Wollongong

Paddy Bostock

A Wings ePress, Inc.
Romantic Fantasy Novel

Wings ePress, Inc.

Edited by: Jeanne Smith
Copy Edited by: Jeanne Howard
Executive Editor: Jeanne Smith
Cover Artist: Trisha FitzGerald-Jung

All rights reserved

Wings ePress Books
www.wingsepress.com

Copyright © 2021 by: Paddy Bostock
ISBN 978-1-61309-551-5

Published In the United States Of America

Wings ePress Inc.
3000 N. Rock Road
Newton, KS 67114

Dedication

To Dani with love.

* * *

One

At around seven p.m. on an evening several weeks BC (Before Coronavirus), Doctors Andy Crane and Sandra Normington were sitting in a consulting room of their GP surgery sipping tea and mulling over the day's events, prime amongst them the enforced absence on "gardening leave" of their colleague, Doctor Quentin Trimble.

"Any idea why?" Sandra asked Andy. "All sounds a bit mysterious to me."

"Rumours abounding," said Andy, popping a Propranolol after a long day trying to distinguish the truly sick from the fantasists and malingerers.

"Best guess?"

Andy grinned. "Heard the one about the collie who was relieved of his duties for worrying sheep?"

Sandra shook her head and rolled her eyes. Andy and his lame jokes!

"Know why?"

Sandra sighed. "No."

Andy chuckled at the upcoming punch line. "For creeping up behind them and whispering 'mint sauce' in their ears."

Even Sandra couldn't resist a smirk. "Which has what to do with Quentin?" she said when the smirking was over.

"Because that, in the view of management as I understand it, is the official reason for him having been given the temporary shove."

"For worrying sheep?"

Andy hoisted an eyebrow, unsure whether Sandra was being funny or just plain silly. It was hard to tell with these Merseyside girls.

"Not sheep, Sandra, *patients*," he said, wrecking what was left of his joke.

Sandra frowned. "Ah. Worrying them how?"

"By exaggerating their conditions. By recoiling from them, saying things to like 'Eeue, yuck, nasty, *that* looks sinister,' when all he was looking at was a wart, then packing them off to histopathology for a biopsy."

"Sensible preventative medicine?" said Sandra.

"Not when ten times out of ten the results came back benign. Not when our histopathologist pals started wondering how come their precious resources were being wasted on faux cases and whether a review of our practice might be in order, and, unsurprisingly, there were the complaints from the patients, some of whom had been so worried they developed cancer-phobia syndromes and had to be prescribed expensive long-term anxiolytics. Little wonder management got twitchy."

"Mmm, medical ethics, eh?"

"Quite, and with them funding, or the potential lack of it, if the case were ever to hit the social or real media. Just imagine the blogs and posts about the 'crazed medic of Battersea terrifies sick people.' Anyway, *any*way, that seems to be why our friend Quentin got sent home to cultivate his garden. I always thought there was something a bit off about him.

"And he went without protest."

"So far as I know. Probably not left with much choice in the circs. He'll be offered help, though."

"Of what kind?"

Andy shrugged. "Advice about how to stop tormenting patients, a spot of CBT, or a dose of good old Freud, who knows? Maybe there's some underlying problem needing attention. Now, how would you fancy popping around the corner for a quick snifter? It's been a tricky sort of a day."

"Sorry, not today. It's a hair-washing evening."

"Some other time then," muttered Andy, as had become the norm in these circumstances. His most ardent current ambition was to remove Sandra's clothes and give her what he reckoned a thorough medical examination, but there was that bloody hair-washing excuse yet again. How many girls in Battersea had cleaner hair than Sandra Normington? None, reckoned Andy Crane, who shrugged, set down his teacup and, theatrically round-shouldered, slowly took his customarily frustrated leave.

"Possibly," Sandra called after him, tantalizingly leaving the door to future assignations if not open, at least ajar.

It really was high time Doc Sandra Normington finally made up her mind about whether she wanted anything of an emotional kind to develop with Doc Andy Crane, and she knew it. The playing-hard-to-get routine was running more than a little thin for both of them.

~ * ~

Andy Crane was right in his diagnosis of Quentin Trimble being beset by "some underlying problem," however, because since his only-child early adolescence, Quentin had been what the French dramatist Molière termed a *malade imaginaire*, which translates literally as "imaginary invalid," hypochondriac in more normal parlance. Any tiny aberration from what he considered the norm, of which there were thousands, and Quentin became convinced he was at death's door. His major medical obsession was one of any number of cancers, although on the psychological front, OCD, bi-polarity and all manner of manias featured prominently, including an abiding fear of pandemics which peculiar mindset was never recognized by his parents. The very *last* thing on earth his consultant neurosurgeon father Doc/"Mister" Frederick Trimble and, under her husband's fierce insistence, his gynaecologist mother Doc Antoinette Trimble were about to admit was to having raised a defective child.

"Nothing wrong with the lad and, as professionals, we should know," they would tell his teachers on parents' evenings when told Quentin refused point blank to join in any sports activities in case he got injured and insisted on a special desk at the back of the class isolated from the other pupils lest they should sneeze, cough, or infect him with otherwise undetectable germs. With hindsight, Quentin might have been seen as some sort of oracle of Covid-19 but, as noted, that nasty little bug was still some way off in the future.

"Won't play with the other kids in the playground. Won't go *into* the playground without a special mask on," said assistant head Muriel Coppell on one such occasion. "And keeps muttering the names of diseases. You're not telling me that's normal."

Doc Frederick shrugged nonchalantly. "He's a hypersensitive chappie, that's all. Probably destined to become a brilliant brain surgeon."

"Reads all the time," Doc Antoinette interjected mock proudly.

"Literature?" asked Coppell. "Novels, plays, poetry and so on?"

Doc Frederick winced. "*Literature?* Good God no. We have an extensive library of medical and psychoanalytical texts at home, and Quentin spends hours poring over those. Doesn't he, Tonie?"

"*Hours*," Antoinette confirmed meekly. "Probably already knows better than most practitioners the names, symptoms, procedures, and outcomes of a whole range of physical and mental conditions," she added, sticking to Doc Frederick's script for the occasion.

Muriel nodded as little tumblers began to fall into place. "I *see*," she said, smiling wanly.

"So don't you go telling us *our* business," Doc Frederick intoned, standing and dusting himself down while Doc Antoinette did the same before they both stalked out of the room.

It was as the result of such parental confrontations with his teachers that between the ages of twelve and fifteen, Quentin Trimble attended nine different schools until Doc Frederick reckoned enough was enough and his precious, gifted son would, in future, be home-taught by either Doc Antoinette or the occasional thoroughly brainwashed tutor. All of which meant that by the age of eighteen, Quentin knew nothing at all of the regular school curriculum, had made no teenage friends to hang out with, had never fallen in love, had no soccer team to support, and no rock 'n' roll band to worship, but *was* possessed of an albeit dodgy brain now crammed brimful with a greater awareness of ailments and afflictions than most medical school graduates. It was this qualification, despite the total absence of all others, that enabled Doc/Mister Frederick Trimble to pull rank over the admissions team at University College Hospital London and ensure his son got the education he fully deserved.

So it was that Quentin Trimble spent the next eight years happily learning of even *more* diseases to be frightened of before graduating with distinction, but little or no trust in medicine's power to heal either him or the conditions that freaked him.

Talk about "some underlying problem."

~ * ~

Mind you, Quentin took his gardening leave seriously—by gardening. Not so long later, when the dreaded coronavirus hit, such activity would be dubbed an aspect of "self-isolation," but for now, it was still innocent of any death threat. Behind his one-bed basement flat in Battersea, there was merely an overgrown stretch of lawn skirted on two sides by strips of soil containing a forest of nameless weeds, plants and bushes, at the end of which stood a rickety fence, a couple of trees, and a wooden potting shed with a door that flapped in even the gentlest of breezes. Until his banishment, Quentin had never set foot in this wilderness, just peeked at it through the window of his kitchenette door from time to time and muttered inconclusively about one day doing something to improve it. But now that day had come and, being a literal sort of a person, Quentin took to cultivating his garden without any hint of the interpretation some Voltaire scholars have attributed to the ending of *Candide*, namely for "garden" read "self." No, no...to Quentin Trimble, garden meant garden. As for the self, neither he nor anybody else had taken to the time to cultivate that, although in the light of his recent problems, the surgery boss Doc Miriam Proudfoot had tentatively suggested the services of a American shrink called Doctor Hank Orlando, who offered a guaranteed therapy called "Release Your Hidden Self." But with such titles—for both the bloke and his therapy—Quentin had assumed him to be a charlatan and gone nowhere near him or his treatment. So far as Quentin was concerned, he'd keep his self under lock and key, thank you very much.

With nothing better to do, therefore, and given the unusually mild early spring weather, despite the recently unpredictable ravages of climate change, out he would go every afternoon—Quentin didn't leave his bed until exactly one p.m.—to potter about, peering at plants and wondering what to do about them. For this purpose, he would be wearing wellingtons, an ankle-length ex-army green overcoat zipped up to his chin, a balaclava above his face mask, and to-the-elbow brown leather gauntlets. After all, one could never be too sure what sorts of poisonous fungi and/or other plants might be out there, not to mention bees, wasps, or snakes, one of whose bites or stings would see him in intensive care before he could say boo to a boa-constrictor. Interested indeed, he would have been in the theory posited by some SARS-COV scientists, that the global mayhem soon to come was the result of deforestation and the consequent release into the human food chain of infected creatures such as bats and pangolins. But Quentin had been too pre-occupied frightening patients to have read any of that.

His first major project was the lawn, shin-high in not only what passed for grass but even more weeds. The latter he dealt with rationally enough by yanking them out, then tossing them into a bucket he sporadically emptied over the rickety fence, which he discovered overlooked a pathway that led to heaven knew where. This activity he found himself enjoying. Maybe it was the mechanical routine he liked, maybe anything, but whatever it was caused him to sing little songs to himself. Not pop songs, because he didn't know any of those, little ditties of his own he made up as he trundled backwards and forwards. One of them went: "Hey-ho little weedies, now off you go. Hope you'll find a better place where you can grow."

The tune wasn't great, in fact, it wasn't really a tune at all, more of a chant, but Quentin liked it and was proud of the rhyme.

It wasn't until the following afternoon's session that he was confronted with the lawn grass itself which initially posed a major problem, namely, how to cut it. No point in pulling bits out stalk by stalk, he reckoned, which in any case would leave it totally bald. After all, a person didn't go the barber to have his hair pulled out, did he?

"Mmm," he mused until part one of his epiphany hit: namely lawn mower.

But where was he to find such an object? Quentin was damned if he was going tramping around Battersea looking for a lawn mower shop. He had enough trouble buying food from supermarkets, never mind negotiating specialist garden equipment outlets. Nor could he order one online from Amazon because, apart from their most rudimentary uses, computers terrified him.

"Mmm," he mused some more, until epiphany part two kicked in.

"Eureka," he said, "The *shed*."

And so it was that, unfortunately in the process pulling the door off its already terminally rusted hinges, Quentin ventured into the potting shed to be greeted by a small white-bearded person sprawled on a heap of smelly brown sacks of horse dung presumably left by the previous tenant.

"Hi there, Quentin, wondered how long it would take you to find me," he said. "I'm Fion. Pleasetameetcha."

"What the...?" said Quentin.

"Am I? An elf but you'll get used to it. Need a hand at all? The mower's over there in the corner," said Fion, jerking a thumb in the direction of the corner in question.

Quentin peered back and forth between the elf and the mower. "Thanks."

"No problemo. I'll show you how it works if you want. It's one of those old-fashioned ones without a motor, so you'll have to push it. And don't forget to fix the tray on before you go a-mowing."

"Okay."

"Here, we'll get it out and I'll show you how," said Fion, rolling off his sacks and hopping over to the rusty old machine.

"Right. Thanks again," said Quentin, following in his wake.

You will be wondering how and why Quentin Trimble accepted without apparent demur the presence of an elf in his garden shed. After all, most of us would have blanched a bit or run away in fright, wouldn't we? Well the answer is this: despite never apparently having read any literary fiction during his education, only ever medical and psychoanalytical tomes, Quentin *had* over the years, secretly under the bedclothes at night with a torch, digested with immense pleasure a dusty pile of books about faerie folk he'd found buried in the depths of an old cupboard. And these were not just kiddies' stories, they were proper analyses of faerie lore for grownups with lists and pictures of different types of the creatures, the sorts of clothes they wore, their customs, and the places they were most likely to be found. It was in this way that Quentin became as firm, if covert, a believer in the existence of the Little People as he was in the evils of human diseases. And where was he most likely to encounter one? At the bottom of his garden, that was where.

To Quentin's mind, therefore, the appearance of Fion was a phenomenon he'd been half expecting for years. Furthermore, as an elf, the little fellow came with a reputation for benevolence. Quentin would have been a tad more suspicious had he been a goblin or a boggart.

And so it was, once the ancient mower had been oiled a bit and had its tray attached, between them Quentin and Fion eventually produced a surface on the once derelict lawn of which a top notch Wimbledon tennis court or Wembley soccer stadium groundsman would have been proud.

Standing back to survey their achievement, Fion said, "You'd have no trouble eating your dinner off that."

Quentin agreed. "Great piece of work, and thanks for your help. Cups of tea in order, don't you think? Care to step into my kitchen?"

Fion was happy so to do, but had in mind a brew of somewhat greater potency than straight tea. Taking from his trouser pocket a small blue phial, he asked if perhaps a few drops of fairy tincture might be added to the cuppas to "add flavour." Which was how Quentin Trimble tasted mind-altering substances for the first time in his life, and slept the sleep of the innocent for the following sixteen hours. Before leaving him to his dreams, Fion pinned a notelet to his duvet reading: "If you ever want another meet-up, all you have to do is whisper the word 'Noif' three times." Then he hopped over the rickety fence at the bottom of the garden and followed the path on the other side to places only he could know.

<h1 style="text-align:center">Two</h1>

When Quentin awoke at nine o'clock the following morning, it was with no intention of staying in bed until his normal one p.m. Why this should have been he had no idea. He just didn't feel like it, that was all, his recent sense of empty lassitude having somehow been replaced with what he could only think of as sprightliness. Which made him chuckle. After all, sprites were fairies too, weren't they? Okay, they were spelt differently from the way he was feeling but what was a little orthographical glitch between friends? Phonetically, the sounds would be the same. He chuckled some more when he sat up and found Fion's message, particularly when he came to the "Noif," which he reckoned he could pronounce "No If," as in 'no ifs or buts.' Nice little word games. And sure enough he *would* like another meet-up with the elf. Such a helpful chap he had been.

"What if?" Quentin muttered as he sprang out of bed and took to doing squats and push-ups, "that stuff he put in my tea had something to do with this?" The "this" being the inexplicable cheerfulness he was feeling. Even weirder—the total absence of the desire to check himself out for bodily malfunctions the way he had routinely done every morning of his life for as long as he could remember. Once the narcissists in the White House and 10 Downing Street had belatedly woken up to the "Chinese bug" and discovered it to be more of a problem than they'd anticipated, Quentin would have to start the old routine all over again. But for now, magically, he was free of it.

"Well, bugger me with a broomstick," he said, which was another first, because Doc Frederick abhorred the use of foul language and would beat him with a slipper if he ever employed it. "P'raps I should give old No If a call and see if he was serious with his message."

Which was what Quentin did and, within microseconds, Fion was at his side in the kitchenette.

"Hey ho and a nonny," said the elf. "So we meet again."

"Yes. I just wanted to tell you how much better I was feeling since yesterday and to thank you for whatever it was you did. Another cup of tea?"

"With pleasure, only this time with a tincture from a different bottle," said Fion, taking from a pocket another phial, this one pink.

"Different how?"

"Oh, you know, *diff*erent," said Fion adding a few drops to each cup before Quentin added the tea bag and boiling water.

"Milk this time?" he asked.

"Tch, tch, no thanks, never touch the stuff. Poor little calves being taken away too early from their mummies so the farmers can make more money."

Quentin had never thought of that. "Okay then. Sugar?"

But Fion wasn't having additives of any kind. "Bad for the teeth, old chap. You don't get to live as long as I have and keep your teeth if you eat sweetie foods."

"And how long *have* you lived?" asked Quentin as they clinked cups and took their first sips.

"Not sure. A *long* time, though. Seems to me I've always been alive."

Fion wasn't fooling with this response. As he went on to explain to Quentin, fairies don't share humans' obsession with time. To them, theories of origin or destiny are meaningless. Where they come from or where they are going does not concern them, they just *are*. In their multiple languages there are no words for yesterday or tomorrow, only today. A timeless present, therefore.

Quentin sipped at his tea and felt a giggle coming on. "So you don't even know when you were born?"

"Nope."

"Or who your parents were?" Quentin continued, thinking ruefully of Doc Frederick and to a lesser extent Doc Antoinette.

Fion shrugged. "Also nope. Didn't know there were such things as parents until I began meeting with you human folk."

"Lucky you."

"Yes. I understand yours have been a tad, how shall we say? Difficult?"

Quentin frowned. "And how would you understand that?"

"Little vibes I get. It's how we elves are. We see things you guys don't. Sometimes they can be useful, sometimes not, but they are always *there*."

"Blimey. So you're some kind of a mind reader?"

"Your term, old chap, not mine. The best way to think of us elves is just different, that's all. There are times when we see *too* much and it hurts, but we always try to look on the bright side and help where we can."

"And you're *always* here on Earth?"

"Some are and I'm one of them. Others are elsewhere across your universe and yet others back home in our own place."

Quentin grinned as he recalled his childhood post-bedtime secret reading. "In Fairyland."

"Exactly. Oh, and while we're on the subject of difference, there is one other thing you need to know, something you humans are finding it difficult to comprehend, although at least you've started to try."

"Which is?"

"I can also be Fion*a*."

"Excuse me?"

"We fairies are both male and female. According to circumstance, the switch is always available and saves an awful lot of unnecessary hassle."

Quentin froze as a result of the fear of gay, trans and bi people he'd carried with him since the age of twelve, when Doc Frederick had delivered his birds and bees speech in which such "creatures" were condemned as "abominations and a shame to humanity."

"A route no son of mine shall *ever* take or he shall be disowned," his father had declaimed before tossing a sex guidance booklet at his son, then beating a hasty retreat from the bedroom calling back over his shoulder, "Any questions, ask your mother."

"You still have a problem with that?" said Fion, intuiting both Quentin's unease and the reason for it.

Quentin swallowed and said nothing.

"No need to be worried about it," said Fion. "Look, how about I give you a demo?"

Quentin blinked as the little fellow with the white beard morphed into a nymphet with blonde tresses and a come hither smile.

"Sorry about the crudity of the appearance, that's just how you humans so often portray our womenfolk. As sex symbols," said Fiona. "If you like, I can do grannies and witches and different sorts of males and..."

That's when Quentin fainted and had to be revived by six drops from Fion's green phial squirted up his nostrils.

"Holy Christ," he mumbled, when seconds later he regained consciousness.

"Afraid not, old chap, can't do *that* one. See where you're coming from, though. When it comes to the grand myths you humans have created all through your relatively short history, the guy can compete with even us fairies."

Quentin was still struggling with the sum of these peculiar concepts of time, space and gender when Fion took to tapping at his pointy ears and nodding.

"Problem?" said Quentin.

"Incoming message," said the elf from one side of his mouth while, with the other side, saying, "Okay, I'm on my way."

"But you haven't got a phone."

"No need, old man. Not with TET."

Quentin frowned.

"Telepathic Elf Transmission," Fion explained. "No need for the silly little plastic things you guys have allowed to take over your brains. *Any*way got to love you and leave you, I'm afraid. Pal of mine's in a spot of bother and needs a chat."

And with that, in the blink of an eye, he was through the door, across the beautifully mown lawn, over the fence, and off down the lane that led to only he knew where, leaving Quentin in a state of some perplexity.

~ * ~

Speaking of phones, it was only moments later that Quentin's took to trilling somebody or another's overture in F-major from the depths of one of his green army-camouflage trouser pockets.

"What the *fuck*?" he said, pleased at the freedoms of his new parlance, but nonetheless angered by the bally thing he believed to have been permanently switched off somehow having come back to life again. Fion was right about phones driving a person crazy. Even so, he couldn't resist the insistence of the racket, dragged the hated instrument from his pants, and swiping the Accept Call icon. Which he soon wished he hadn't. The last person on the planet he needed a call from right now was Doc Frederick, but that's who it was and, as usual, up to the gunnels in righteous indignation.

"QUENTIN?" he shrieked as an introduction.

"Speaking."

There followed a big long diatribe about the irresponsibility of somebody, i.e. Quentin, having had the audacity to leave his phone on call-minder mode for days on end and not called back when a busy person of Doc Frederick's standing in life wanted to talk to him about a *very* important matter. Now aged sixty-five, and close to being retired because of the hand tremors ironically caused by one of the neurological diseases he was meant to cure, Doc Frederick had become obsessional about his "standing in life" and the need for it to continue being respected.

"So what's all this crap I hear about 'gardening leave'?" he bellowed when the big long diatribe had more or else fizzled out.

Because Quentin had told neither of his parents about his removal from the GP practice and looked at none of the messages that pinged into his in-box, the only way Doc Frederick had discovered this inconvenient truth had been by phoning the surgery and being told by a receptionist called Maggie that Doctor Trimble was temporarily on gardening leave and might or might not be back soon.

"So *what* in the name of tarnation was *that* all about?" he now wanted to know.

Under normal circumstances—i.e. those obtaining in his adolescence if ever caught out for some trivial blunder—Quentin would have made up a story or, to put it more bluntly, lied. But something about his recent dealings with Fion, possibly the little blue, pink and green tinctures, or equally possibly merely the elf's frankness about *his* self must have had a much greater impact than anything Hank Orlando could have offered, because without hesitation Quentin told Doc Frederick the truth, the whole truth, and nothing but the truth.

"Scaring *patients*?" his father ululated.

"Yes. And when I look back on it now, I probably was," said Quentin, going on to detail the ways he'd so frequently said, "Eeue, yuck, nasty, *that* looks sinister," when examining a wart and sending patients off for biopsies after which process the patients had nervous breakdowns.

"Not *your* bloody fault. Perfectly sound preventative medical practice," opined Doc Frederick, echoing the views of Sandra Normington.

"Not when they *always* came back from histopathology benign. Not hard to understand the surgery's worries about me, wouldn't you say?"

"No...I...would...*NOT*...say. Some trumped up hoo-ha, some plot designed to tarnish the Trimble family's good name is what I *WOULD* say."

Which was when, to his astonishment, Quentin said, "Bollocks."

"*WHAT* DID YOU SAY?"

"Bollocks. Conspiracy theorizing. What I told you is the truth."

"HAVE YOU GONE RAVING *MAD*, BOY?" said Doc Frederick before a whisper-filled hiatus after which Doc Antoinette came on the line taking much the same approach as her husband, only with marginally lower decibels.

"What on *earth* is this all about, Quentie?" she said, employing the diminutive he had loathed since he was five but never dared reproach his mother for. "Your poor father's be*side* himself."

Momentarily, Quentin imagined two versions of his father standing alongside each other and had to suppress a chuckle before telling Doc Antoinette the same story he'd told Doc Frederick.

"And they sacked you for *that*?"

"No, Mother. Just gardening leave with full salary until...I don't know...I recover, I suppose."

"From *what*?"

"Hypochondria would, I think, be the technical term. You never noticed?"

"No, darling. You were just hypersensitive, that was all. Which was why we saved you the agonies of being bullied at school and taught by oiks who couldn't tell a scalpel from a penknife. Gave you the best home education money could buy and..."

"Wrecked my mind," said Quentin, who in his new state of total honesty was beginning to enjoy this. "How's it going on the foetus production line by the way? Still helping them pop out by the cartload?"

That was when there was a lot of spluttering and gurgling down the line before it went dead because, listening to Quentin's words on the speaker system, Doc Frederick had clamped a hand over her mouth with one hand and wrested the phone from her with the other.

"How *DARE* you speak to your mother that way?" he hissed. "You will live to regret this conversation, my boy. Trust me, you will."

Three

Attributing his father's fury to age and bad chemicals in his brain, Quentin thought nothing more of Doc Frederick's bile and slept the sleep of the just with a little help from one of Fion's tinctures. The sweetest of dreams he had, dreams in which he began to speak all sorts of truths he had previously concealed.

His nirvana-like state was, however, shattered around noon when a police car arrived at his door with blue lights flashing and sirens wailing and Sergeant Jim O'Cafferty and PC Betty Withenshaw broke down his door, charged him with matricide, read him his rights, and handcuffed him before marching him to the car, folding him into the back seat and speeding away to the cop shop.

Bleary-eyed and writhing in the back seat, Quentin tried over and again to ask what the hell this was all about, but all he heard from O'Cafferty and Withenshaw was, "Shut the fuck up, mother killer."

"*What?* I didn't kill my mother? I love my mother," he persisted.

It was Withenshaw who finally turned in her seat. "Not according to your father, otherwise why would you have broken into their home in the small hours and in a fit of jealous rage throttled your mother for having loved him more than you? Now shut your face, if you know what's good for you, sonny. Any story you've got, keep it for the judge."

After that, silence fell, a silence which continued all the way to the police station where Quentin was checked in with the desk sergeant before being led away to his cell, shoved inside and left to ruminate existentially on the consequences of telling the truth and how life could have in store outcomes even worse than mere fantasy diseases.

Mercifully, however, Quentin didn't have long to spend incarcerated at the police station. In fact he was released with apologies the very same evening. Why? Because Doc Antoinette wasn't dead, that was why.

"*What?*" I hear you gasp. "But there must have been a body. The cops wouldn't have just arrested a person on hearsay."

Which was true enough. The problem was there was a corpse all right, only it wasn't that of Doc Antoinette. Instead it belonged to part-time streetwalker Fanny Flint (not her real name) who'd been strangled by a client during rough sex. Doc Frederick had stolen it from the hospital morgue at the dead of night on the pretext it needed urgent analysis at an adjacent laboratory facility and, given his seniority, had been waved through without question. Once back home with Fanny in the boot of his car, he dressed her up in Doc Antoinette's clothes and while his wife, distraught after the argument with their son, was sleeping off two melatonin tablets and the better part of a bottle of *Asti Spumante*, called the cops. And what a show he'd put on. Weeping, tearing his white hair and cursing Quentin for committing the dastardly act.

"Ungrateful little bastard has his own key to the house and must have let himself in while I was upstairs engrossed in putting the final touches to my latest article for *The Lancet*. Didn't hear a thing from up in my study at the top of the house until the front door slammed and, looking through my window, there was Quentin running away down the drive. I called after him to stop, but he just turned around, laughed, and gave me a V-sign."

It was by this performance, plus the clearly strangled dead body of the person they took to be Doc Antoinette even though they'd never met the woman, that Sergeant Jim O'Cafferty and PC Betty Withenshaw were easily persuaded. Hence Quentin's arrest, which would have entailed an absence from normal life somewhat more extended than gardening leave had it not been for the intervention of Fion the elf.

Yes, folks, for it was Fion, whose psychic fairy intuition had alerted him to the entire episode, who morphed into Detective Inspector Malcolm McPhee of the PSCU (Possibly Spurious Case Unit), headed off to the police station and, suspecting a miscarriage of justice, urgently advised O'Cafferty and Withenshaw to re-check the evidence.

"Something's off here, I smell a rat," he told them. "Specifically regarding the identity of the dead person."

And a rat he surely had smelt, because it transpired on further examination that Fanny Flint's corpse shared none of DNA swabbed from the mouth of an hysterical Doc Antoinette, and that Doc Frederick must therefore have concocted the entire narrative for his own malign purposes. Mind you, the spurious case hypothesis had been given wings even earlier when O'Cafferty and Withenshaw returned to the Trimble homestead, knocked on the door and it was Doc Antoinette—still somewhat hungover but clearly not dead—who opened it.

*Any*way, what with one thing and another, it was thanks to Fion that Quentin was so quickly released from the local nick, some days later to be replaced by his father on suspicion of faking a death and deliberately misleading the police which, if proven, carried with it a lengthy term of imprisonment. It was Fion, still in the guise of DI Malcolm McPhee, who accompanied Quentin back to the Battersea flat where he morphed back into elf mode and the pair briefly celebrated in the garden with dancing and whooping of the kind inspired by Fion's purple tincture.

~ * ~

When the dancing and whooping were over, Quentin asked Fion for an explanation of what had happened to him over the past eight hours, so Fion gave him a thumbnail sketch after which a quivering Quentin said, "You mean my own *father* set me up for killing my *mother*?"

"Afraid so."

"The old *bast*ard. He said I'd live to regret what I told him on the phone last night. Or was it the night before...my head's all over the place. But *why* would he do that?"

"To teach you a lesson. Or more precisely, to prevent you from ever understanding the truth of his influence over you."

"And if you hadn't saved me and I'd been found guilty?"

"Let's not go there, Quentin. Maybe he'd have owned up to his own game, maybe all kinds of things. In any case, that would be a whole different story."

"And how *did* you save me? I still don't understand..."

Fion shrugged. "It's just something we elves can do."

"What? Foresee a whole situation and then resolve it?"

"With luck, yes. If we spot injustice and there's something we can do about it then..."

"You do it."

"Also yes."

"And you can turn yourselves into anything you want?"

"Anything that fits the circs. This time it was a copper. Other times it's been other things," said Fion, raising a warning palm. "But please don't ask me for examples because, as I told you, the past is another country we elves don't tend to remember much about. If we spotted disagreements you humans were having that might have led to big time disputes and possible bloodshed, we did our best to sort them out. It's all a bit fuzzy in my head. To be honest, even your little problem is already starting to drift away."

"Want me to remind you?"

"Not really. What's done is done."

"Well anyway, I owe you a huge debt of gratitude."

"*Pas de quoi*," said Fion, who spoke all the six thousand five hundred human languages in the world but, for reasons unknown, from time to time favoured French.

Quentin cocked his head to one side, raised an eyebrow, and winked winningly. "No chance you might teach *me* some of your tricks?"

Fion winced. "If memory serves, which as I told you it normally doesn't, you guys don't have the mindset for decent results, but..."

"We could try?"

Fion stared off. "We could, but let us be clear...results would not be immediate or conclusive. Sure, I could change your outside *appearance* into almost anything you wanted, but it's the inside that's the problem. As I said...the mindset."

"Meaning?"

"That for however long it is my friends and I have been amongst you humans, we have remarked on certain tendencies that run fundamentally counter to ours. And in the few experiments we have conducted with you guys, these seem *very* hard to overcome."

"For example?"

Fion shrugged again. "There are many, but let us take the primary one, shall we? The one from which all the others in one way or another follow like a trickle-down effect."

"And that is?"

"The belief that you are the sole centres of the universe, either as individuals or as an entire species. Ever since your god or gods apparently created you, there has been the innate belief you are somehow superior to all other living creatures on Earth and have the right to use them at will. As a pal of mine once said, it seems you'll eat practically anything on four legs or you can catch from the seas. *In extremis,* you will also eat each other. A wonder such behaviour has been tolerated for so long. Who knows, some day there may be a backlash," said Fion, who knew exactly what that backlash would be.

Quentin swallowed hard and nodded. Put in that context, it was hard to deny.

"And furthermore," Fion continued, "in blind pursuance of personal and communal greed, you have polluted your planet with poisonous gases to the point it will soon no longer be able to sustain life of any kind, including your own. How dumb do you have to be to commit mass suicide and inflict genocide on innocent creatures who have no say in the matter?"

Quentin dropped his head and massaged his brow. "Christ," he said, aware of the Extinction Rebellion and the scientific analysis that underpinned it, but having been too preoccupied with faux diseases to pay such matters much attention.

"Not a bad bloke in his own way," said Fion, "but, as I said once before, sadly not what you folk have imagined him into being. And that's before we come to all the other fantasy messiahs around your globe and the wars that have ensued between the followers of the different faith systems. You guys sure like a fight."

There was no denying it, and Quentin didn't try.

"And all that's in the big picture, the international one that continues till your present day," Fion went on. "But it's mirrored in the small picture, too."

"Small picture?"

"The everyday one. It's not only that humans as a species think they're superior to other animals, or that some *groups* of them claim truth dominance over others, you even have strict rules about which indivi*du*als are top of the pecking order and which at the bottom."

Quentin frowned, so Fion clarified the point.

"The rich are stronger than the poor, men are stronger than women, parents are wiser than children, white humans of both genders are more deserving than brown or yellow ones, heterosexuals are normal, homos, bis and trans are not...the list goes on. Yet the powerful remain fearful of anything *other* that challenges those prejudices and will lie through their teeth to protect their position. Do I make myself clear? Have you not observed any of this in your leaders?"

"Yes," said Quentin in a very small voice, the description so clearly matching the solipsists in charge of the White House and 10 Downing Street.

"So perhaps you will now recognize my difficulty with the inside and the outside problem when it comes to trying to morph you guys into something you are inherently not. Unless extreme circumstances require such an intervention, of course."

"I do. Sorry for asking. But may I ask how you elves so radically differ?"

"Essentially because we neither recognize nor tolerate hierarchies. Where I come from, everyone's equal," said Fion. "Do I need to go through the whole list again and give you examples?"

"No, I guess not. So you have no rulers? No kings or queens?"

"Only the ones you humans invented for us in your fairy stories, which translate as lies."

"I read some of those when I was a kid."

"I'm sure you did and much good they will have done you. Normally they just portray us as funny little non-existent meddlesome nuisances."

"True enough, but there is one sense in which they were very helpful, to me at least. Because without them I would never have found it so easy to get along with *you*."

"Well at least there's *that* bonus. And look, Quentie, I'm sorry for the lecture. I was only aiming for a little clarity."

"No problem, but just one last question if I may."

"Fire away."

"Can you and I see each other as equals? It would make me happy to think so."

"Of course we can. You seem to me a rather special type of human, one who appears able to think metaphorically, to make connections where others may not. *Now* how about we leave the whole subject alone for the moment and try a squirt each of my orange tincture? I find it helpful when it comes to returning to reality."

Quentin laughed. "Re*ality*?"

Fion shrugged. "A tricky concept, I agree. But hey ho and a nonny, eh? On we go."

"Onwards and *up*wards?"

"I wouldn't know about the upwards. Onwards is good enough for me."

<h1>Four</h1>

Docs Frederick and Antoinette Trimble—a weeping Doc Antoinette having subsequently been arrested on suspicion of criminal complicity—were having a tough time at the cop shop despite being represented by top defence counsel Percival Peterson, whom they'd employed in accordance with their rights after twenty-four hours of detention without charge.

Given his views on humankind, Fion would have shaken his head and grinned in recognition of Doc Frederick's explanation of events on the night in question. Which was that the whole thing had been a mere charade to teach his ungrateful son a lesson he would never forget, something people of such social and medical standing as Doc Frederick had every right to do within the privacy of their own homes. Okay, it had got slightly out of hand in the explicit accusation of Quentin having murdered his mother but, "you dim-witted bally rozzers" ought to be able to tell the difference between "actual" murder and its "staged" equivalent.

Detective Inspector Derek Wilde, to whom the case had been consigned, eyed the pair and their lawyer with a disdain coloured largely by such wet-nelly posh people having the brass neck to describe policepersons as "dim-witted bally rozzers" to his face, but did his best to mask the revulsion with what he thought of as an ironic smirk.

"And the already dead body of the whore, Doctor Trimble? A somewhat elaborate measure in what was merely a family punishment charade, would you not say? The sort of thing my dim-witted colleagues might be expected to take with a little more than a pinch of salt? And, of course, the accusation that your son had been seen running from the property at the dead of night."

"I am a professor of medical science, my man," said Doc Frederick. "Cadavers are my business. If I want to bring one home for private examination, that is my business."

Percival Peterson winced at Wilde as imperceptibly as he was able. After all, *his* reputation was on the line here. But, locked into what he reckoned as his fully justified Detective Inspector mode, Wilde took no notice. Such a pain in the arse overpaid poncy lawyers could be.

It was all getting very alpha-male-ish until Doc Antoinette, weeping and spluttering as she tried to defend her crazed husband, interceded with the lie that cadavers dressed up as her had on occasion been employed to enhance the couple's dwindling sex lives.

"For fuh-fun, if you know wuh-what I muh-mean," she said, at which Peterson winced again and took an unnatural interest in the ceiling.

Everything got all alpha-male-ish all over again at that point, because that was when Doc Frederick told Doc Antoinette to shut her fucking trap if she knew what was good for her and DI Wilde was barely able to restrain himself from punching Doc Frederick on the nose.

Instead, he asked the pertinent question: "And your report to the police of seeing your son Quentin running away down the drive while you were finishing an article for *The Lancet* was?"

"A fabrication whose consequences were intended to purge his troubled soul," admitted Doc Frederick. "The means of giving him a little thinking time in choky for his own wellbeing. The duty of any father when the father's words of obvious wisdom have been perverted and distorted."

"So Quentin was *never* actually seen on the driveway?"

"As I said. No."

"And *who*, one wonders, killed Fanny Flint?" Wilde wondered aloud.

"Not *me*, that's for sure," declared Doc Fredrick.

"Well, we shall see about that," said Wilde, calling the interview a day *pro tem*, but insisting the Doc Frederick Trimble be kept in custody for what he termed "further investigation." Doc Antoinette, would be allowed to return home without any stain on her character.

And Quentin, of course, was completely off the hook because of not only the intervention of Fion/DI Malcolm McPhee, but also the tardy confession of his own father.

~ * ~

It was unfortunate that PC Harry Pertwee knew nothing of this absolution when, the morning after Quentin's arrest and release, he went for a consultation with Doc Sandra Normington suffering from what was then thought of as flu—a persistent temperature and a hacking dry cough. Had this indisposition hit a mere six hours or so later than it did, the constable would have still been on duty at the cop shop and known Doctor Quentin Trimble had been released without charge, not to mention that nobody had actually been killed. Well, except for poor old Fanny Flint, who was dead already. But no, illness had to strike him down only fifteen minutes after Quentin Trimble had been dragged in and locked up, loudly protesting his innocence, for such are the chaotic workings of malign fate, and in his flu-inspired delirium, Pertwee was unable to control his mouth.

"Say that name again," said Sandra taking Harry's temperature with an ear thermometer as he sat before her, teeth chattering and perspiring sufficiently to fill a washing-up bowl.

"Tuh-tuh-Trimble. Duh-duh-Doctor Trimble. Huh-heard of huh-him, huh-have you?"

"Rings a bell," said Sandra diplomatically. "And he was arrested for?"

"Kuh-killing his muh-mum wuh-with a pair of suh-scissors," Harry garbled, thereby becoming the first on the rumour mill to the inflate the crime into the myth that would later blossom into the ill-fated but anonymous mother in question having been offed with secateurs, pinking shears, a carving knife, a dagger, a sword, and ultimately an axe. Quite *who* had been the deep throat to divulge the story, albeit with no mention of the name Trimble, is a mystery, certainly not Sandra, although Doc Andy Crane was to become a potential candidate for the leak. Blossom the story soon did, however, hence *The Battersea Gazette's* horrifying headline "LOCAL DOCTOR DECAPITATES MOTHER WITH AXE." Had he known Quentin's name, the *Gazette's* editor would have blazoned it all over the piece but he didn't, because even Deep Throat must have had the decency to keep schtum over that detail. Not that the omission made all that much difference to the number of local doctors who—as innocent as Quentin himself—suddenly found media morons crawling around their premises looking for blood-stained axes. *Very* pissed off were said local doctors/matricidal maniacs.

Anyway, back to Sandra packing Pertwee off with a prescription for a week's supply of blue pills, after which she immediately buzzed Andy Crane to put appointments on hold and get his arse into her room pronto and thereby, in the light of subsequent events that same evening, raising the potential for Andy's rumour mongering.

"Bloody *hell*," he said after Sandra had recounted PC Pertwee's story. "Didn't I tell you there was some underlying problem with the bloke?"

"Enough to kill his own mother with kitchen scissors?" said Sandra, already further distorting Pertwee's account by the addition of 'kitchen.' "Hypochondriac, I thought you had him down as."

Andy shrugged. "Yeah, but who knows where that may lead? When the mind's off kilter, Sandie, all sorts of stuff are possible. Maybe Trimble blamed his mother for faulty genes. Maybe anything."

"But why not murder his *fa*ther? Fathers have genes, too, you know."

"Tell me about it," said Andy, whose own father was last heard of in Australia having divorced his mother and, by all accounts, a further three women from Sydney, Wollongong and Perth who had between them produced five half-brothers and sisters Andy had never seen. It was a murky history he had no intention of sharing with Sandra in case she might think such fecklessness ran in the male line of the family and render his attempts to get into her knickers even less likely.

"Mother fixation seems the most likely in my view," he therefore quickly concluded. "*Now* if you'll excuse me, I'd better get back to my patients. Fancy a snifter after work?"

"Not tonight. Got to wash my hair. See you tomorrow."

Maybe it was the disappointment of Sandra, yet again, having to wash her hair rather than submit to Andy's charms that caused him to drown his sorrows so thoroughly in The Queen's Head that night as to start whispering stories to fellow topers about knowing personally the bloke who'd killed his mother with a carving knife. Hence the Deep Throat suspicion, but as noted, even though thoroughly soused, Andy must have had the decency not to mention the name Trimble. Either that or, after five pints of Special Brew, it had slipped his mind.

Anyhow, *any*how, that's one possible explanation for how the stories began proliferating. And you know how it is with stories... how fast they can grow legs and with each re-telling be garlanded with new and improved scenarios. Who would have guessed, for example, that when committing the dastardly deed, the murderer would be dressed in garb ranging from a steel-reinforced red lacy bra over purple lace panties to the costume favoured by Superman in the original 1938 Action Comics? And those were only two of sundry other fictions, some of them so grotesque as to challenge even Stephen King's notion of "gross-out."

Thankfully for him, Quentin was protected from any contact with this media frenzy by Fion, who suggested the pair of them take a little walk down the path across the fence at the bottom of the garden. He knew perfectly well it was only to Docs Normington and Crane the Trimble name had been divulged and neither had mentioned it in public, but reckoned the very last thing the boy needed right now was exposure to vicarious guilt at the merest hint of the public outrage for a crime he hadn't committed.

"Nothing like a breath of fresh air in difficult times," he told Quentin, who jumped at the prospect and thus remained blissfully unaware of the fictive vipers' nest, which in any case would be replaced for goriness only three days later by reports of the "brutal assassination" with machetes of an ex-anti-Brexit campaigner in Tooting.

To Quentin, the visit to Fion's fairy glade at the end of the path seemed a lot longer than a mere three days, more like three months, but that's the sort of effect fairy glades can have on a person. By the end of even the first day/month, he was almost a new man. By the time he and Fion returned home, the process was complete.

Five

Quentin's call to the surgery's head honcho, Doctor Miriam Proudfoot, to see if he could quit gardening and have his old job back seeing as he was feeling like a new man might have met with a greater degree of sympathy had Sandra Normington not felt duty bound on the very same day she'd told Andy Crane, and without Fion noticing, to inform her boss of the matricide suspicion. At that point, remember, there had been no evidence of Quentin's early release, because the last thing DI Wilde & Co wanted was egg on their faces for his false arrest, let alone the freedom he'd been granted on the clear understanding he would never under *any* circumstances mention the incident to *any*one. To which Quentin had happily agreed, on the assumption, of course, that Fion wasn't an actual person, so telling him would be okay. *Sub rosa* also had been kept any subsequent leaks of Docs Frederick and Antoinette having been hauled off to the cop shop instead—Percival Peterson had make very sure of that—*or* indeed the fact that nobody had actually been killed. So far as Proudfoot and everybody else in and around Battersea knew, Flonk The Axeman, which was what the killer had been dubbed by a scurrilous reporter from *The South West London Enquirer* named Bryan O'Leary, was safely behind bars and awaiting trial.

"Lock him up forever and throw away the key," O'Leary concluded in a vitriolic piece railing against all more recently liberal views on the nature/nurture debate, in which he returned to the Victorian principle that people were born mad, bad or both, and there was nothing to be done about it except keep them in asylums of one kind or another safely away from "normal" society, hence Bedlam and so on.

"It's all about genetics," O'Leary claimed. "And what are we supposed to do? Find all the nasty genes and transplant them? Fat chance. And don't tell me shrinks' talking cures can do anything about it. No, no, if a person's got screws loose, he's got screws loose, and that's *that*."

Which opinion, of course, was met with told-you-so glee by a readership which, locally and nationally, had recently elected a Tory party of much the same persuasion, led by a person who was very clearly off his trolley but would never be locked up because he was "a winner." Much the same could be said of the criminal madman in the White House currently standing an excellent chance of re-election to a second term, given the House of Representatives' impeachment attempt had been quashed by the Republican toadies in the Senate.

And what is the relevance of this apparent digression to the story in hand? To demonstrate how *genuine* fake news can impact on an entirely innocent person, for this was the factor that explained why head honcho Miriam Proudfoot screamed, swooned, and fell off her chair when she heard Quentin's voice down the line telling her he was feeling like a new man and asking if he could have his job back.

"Hello. *Hello*?" said Quentin, jamming the phone closer to his ear.

"Problem?" said Fion, who had accompanied Quentin back to his flat in case of further developments.

"Proudfoot."

"What about her?"

"As soon as she heard my name, she screamed. Then there was this thud. After that, the line went dead."

Which was because Sandra Normington had heard the thud, too, rushed to Head Honcho's aid, and kicked the phone out of her limp hand.

"Shit," said Fion, unusually for him, for elves very rarely swear. But he was cross with himself for having neglected a link in the puzzle. And sure enough, as he backtracked through his ElfVision files, he first witnessed Proudfoot's recent horror at hearing the name Trimble then, rewinding even further back, there it was: the scene he'd somehow overlooked in which Normington tells Proudfoot about Quentin's arrest for suspected mother murder.

"Shit, shit, *shit*," he repeated. "I'm *sooo* sorry, Quentie, must be losing my touch. *Mea culpa, mea maxima culpa.*"

"Pardon?" said Quentin, who didn't speak Latin.

"This is all my fault, *entirely* my fault. I should have *known* Normington would tell her boss."

"About?"

"You being accused of the killing. No wonder she fell off her chair when she heard your voice. Mind you," said Fion tuning back into the current scene, "she seems to be okay now. Up on her feet anyway."

"Don't blame yourself, Fifie. Nobody's perfect. By the way, while we're on the subject, do a lot of people think I killed my mother?" said Quentin.

Fion shook his head. "Only Normington, Crane, and as it turns out now Proudfoot. Silly, *silly* me," he said before giving Quentin a brief rundown of events during their sojourn in the fairy glade, including the Flonk The Axeman invention and all the other gruesome narratives, including the stolen corpse of Fanny Flint.

Unsurprisingly, Quentin was gobsmacked. "You're telling me that...?"

"As I told you on the night you got out of jail, the whole thing was a trick, a 'charade' as your father called it, dreamt up by him to correct and improve your behaviour. *Nobody* was killed, but the media made a proper meal of it."

"And now he and Mother are in jail instead of me."

Fion nodded. "Not your mother. She was set free because it was obvious she knew nothing of what happened. But your father, yes, although nobody knows it, seeing as a cloak of secrecy has been wrapped around the whole episode. The media have had quite enough fun with that story."

That's when Quentin briefly blacked out and had to be resuscitated with Fion's yellow tincture, a potion infinitely more effective than the merely mortal potions being used to return Doc Miriam Proudfoot to something resembling consciousness.

~ * ~

When he awoke from his blackout, Quentin was light years away from the sort of new man he had been when phoning Miriam Proudfoot, the new man full of confidence and self-belief he had briefly been. This is not to say he wasn't new at all, just that the newness was of an entirely different order, a terrifying one occasioned by the epiphany he'd experienced while elsewhere in dreamland. For, as is supposedly the case with humans close to death, the whole of his life so far had flashed before his eyes, and he hadn't liked what he saw, not one bit he hadn't—Quentin the dominated child, Quentin the wimpish freaky adolescent who'd never played football, the gender-neutral Quentin who hadn't the least idea why his willy sometimes went hard and poked out of his pyjamas and squirted...the list went on and on and *on* into his twenties, and now, early thirties, and none of it was soul enhancing. No wonder he had drown into the hypochondriac who had spent his sheltered life in fear of deadly diseases, he now saw. What he saw, in addition, was that this was just a displacement activity to shelter him against the real terror, which wasn't of death but of *life*. Being *alive*, he now understood, carried with it the prospect of hidden traps and dangers infinitely more horrifying than measles, chicken pox, or even cancer. Like being set up by his own father for murdering his mother, for example. And all this occurring merely as punishment for the innocent phone call in which he'd told the pair of them the truth for the first time. If this was *life*, Quentin wasn't sure he wanted anything more to do with it.

Intuiting this conclusion, Fion was unsurprised. Having been around for more centuries than even he was aware of, he knew only too well the dilemmas and tragedies humans exposed themselves to and the misery to which they could lead. Put simply—how frequently they could screw up either individually or in groups and yet on they went deluding themselves into believing they ruled the world. Amongst all the literary figures he had known, it was perhaps only Willie Shakespeare who had so consistently understood this, but even Willie had needed a little help from his friend Fion when the muse temporarily deserted him, and the way forward looked all but bleakly impossible. At which point Fion would remind him of the gift of irony when penning his plays, by which he meant not only the supposedly witty trope, but also a way of being in the world. Which in turn meant that audiences might be amused at the word play while still in their seats, but on reflection when reaching home found themselves conflicted by the irresolution of apparent opposites, for that was the message most likely to help them understand the persistent and often irresolvable contradictions that were the precondition of their existence.

"An essential tool if your little dramas are to survive your death by more than two minutes," he'd told Willie during a bibulous night on the banks of the river Avon. "Always a good idea to add a fairy or two if the going gets really tough," he'd said as the pair shared a mug or two of his pink tincture. "Nothing like a fabulous metaphor to jar the mind into a new awareness of the necessity of difference and irresolution."

"Gosh, well said, young sprite, what a spiffing idea," said Willie, the germ of *A Midsummer Night's Dream* popping into his head uninvited.

The rest is a history of the ongoing debates in schools and universities over the true meaning of Willie's plays and their endless recycling into even such oddities as *West Side Story*. Better that, though, than them dying their death along with their author on April 23rd 1616. Always assuming Willie *was* their author, that is.

"Quentie, *Quentie*, wake up," Fion whispered as the despairing Quentin held his head in his hands wondering how best to depart this life. "We need to talk."

~ * ~

Back at the cop shop, DI Wilde had been obliged to give up on the notion of Doc Frederick having murdered Fanny Flint (real name

Irene Irons), seeing as only a little research into police files confirmed the person who'd killed her during rough sex (Kenny Ramsbottom) was now imprisoned for the next seventeen years, although with good behaviour he might be back on the streets in ten. That wasn't likely, though, because even in jail Kenny continued to behave badly, furiously maintaining to any fellow cons or warders who cared to listen—of which there soon became very few—that if it was rough sex you paid for, then rough sex is what you got. And if they answered back, he normally broke their noses. Furthermore, the only reason he'd fastened the dog collar around Irene's neck then had her crawl round naked on hands and knees like a bitch in heat and knocked her around a bit if she disobeyed his orders was she wanted him to. Said it was her favourite thing and how the fuck was Kenny to know the collar was too tight when he yanked on it? *No* way, that was how. He'd just thought she was having fun as she spluttered, gurgled then went all limp and collapsed. All part of the act, he reckoned. And not even worth the money because he hadn't even ejaculated yet. In other words, the *WHOLE FUCKING THING* was *her* fault and should have been regarded as suicide rather than murder. That was whores, and women in general, for you. Always up to their nasty tricks, then putting the blame on *you.*

Unsurprisingly, neither the judge nor the jury nor indeed Kenny's lawyer had bought this line of defence. Neither had they paid any attention to Kenny's claim to having been sexually abused by his sister when he was a baby, especially seeing as his sister had grown up to become the policeperson reputed to have shot stone dead two Guy Fawkes-type ISIS terrorists attempting to blow up Parliament. No, no it was a life sentence for Kenny all right. As for poor old Irene, it was decided her body should be left to medical science, seeing as nobody came forth to claim it.

All of which left DI Wilde with little reason further to question the version of events presented by Doc Frederick when it came to the presence of Fanny Flint/Irene Iron's corpse in his home on the night of the charade, at least where the murder of his wife was concerned. Most likely the excuse of sexual titillation had merely been a desperate attempt by Doc Antoinette to get her deranged husband off the hook, which was essentially why she had been released without charge. Even so, DI Wilde wondered, from where would such a clearly blameless woman have derived such an idea, unless, indeed, she had known her husband's little peccadillos with corpses to be true? In which case, Doc Frederick might be kept in pokey for entirely different crimes.

But top defence counsel Percival Peterson was having none of that. "Difficult to see you keeping your job should you make any such specious allegation, old chap," he told Wilde when the suspicion was aired. "My client is a highly respected member of the medical community about whom nobody would believe such scurrilous assertions and you would merely be left with egg on your face."

At which Wilde sniffed a bit, but then relented. Not only did he wish to *keep* his job but indeed, hoped in due course to be promoted to *Chief* Detective Inspector.

And so it was that Doc Frederick paid Peterson his five-thousand-pound fee and walked free from the cop shop without the least blemish on his character or reputation.

Six

Doctor Miriam Proudfoot's until recently glittering career as head honcho at the Battersea surgery was teetering on the brink of collapse. Fighting the battle with the histopathologists pissed off at "Doctor Death" for his persistent referral for biopsies of patients suffering from little more than bunions had been taxing enough, even humiliating when it came to acceding to the higher prestige they claimed as "experts in the field," and being obliged to pack Quentin off on gardening leave. Neither had her credibility been enhanced by repeated enquiries from her CCG (Clinical Commissioning Group) when they heard of the histopathologists' beefs as to how she had managed to employ such an evidently disturbed individual—possibly a bipolar hypochondriac—in the first place. Difficult days indeed for Doc Proudfoot, but somehow, she'd managed to muddle through in the time honoured fashion of British double standards by on the one hand obfuscating politely and on the other, lying through her teeth. Which magically had worked, at least as far as keeping the CCG off her back pro tem was concerned.

But then, out of the blue, the bloody mother killer had phoned her, hadn't he? And she'd swooned, fallen off her chair, and had to be revived by underling Doc Normington. Which had been demeaning. Not at all the sort of thing head honchos should be expected to have to undergo, although she had been comforted to hear from Normington—who didn't know anything different—that Quentin was *indeed* suspected of being a matricide, and she had every reason to fear his probably psychotic call about being a new and improved man. So back she went to the grindstone, albeit with some difficulty. Until the third career-blighting whammy came that was, namely, the accusation by several female patients of having been "tampered with" by Doc Crane.

"Made me strip to the waist just to take my temperature," complained thirty-three-year-old Hannah Harbottle, for example. "It wasn't like I was having an ECG or anything," she added, because Hannah knew her medical onions. "All I had was a sore throat."

And Hannah wasn't the only one to object. Into the same category fell twenty-seven-year-old Norma Hancock, a potential bronchitis patient, thirty-eight-year-old Suzie Williams complaining of suspected psoriasis, and nineteen year-old French student of English literature Annie Duchamps suffering from acute exam anxiety.

Those of you who still believe in the old chestnut that, as sacrosanct custodians of our corporeal welfare, doctors have the right to unquestioned trust in doing whatever they want to our bodies and still expect high social status might feel a little challenged by this alleged unethical behaviour. After all, doctors aren't rock stars who can get away with *any*thing they want, are they? But let us not run away with the idea they are somehow superhuman and therefore immune to the same perversities as demonstrated by such sex pests as those in the White House and 10 Downing Street, men who revel in the reputation of grabbing pussy and may well have become role models for behaviour as deviant as even that of Kenny Ramsbottom. So no good burying our heads in the sand here, folks. Emerging reports from the hospital zone, like that of Adam Kay's book *This Is Going To Hurt*, suggest it is far from unusual for consultants to have sex with drugged patients in their cubicles at the dead of night.

*Any*way, back to Doc Proudfoot's extra little headache after all these years of running a perfectly respectable practice with barely a hiccup. And a fat salary she enjoyed after the NHS reorganization that had placed GPs at the centre of health care in order to reduce pressure on hospital A&E services. Which had been a total failure, but that was none of Proudfoot's concern. In the winter break, she went skiing in Chamonix, in the spring hols she cruised the Mediterranean, and in autumn she relocated to a rented villa in the Alps. What could have been nicer? Nothing, that was what. And now there was all *this* hoohah.

Andy Crane was the *last* of her doctors Miriam would have suspected of morphing into a sexual predator. A nice enough boy, she reckoned. How was she to know he was the son of a father who serially philandered with women in places as far-fetched as Wollongong, and worried about the possibility of having inherited some rogue gene as a result? No way, that was how. Such information had been kept well under wraps. As, obviously enough, had been the manner in which Sandra Normington's repeated hair-washing excuses had jangled some nerve deep buried inside him, the one that feared the truth of his persistent failure in the boy-meets-girl-and-shags-her department, and caused him to take out his frustrations on innocent young patients. Which *was* the truth, seeing as Sandra had finally given up wondering about her feelings for Andy, decided she didn't have any, and focused her desires instead on the American psychiatrist Hank Orlando, whose services Quentin Trimble had spurned.

Anyway, *anyway,* the upshot of all this confusion was the painful interview Proudfoot—yet again, with the CCG snapping at her heels over accusations brought by Hannah Harbottle and friends—was obliged to conduct with Doc Crane, the one in which he first melted into floods of abject tears then took a scalpel from his trouser pocket and began experimental slices at his wrists.

It was just as well in the circs Miriam had an emergency button under her desk...otherwise Andy might have been a goner. Mercifully for him, however, it was mere seconds after the purple lights started flashing and the wah-wahs started up around the surgery before six-foot-three ex-wrestler-turned-receptionist Max "The Mangler" Morgan burst into the room and swiped the scalpel from Andy's quivering hands.

It would have been better for all concerned had the ambulance arrived in the seven minutes guaranteed by the NHS, otherwise Max wouldn't have needed to restrain Andy in a full nelson and dislocate his left shoulder, but you know how it is with hospital overload—and London traffic.

~ * ~

It took Quentin Trimble a little time to process Fion's words as he contemplated the pointlessness of existence, but jarred by elvish shoulder-shaking, he finally looked up.

"Need to talk about *what*?" he muttered grumpily.

"You."

"Nothing to talk about. Unless you think it would be fun to talk about a thirty-two year-old failure whose father set him up as a mother killer. You're telling me *that* would be a fun subject for a chat?"

Fion shrugged. "Not fun perhaps, but necessary."

"Who for?"

"Me. I'll do the speaking, if you want. Or else I could listen too, I have big ears," said Fion, waggling his pointy elf ears one by one in a little dance. It was one of his favourite tricks.

Despite himself, Quentin grinned a fraction.

"And just to be clear," Fion continued. "I already understand your feelings about your situation, so you won't need to say all that much about it. Just maybe nod from time to time."

"Funny kind of a chat."

"I'm a funny kind of an elf."

"So you talk while *I* listen? Fifie, you've been a friend to me, maybe my only friend. But I've spent my pointless life listening to other people then doing what I'm told, and I've had enough of that. Look where it got me. To *this*."

"Okay then, so *you* talk and *I*'ll listen. In which case, there are only a couple of things I would ask of you."

"Which are?"

"You don't ask for pity and you do speak your mind. In such a discourse, there is no place for flabby and repetitively self-defeating histories, only for distilled thought. D'you think you could manage a spot of that?"

Quentin stared into Fion's narrowed green eyes from which emanated arrows of unspoken and unspeakable wisdom.

"I s'pose I could give it a go."

"Good man. And remember, this is all about who you *are* and might go on to be, *not* about who you were or were hoodwinked into becoming."

Quentin frowned like a child asked to solve a quadratic equation with no prior knowledge of maths.

"That's too hard," he grumbled.

Fion shrugged. "Take your time. There's no hurry."

"But how can a person speak about who he is *without* referring to his past?"

"By contemplating essence," said Fion, in what would develop into a radically different take on the nature/nurture debate from Bryan O'Leary's in *The South West London Enquirer*.

"Huh?"

"Let me ask you just one question."

"All right then."

"Do you consider yourself a bad person?"

Quentin winced. "Must be, mustn't I? Sad, mad, bad..."

"And where does the 'must' come from?"

"What's been happening my whole life. Must've been something wrong with me, mustn't there?"

Fion shook his head and placed a forefinger over his lips. "Tch, tch, what did I say about the past?"

"Yes but...what *else* is there when it comes to working out who you are?"

"You, the *inner* you."

"Oh, for Christ's sake, this is starting to sound like what the Orlando fraud had on offer. What the hell're you talking about?"

"The belief I, my fairy friends, and even the more enlightened of you humans have that *no* child is born sad, mad or bad, although there may be some genetic contribution to the first two. But as for badness, that can never be hereditary. In any case, it is normally only the definitions of contemporary society that nurture and determine the conditions for such an idea. In his time, my old pal Galileo Galilei was considered off his trolley for going on about your Earth being round and not the centre of the universe. Interestingly, by the way, it was also he who said, 'You cannot teach a man anything; you can only help him find it within himself.' Before and after him, your human history is littered with folk thought by their fellows to be crazy. Ever read *One Flew Over the Cuckoo's Nest*? Or seen the movie?"

Perplexed, Quentin shook his head.

"Well, one day you should. These things help to shake up *idées fixes*. You might check out what Michel Foucault had to say about crime, punishment, madness, and sexuality. Rather good at philosophy, the Frenchies. Mind you, Scouser John Lennon's 'Working Class Hero' is worth a listen, too, when it comes to being failed by parents, school and society in general till he was so fucking crazy he couldn't follow their rules."

Quentin yawned. "Any chance of getting to the point, Fion?"

"Sure. Madness and, worst of all, badness are not absolutes but constructs of your human society open to revision from generation to generation. This is particularly true of badness. You may recall a time back in the last of your centuries when homosexual people were jailed for being bad, now they can marry each other. Albeit not always in all churches because of the head-in-the-historical-sand pig-headedness of most of your religions on almost all subjects, but still it's a small step in the right direction. As it would be if a person's colour were no longer to be the determining factor in his or her place in society."

Quentin sighed and scratched an earlobe. "And all this has *what* to do with me?"

"I'll just ask you my first question again, this time to be answered in light of what I've been saying. Do...you...still...consider...yourself...a... bad...person?"

Quentin took a deep breath and an unusual interest in his shoelaces.

"Well? Deep down, *do* you? Never mind your parents and your childhood and your education and recent events, during all of which I regard you as having been more sinned against than sinning."

Silence as Quentin fiddled with the bow on his right shoe.

"Quentin? Answer please. *Hon*est answer."

"Nuh-no," Quentin muttered head still bent. "And there's another honest answer, if you want that too."

"Please."

"Until the recent events you mentioned, I'd never really thought about myself at all. I just sort of *was*."

Fion smiled, recalling his own description of himself albeit for radically different reasons. "Understandable. That was how you'd been conditioned. To be just a cog in a machine whose workings were never explained."

"If you put it that way."

"I do. And now's the time to change all that."

"At *my* age?"

"Learning never ends, old chap. I'm sure you're perfectly able to find it within yourself, as old Galileo said."

"Mmm," mused Quentin, chewing at a hangnail.

"Can I take that for a yes?"

Quentin shrugged and nodded.

"Okay, at least we seem to be getting *some*where. So, my friend, the next time you think about yourself, think: 'Who am *I* beneath all the layers of other peoples' opinions?' Do we have a deal?"

"Deal," muttered Quentin, extending a tentative hand for shaking.

Instead of returning the shake, Fion sprouted several feet in height and took Quentin in a bear hug.

"Good man," he said. "It's only the first baby step, but who knows what might follow? By the by, have we yet tried my special indigo and scarlet tincture?"

"Not that I remember."

"So let's give it a go, shall we? As I recall, it has rather a pleasant effect on a person's general outlook on life."

Seven

Doc Frederick was incandescent when he was finally returned home from the police station to re-join Doc Antoinette. From behind the front door after he'd flung it open, he flipped the departing cop car a covert V-sign, then headed straight into the lounge where he attacked the drinks cabinet, poured himself a glass of twelve-year-old Glenkinchie whisky, downed it in one, then poured himself another.

"A drop for me, too?" said Antoinette trailing in behind him.

"Get it yourself, bitch," spat Doc Frederick, who had for so many years vented on Doc Antoinette his spleen at what he considered his maltreatment by the world in general. That was the convenient thing about wives: they were always around and could be treated the way others could not. Mind you, it was true in this particular instance, as he'd reflected while in custody, that *she* had been the one who'd been kind and friendly to her rude and mouthy son in that fateful phone call, meaning *he* had needed to take over the conversation. If she had only had the good sense to play the game according to *his* rules, there might never have been the need to cook up the *faux* murder story and get arrested. But that was the story of his marriage to the woman who had never fully understood her rôle as a dutiful wife who, it seemed to Doc Frederick, had loved the idiot child more than she'd ever loved *him*. Okay, she'd gone along with the teachers' misreading and the home schooling and all that, but only because she'd believed the boy to be "special." Probably because of faulty ovaries, he now reckoned, there sure as shit being nothing wrong with his sperm.

In short, Doc Antoinette was the most convenient target for Doc Frederick—"Raging Bull" as unbeknownst to him he was dubbed by hospital colleagues—who was losing the few remaining marbles he possessed and needed someone else to blame for it.

"There, there darling," said Doc Antoinette, edging past him towards the Glenkinchie bottle, from which she poured herself a couple of fingers. "Let's just calm down, shall we? I'm sure everything will be all right," she added, employing the phrase second nature to her after all the years of soothing jittery expectant mothers while wheeling them into the delivery room.

Fat chance of it working with Doc Frederick though, not in his current state of dislocation from the world he'd enjoyed for more years than his failing memory could count, the one in which as a top neurosurgeon, he expected to be worshipped and obeyed unquestioningly as a *sine qua non*.

"CALM DOWN, CALM *DOWN*?" he said.

"Yes, you know this is doing your heart no good."

Doc Frederick had recently been diagnosed with the stress-related atrial fibrillation that sometimes caused his hands to go wonky during surgery.

"BAH AND BALONEY," was his response to those soothing words while, yet again, topping up his Glenkinchie glass, after which he misquoted the only lines of Willie Shakespeare's he ever registered: "Get thee to a fucking nunnery. Wise men know well enough what monkeys you bitches make of them."

At this, Doc Antoinette sighed, turned on her heels, and headed to the fifth bedroom, the one at the very top of the house where Doc Frederick never went, the one Quentin had slept in until he went off to medical school and never came back home.

"Just as well, poor boy," she reflected as she undressed and groped her way beneath the duvet.

Not that she slept well, or indeed much at all. Not with Doc Frederick rampaging about the lower floors and the fury *she* was beginning to feel at having for so many years kowtowed to his wishes instead of concentrating on her needs—and indeed those of her son.

"Forever dancing to someone else's sodding tune and moving to the rhythms of others," she muttered round and around to herself in the dark until around four a.m., when something resembling sleep hit her and she became feverishly comatose.

~ * ~

It was ironic that the shrink Andy Crane was obliged to consult before he could return to work should have been Hank Orlando, the object of Sandra Normington's desires, but such is the nature of chaos theory. Sandra herself knew nothing of the referral, which had been made by head honcho Miriam Proudfoot under extreme pressure from the CCG's chief exec and one-time doctor Professor Finian O'Toole, who had this time insisted on the "Release Your Hidden Self" therapy Quentin Trimble had managed to avoid.

"From here on in," O'Toole had written in a stern email, "I'm tolerating no more loonies in your surgery, which you may consider under threat of closure until I'm satisfied beyond reasonable doubt all its practitioners are sane."

So it was, after getting his dislocated shoulder relocated by a tired nurse called Betsy and having his mental condition appraised in a fifteen-minute session by an overworked and underpaid junior psychologist called Ben Casey, who confirmed his mental health, "left a lot to be desired," that Andy was obliged to attend Hank's clinic. With which Hank was happy enough, seeing as he ran what he termed "a tight ship" with a fast "turnaround time" for practically any form of lunacy as long as the cash came up front, the cash amounting to five hundred pounds per fifty-minute session for private patients with a ten percent "knockdown rate" for NHS-recommended clients. And it was a thriving business, particularly amongst female clients, given Hank looked a lot like Robert Redford in *Butch Cassidy and the Sundance Kid*.

"Hi there, you'll be Doc Crane, right?" he said when Andy was ushered into the room by a *Playboy* sort of a girl called Sabrina. "Come in and make yourself comfortable. Okay if I call you Andy?"

"Sure."

"Ookey dokey then. Take a seat, Andy," said Orlando, gesturing at a straight-backed dining chair across the mahogany desk behind which he sprawled on a red-leather swivel. "This shouldn't take long," he added scrolling down his computer screen till he came to the notes on Doctor Andrew Crane.

Andy sat uncomfortably where indicated and waited.

"Ookay, right, gotcha. Mmm, inneresting," said Hank, checking Ben Casey's scribbles. "Sooo, lemme ask ya straight up front, Andy. What do *you* figure is the matter with you that would make you take lady patients' clothes off then wanna slash your wrists when you were asked about it? I got time, so tell me about it."

Hank lay back in his red-leather swivel and adopted his concerned look, the one that had earned him all those mega-bucks in Hollywood until he was given the boot for running a clinic under the name of Robert Redford Jnr. The real Robert had been very pissed off when he found out, hence the court case, the hefty fine, and Hank's hasty midnight flitting to the UK where nobody knew him from the mailman.

"That was what I was hoping *you* would tell *me*," said Andy, recalling with some embarrassment patients using the same line after being asked by him what was the matter with *them* today.

"Comin' to that. Inneresting the sex and death angle though, huh?"

Early in his career back in NYC before the move to LA, Hank had taken a crash course in Freudianism called KYS (Know Your Sigmund).

"If you say so."

Hank said nothing. Just stared at the wall behind Andy's chair as advised by his teachers' mantra to "make the client do the work."

Andy shrugged and said nothing, so Hank was finally obliged to say *some*thing to get the show on the road before the clock ticked down to session end. Staring at Ben Casey's hurried notes on his screen, what he went for was, "Some worries over your daddy's sex life?"

Andy twitched. Had he *really* said anything about that in the hospital? He didn't think so, but the morphine he'd been given while Betsy relocated his shoulder might have befuddled his memory of the later interview with Casey.

"Well?" said Hank while Andy went on twitching encouragingly. "We ain't got all day."

And then out it all spilled, the whole story up to and including Andy's persistent fear of failure in the boy-meets-girl-and-shags-her department, after which he hung his head and went on twitching.

Hank nodded and smiled a bit. "You wanna sit up straight on your chair? Can't afford to have you falling off and hurting yourself."

Andy straightened up as best he could.

"And how did you *feel* about that?"

"Bad."

"Like bad as in 'ill' or bad as in 'naughty'?"

"Both."

"Uh-huh, inneresting," said Hank. "Any dreams?"

KYS had been heavy in the dream department.

Andy nodded.

"Wet ones?"

Andy nodded again.

"Uh-huh, inneresting," said Hank tapping at his computer keyboard. "Ever wanted to *kill* your father?"

"Huh-he wuh-was nuh-never around to kuh-kill."

Which was true because Andy was only two when Crane Snr did his runner to Australia.

"Mmm," Hank mused, tapping his pearly white front teeth with a pencil carrying up its barrel the gold-lettered logo BANK ON HANK. "But you had the desire?"

That was when, at exactly the moment the fifty minutes of the session were up, Andy took to screaming and tearing at his hair.

"Mmm, inneresting," said Hank, buzzing Sabrina on the intercom to come assist the patient out of the consulting room.

"See you next week, same place, same time," he told Andy as he was being soothed by Miss Playboy 2017, "and you try taking Sabrina's clothes off, you're facing trouble, lemme tell ya. That gal has a real nasty karate chop."

Andy was escorted on wobbly legs to the payment desk to confirm his NHS status for billing purposes before being released out onto the pavement where Sabrina at least had the decency to call a cab to take him home.

Eight

Fion shook his head as he reviewed the whole convoluted and messy story so far by plugging his eidetic memory banks into an EiP (Elf iPlayer) and watching episode after episode, beginning with Sandra and Andy discussing the possible reasons for Quentin's gardening leave in their after-surgery chat, and ending with Andy tearing his hair out in Hank Orlando's office.

"In the name of Oberon, you couldn't *make* it up," he muttered.

Mind you, after all the centuries spent liaising between Fairyland and Earth, he shouldn't have been all that surprised. Despite the persistent self-delusion they were making what they called "progress," never had he witnessed humans taking more than two steps forwards before they took six steps backwards and returned to their habitual states of confusion, bitterness and disillusion. Revolutions in governance the supposedly most civilized ones had conducted, an "Enlightenment" they'd had, "sciences" and "economies" they'd developed, "literature" they'd written, social media they'd invented, other planets they'd visited and so on...and on...and on. And where had it led them? Nowhere, that was where. In Fion's view, it was the *un*civilized ones who were the happiest, those who still lived peacefully according to ancient tradition in their forests and other shelters until the "civilized" ones came with their machines and tore them down to make roads and towns, and in the name of what? "Progress" of the kind, as Fion had told Quentin, that would eventually render their whole planet uninhabitable, that was what. The only human in whom he had *any* faith was a young autistic girl who was single-handedly taking on the world of "grown-ups" busy consigning her generation and all future generations to extinction.

"Love you, Greta," he said switching off his EiP. "Let's hear it for Aspergers."

Added to *that* extinction concern, though, was the Covid-19 pandemic Fion was expecting anytime soon, which, in his view would be the result of the disruption to natural habitats and the subsequent eating of ancient animals which had for centuries survived the virus that would be indiscriminately killing humans in their hundreds of thousands and wrecking their proudly built economies. Nature's revenge for mindless meddling was the way Fion read the situation.

Anyway, what with one thing and another, he reckoned now would be as good a time as any to take a break from the predictable insanities of the human zone and recharge his batteries. With this in mind, he headed off to the fairy glade for a heavy dose of different coloured potions, dancing, singing, the telling of tall tales and...sanity. After all, of what use to anyone was an elf so mired in human misery he could no longer think straight or, as Fion preferred, ironically. After all, he'd got along well enough with his old pal Socrates. A pity his elenchus hadn't caught on, because Fion had warmed to it but evidently such dialectics had been, and remained, far too sophisticated for the normal human brain, which brought Fion back to square one in his need for a little head space. So off he went to the grassy glade.

It was during a break in these jollies, he took his oldest friend Bert(ha) to one side and sat with him/her in the sunshine puffing at a shared pipe of FairyBac beneath the branches of a tree unknown to humans, although it vaguely resembled their weeping willow. Not that fairies cared *what* it was called seeing as they believed the naming of things to be just one more human fallacy, yet another way of classifying and colonizing their environment by nailing down identities that had the right to remain fluid. They only gave each *other* names for the sake of jolly social intercourse. How miserable would it be to live in a world where you met a pal and just said "Hi there, Fairy"?

"You're looking a mite glum, Fifie," said Bertie. "Ever tried sticking a finger up your bum?" s/he added, stealing the joke from a one-time English satirist pal called Willie Rushton.

Fion giggled. "Smelly!"

"Yeah, but sometimes it helps. Seriously though, you're not looking your usual chirpy self."

"Been over on Earth too long."

Bertie nodded. "Loonyland, eh? Yeah, it never helps, does it? I got lucky with a homeland job for a few moons. Feel like a new wo/man now. Would do the same for you. I could pull a few strings if you wanted."

"Thanks but nah, there's still stuff I've got to do, loose ends to tie up. Pass the pipe, would you?"

"You're not still thinking you can *cure* those crazies, are you? said Bertie, taking a luxuriant toke at the long thin pipe before handing it over. "We did our best, but look where it got us. Thought we'd given that idea up many, many, *many* moons ago."

"You're right, we did."

"So?"

"There's always the one who might benefit from a little help, who shows promise. What was that line about thieves in the Christ crucifixion story?"

"One of them was saved. But the other one *wasn't*. Anyway, don't tell me you've bought into *that* fiction after all the killing humans have done in its name."

Fion took his drag at the pipe, blew the marijuana-scented smoke across his shoulder, and passed the pipe back. "No, but out of all the trillions of humans, there must be *some* who are still worth helping."

Bertie shrugged. "I suppose. Who've you got in mind?"

So Fion told him/her Quentin's story, adding as an endnote, "I've got him a little way down the road, but not far enough. It'd be sad to just leave him hanging."

Bertie lay down the pipe on a tree root, took his oldest friend in a tight embrace, and said, "You silly old fool, you'll never learn, will you?"

"No."

"And it's soo good to see. You want my advice…go for it. And, look, if you need a hand, you just call out my name, you've got a friend."

Bertie sang the final phrases to the tune of the song by two American humans called Carole King and James Taylor s/he'd helped through some hard times back in the last of Earth's "centuries."

"Thanks."

"Any ideas in mind for this help? And puh-*lease* don't tell me you're planning to turn him into some superhuman who rescues the planet from apocalypse. That yarn's been spun enough times already."

Fion shook his head. "No, I've seen those movies, too. No, what I was thinking was personal help only, nothing political. Of him spending a little time as one of us, for example."

"As one of *us*?"

"Yeah. He's already spent a few human 'days' with us and seemed to benefit from it. Now maybe he could *be* a fairy for a short while. I left him pondering on who he really was, but I'm not sure he has the capacity or the experience to do that, so perhaps something more radical? A genetic transfusion, you might think of it as."

Bertie nodded. "See where you're coming from. He'd have to be both of their 'genders,' of course."

"Sure, but might that not be a good thing?"

"It is for us."

"My point. It would perhaps wipe him clean of the human preoccupations with origin and destiny. So *much* time they devote to their pasts and their futures and hardly any to their presents."

"True enough. But two questions, Fifie."

"Fire away."

"Number one: won't he *know* this is being done to him?"

"Not if it comes to him as a dream. I give him one of our little potions before I bring him over to the glade and another when I wake him up back home, and just a splendid rest is all he'll know he's had as well as the epiphany he'll have experienced, of course."

Bertie nodded. "Okay. And question number two? Although I believe I know where you're going. What *use* will all this be to him when he's back with the human tribe? Surely they'll just brand him crazy and walk all over him."

"Not if, like us, he knows no prejudice, no identity issues, no greed, no lust for power...and above all, no fear."

"But in his world that will still make him a loner, an outsider."

Fion smiled. "And if I were to ask you to name the only humans for whom you have the least respect, who or what would they be?"

A now more masculine Bertie shook his hirsute head, pulled at his beard, and chuckled. "Loners and outsiders, some of them termed geniuses by their fellow earthlings."

"Quite. Soo, you still on board for a little help should I need it?"

Bertie smiled. "You just call out my name."

"Good man. *Now*, enough of this philosophizing, my brain's starting to hurt. You dancing?"

"You asking?"

"I'm asking."

"Then I'm dancing."

So it was that Fion and Bertie took final puffs at their wacky baccy pipe, sprang to their feet, and re-joined the massed fairies cavorting gleefully to tunes provided by an elf folk band playing nameless instruments unknown to human musicians, including one consisting of cymbals attached to the knees which were clapped together whenever the wearer felt like it. It was all very random, but the fairies didn't care. They didn't dance to preordained routines either. Just hopped about at will, some on their feet, others on their hands. Fion and Bertie chose feet and pranced about yodelling, "Fiddle-di-di, fiddle-di-*dah*" while slapping their bottoms with one hand and punching air with the other, a dance soon adopted by other elves such that in the end everyone was doing it in a sort of conga all around the grassy glade.

When it was over, they all went to sleep until the next sun-up.

Nine

Had Sandra Normington not discovered the name of Andy Crane's analyst from a slip of the tongue by Miriam Proudfoot, Andy wouldn't have found himself back in hospital with concussion, a broken nose, and several loose teeth, but we've already seen what a trickster chaos theory can be.

What happened was this: having dolled herself up to the nines for her visit to her longed-for lover Hank Orlando on the pretext of checking how her "much valued" colleague "poor" Doc Crane was getting along with his therapy, Sandra found herself so enthralled by Hank's charms she agreed to sit next to him on his psychiatrist's couch while he explained.

"Damn tricky case," Hank told her, breaking all the rules of confidentiality on the excuse the Sandra babe was herself a doctor. "But I'm working on it and when I git my teeth into a problem, I kinda always work it out."

"I bet you do," said Sandra, gazing into his Robert Redford-ish blue eyes.

Sandra was wearing red Gucci pumps and a pink Stella McCartney sheath dress over an expensive sunbed tan.

Hank shrugged in his idea of modesty. "Comes with practice, and I had a lotta that back in NYC and LA and other places."

"I bet you did," said Sandra, hitching the Stella McCartney number a little higher up her thighs. "Poor Andy."

"Yeah. Just between the two of us, guy needs to get his rocks off more often."

"And you can arrange that?"

"I can tell him how if he don't know already."

"I bet you can," Sandra purred. "Sex therapist as well as shrink, eh?"

"You might say so," said Hank, getting up to ensure the door was firmly closed. "Hey, you thirsty? I got cawfee or I got tea. I got stronger stuff, you wanna go that way."

"It's a little early but..."

"How about a Manhattan? I'm betting you never had one of those."

"You're betting right."

"Ookay, comin' right up."

The next Sandra Normington knew after three sips at the laced Manhattan, was she was flat on her back on the couch with the Stella McCartney number and her knickers around her ankles while Hank was looming over her stripped to the waist, yanking at some obdurate Levis fly buttons and saying, "Goddammit."

"Oooh, Hank, need a hand?" Sandra murmured.

Which was *not* the most propitious moment for Andy Crane to have dismissed Sabrina's protests Doctor Orlando was with a client, brushed past her, and come storming into the office, saying he needed advice on a matter of the utmost urgency. Which was to have been the declaration of his love for Sandra Normington, and what he should do about it, but in the circumstances, those words were never to pass his lips.

The words that passed them instead were: "What the *FUCK*?" yelled only moments before Andy charged Hank and rugby tackled him around the knees, causing Hank's erection to wilt as he tumbled over and Sandra to scream like screaming had only just been invented.

"*AAAAAAAAAGGGGGHHHHH*," she said as Andy took to pummeling Hank around the head.

The trouble was Hank was a brawler from way back, which Andy wasn't, so the few blows he landed were easily brushed off and it was only seconds before Hank was back on his feet, his pants were back in place, and he was beating ten kinds of shit out of Andy. So that was how Andy Crane found himself back in hospital with concussion, a broken nose, and several loose teeth. It explained why Sandra Normington re-dressed as fast as she could, fled the office past an angry-looking Sabrina, and without the trace of a resignation letter to the surgery, took the first train she could to Liverpool Lime Street and thence back home to Birkenhead on the banks of the Mersey.

This left Miriam Proudfoot minus three doctors and reliant only on only sixty-four-year-old Doc Patrick Sewell, whom she suspected of early onset Alzheimer's, and a newly qualified part-timer called Milly McDougal. No wonder she relented three weeks later when Quentin again phoned to see if he could have his job back. Given the whispers over his being a potential matricide appeared to have been no more than that, a passing fantasy on the lips of the now vanished Sandra Normington, why not? The papers were saying Flonk the Axeman had killed himself by leaping from the London Eye at midnight, so it looked very much as though Quentin was in the clear and Miriam needed doctors, so...What was more, there was something new, something mellow she heard in the voice down the line, a certain *je ne sais quoi* that persuaded her perhaps he had indeed become a new man.

Which was the truth, after all, for it was only days since Quentin had returned from the fairy glade "genetic transfusion" promised by Fion that had morphed him into the calm and gentle man who feared nothing on Earth. He still occupied the same body, but internally he was a far cry from the fully negative neurotic hypochondriac he had so recently been.

~ * ~

After the night in which she realised she'd spent her life singing from other people's hymn sheets—particularly Doc Frederick's—and during more or less the same period as her son's fairy rebirth, Doc

Antoinette was well on the way to becoming a new woman. Not for her the old-fashioned bra-burning feminism of Germaine Greer, Kate Millett and company though, no siree. Not only was it in her view outmoded, it eerily resembled the very same crass populist sloganeering that had got misogynistic madmen elected to both the White House and 10 Downing Street, no more than a demeaning version of the same, albeit inverted, version of gender dominance. And Doc Antoinette wasn't falling for *that* crap. She wasn't some madwoman in the attic or the poor downtrodden heroine of a romance novel who needed a hero to fall in love with. No, she was not only a qualified doctor but one who knew deep down inside her there were reserves she'd never explored. Now it was only a matter of tapping into those reserves, feeding them, and allowing them to blossom into a *person* irrespective of gender. In this peculiar way, her resolution echoed much of what Fion had bred in her son.

Unsurprisingly, Doc Frederick didn't like this metamorphosis, not at all he didn't. At first, he barely noticed, but once the cups of tea stopped being made for him and the dinners served, he became resentful. He liked it even less when his views on medicine, parenthood, politics, and the world in general ceased being parroted by the wife he had for so long regarded as some lower form of life.

"What the hell's the *matter* with you, woman?" he asked her one evening, while poking at a lasagne ordered in from a local Italian outfit called *Trattoria Lucca*.

So for the next forty minutes, Doc Antoinette told him and didn't mince her words. The bottom line was ever since med school where they'd met way back when, she'd towed his line but, after recent events and her reflection on them, she'd run out of rope.

"It's not that I *hate* you," she said, prodding a chunk of meaty cheese and poking it into her mouth. "I've just sort of outgrown you, that's all. And from here on in, I shall plough my own furrow."

"You mean we're to be div*orced*?" said a newly fearful Doc Frederick, who had no idea of housekeeping and was starting to wonder how he might survive wifeless. His rôle had always been to be the brains of the outfit with no need ever to worry about the trivial domestic arrangements that kept him comfortable. And now, out of the blue *this*. Always assuming it would be *she* who moved out to some chichi apartment, that was. And what was *he* to do? Stay here all alone in this big house? Sell it and move to God knew where? Prepare his own breakfast? Go shopping? Get the central heating fixed when it broke down, which was often. So *many* terrifying questions all of a sudden.

"Up to you, sweetheart," said Doc Antoinette. "I can play it any which way you want."

"And what about poor Quentin?" said Doc Frederick, hoping for a little emotional blackmail to twang the maternal heartstrings. "Where will *his* home be if you're gone?"

Doc Antoinette laid her fork down on the tablecloth. "And this coming from the father who set up his own son on a fictitious murder charge?"

"For his own good!"

Doc Antoinette shrugged. "Which was bullshit and you know it."

On the tip of Doc Frederick's lips were the words, "How *dare* you, woman?" but in his current parlous situation he sucked them back, albeit too late to fool Doc Antoinette. She read the unuttered words clearly enough behind the familiar grimace and merely raised an eyebrow.

"Get used to it, Freddie," she said. "There's a whole lot more where that came from. Nothing vindictive, arbitrary or capricious, nothing without a solid base in reason, mind you. Put it this way, you are simply no longer the author of my scripts. Those days are long past and gone."

Doc Frederick blinked. "Buh-but I nuh-never..."

"Oh yes you did. For all the years we've been married. How many is it now?"

"Nun-no idea."

"Thirty-seven. I was a mere child and happy enough to play along. Until the idiocy with my 'murder,' that is. That changed everything. Now I see the world, and you, through different eyes. And, just so we're clear, I do not care about the consequences. *Those* are now pretty much up to you."

"*Me?*"

"You. Should you too begin to see the error of your ways, I would be only too happy to help you along. Should you refuse, well..."

"Well what?"

"I shall need to take matters into my own hands and let the devil take the hindmost."

"Holy Christ," said Doc Frederick, thumping at his brow with a loose fist.

"I doubt he's going to help you, but you can always ask. Oops, that's my phone," said Doc Antoinette, rising from her chair. "Gotta love you and leave you, so to speak."

Which was how it came to pass that Doc Fredrick was left staring at a plateful of cold and half-uneaten lasagne, while Doc Antoinette took the first call she'd had from Quentin since the terrible one that landed him in the cop shop.

Ten

Back in Birkenhead, Sandra Normington stayed with her elderly parents in their little two-up-two-down terraced house in Neptune Street only a stone's throw from the Mersey tunnel entrance. It was cramped and chilly, but Sandra didn't care, such was her relief to be away from "The Smoke," as folk around there referred to London. The only good things to go south, they reckoned, were rain clouds, and only too glad, therefore, were Henry and Mildred Normington to welcome their daughter back home. Okay, so she immediately caught a cold, but the cough and the catarrh it caused were nothing to worry about, according to her mother.

"Just the draught up the tunnel, girl. You'll get over it," she said, and Sandra laughed for the first time in a long time, remembering the old Liverpool adage that if you didn't laugh you cried.

So Sandra laughed. Some weeks later, when such symptoms would be greeted with fear and trepidation she might not have, but at this point, coronavirus was no more than some weird bug killing people way off in China, so no worries there. Anyway, it was so good to be home, and she began to wonder why she, like her two brothers, had ever left the place, although back then the reason had been obvious enough: i.e. no work. Cammel Lairds, the builders of such ships as the Ark Royal, were struggling to survive, likewise the Ford motor company. Okay, the Sixties Mersey Beat tourist industry still flourished, but her brothers Ronald and Alfred had bigger ambitions and, like the emigrants from the Pier Head all those years ago, had headed west to the New World to seek their fortunes. Ronnie now ran a computer outfit in Silicon Valley, and Alfie was up north on the same coastline in Vancouver where he taught Beatles Studies at the University of British Columbia. Both would have stayed on Merseyside if they'd been picked to play for Liverpool or Everton FC, but neither was.

And then there was the youngest, Sandra, who'd wanted to be a doctor since early childhood, had the brains to win a place at Liverpool University, but on graduation had headed for the big city lights on the grounds Neptune Street was "too parochial" and she needed to "spread her wings." How she now regretted having not listened to Henry and Mildred when, on the platform at Lime Street as Sandra was boarding the train to London for her new job, they'd wished her well, but wondered if this was *really* the best move.

"Any time you change your mind, just give us a tinkle, and I'll come and pick you up, love," said Henry who earned his crust driving eighteen-wheeler trucks up and down the M6 and the M1, mainly at night.

He and Mildred stood and waved as the train pulled out. When it was out of sight down the tracks, Mildred had cried but Henry just shrugged, hugged her, and said, "Okay, so that's the last one gone. Now it's just you and me, Missus. C'mon, let's go home. At least we'll have the place to ourselves now. Tell you what...I'll make you a cup of tea when we get back. And then tomorrow we can start making plans for the attic like we said we would when Ronnie and Alfie tootled off to greener pastures."

The attic was where the two boys had slept and, as Sandra found on her return, was a little palace. Why, oh why, had she ever left? Surely she could now find a local job with sane doctors interested in community support. But still lingering in the back of her mind and in her dreams was that awful vision of Andy Crane getting his what for while she lay, near naked and helpless on Hank Orlando's shrink couch.

Sometimes, to empty her mind she would take the bus over to New Brighton and walk the sands for miles towards Hoylake, all the while staring out across the Irish Sea and listening to the birds cawing. But even then, the mind-emptying routine didn't always work because Andy's mashed face kept coming back to her.

"Poor bloke," she would think on those occasions. "All he wanted was to be nice to me and what did *I* do? Kept on making the hair-washing excuse, then laid myself out like a doormat at the bastard Orlando's feet."

It wasn't as if she could gain any relief from the guilt she'd started to feel by opening up to Henry and Mildred either. Nice people they were, always there to help their children and genuinely over the moon whenever they succeeded at anything. Henry was forever on the touchline cheering the lads on when they played soccer for local teams, and Milly had been a constant source of encouragement for Sandra's university aspirations, even though it would mean her rising above her working-class roots.

"Just image, lass, you'll be the first Normington *ever* to go to university," she'd said on the day Sandra received the A-level results that would secure her place to study medicine over the water in Liverpool. "*And* to be a doctor! We'll know who to come to when *we're* sick, won't we, Henry?"

Henry the lorry driver had taken his daughter in one of his "lung squeezers" and patted her so hard on the back she'd almost fainted, but it was a good kind of almost fainting despite the coughing bout it occasioned Henry to hold her upright. "No more ciggies for me or I'll get told off good and proper," the twenty-a-day man said, although that was one promise he hadn't kept.

Nice people then, but not the sort to discuss your romance life with, especially not when you'd practically asked to be screwed by some knobhead just because he looked like Robert Redford when younger. What the *hell* had she been thinking?

It was partly in search of some answer, *any* answer, to this question that Sandra got back in touch with her old school pal Lucy Lomax, who she hadn't seen for all the time she'd been down in The Smoke. Like Sandra, Lucy had been the first of her family to go to university—*Cam*bridge on a scholarship!—and now taught English literature at Liverpool University.

"*Sandie*, nice surprise! How're you doin' babe?" she said when Sandra called. Same old husky voice and same old Scouse accent, which not even Cambridge had apparently managed to shift.

"Okay-*ish*."

"Only ish?"

"Yeah."

"Where're you calling from anyway? Thought you were down in Shit City."

"I was, but I'm home now."

"But you got doctored, right?"

"I did. It's a long story. Look Luce, how'd you fancy a meet-up?"

"To talk over old times and like that?"

"And like that."

"Great, I'd love it. Name the place and time."

~ * ~

It was a Wednesday morning when Sandra took the ferry over to Liverpool's Pier Head, now dominated by The Beatles museum the way it had once been by transatlantic Cunard liners.

"Hey, girl!" Lucy hooted, running up to join the old friend who was staring about looking perplexed. "Look at *you*. You don't look *any* different."

"You neither," said Sandra, falling into Lucy's embrace.

"So what d'you fancy doing? Staying here for a coffee and a look around? Going uptown, what?"

Sandra decided on uptown. It was so long since she'd been there.

It was at the Walker Art Gallery's canteen after a quick squint at the Pre-Raphaelites that Sandra told Lucy her whole story, beginning at the beginning with her conversation with Andy Crane about Quentin Trimble's gardening leave and ending up with Andy getting beaten senseless by the arsehole Sandra had been daft enough to throw herself at.

"Holy shit," said Lucy when the story ended with Sandra dabbing at her leaky eyes. "Mind you, I told you to watch out for the creeps down there in London, didn't I?"

"Ay, so you did. But you know how it is. You've always got to find these things out for yourself, haven't you?"

"True enough. Cambridge taught me that, if not much else."

"I'll bet it did."

"Bit of a laughing stock I was at first, like all the dialect characters in the 'great canon of Eng. Lit.,'" said Lucy providing the inverted commas with two fingers. "Had my foot in my mouth practically whenever I opened it. But I got over it."

"How?"

"By turning the joke back on the chinless wonders who thought me so hilarious."

"By taking the piss?"

"Taking...the...*piss*, a concept unknown to the sons and daughters of the great and good, against which they had no defence."

Sandra nodded and smiled. "Same as at school, never one to kiss ass, our Lucy, eh? Still swatting off the blokes, are you?"

Lucy grinned. "Mainly. There've been a couple I strung along for a bit, but you know how it is with blokes, how *thick* most of them are at the same time as thinking they're the best thing since sliced bread."

"So no Mister Right for you."

"Not as yet, but listen our Sandie, that's quite enough about me. Tell me more about you and this Crane fella. Fancy him, do you?"

Sandra shrugged. "That's the thing. I didn't think I did till I got jumped by the Yank ape, then I don't know...I just sort of..."

"Did."

"Yeah."

"And it's not just pity for him after he got beaten up?"

"That's what I don't know, Luce. What I just...don't...*know*," said Sandra, wringing her hands. "After all, he got beaten up saving *me*."

"Like some romantic knight errant."

"That's what I can't decide."

"Well, there's only one way to find out for sure, isn't there?"

"Which is?"

"Get back there and find him. And listen, if you want someone to hold your hand, I'm up for it. There's a PhD student of mine just longing to take over my classes, and I could use a change of scene. Yeah, it's great around here, but things always look even better if you go away for a bit then come back."

Sandra's eyes widened. "You'd come with me to Shit City?"

"Could be a laugh, you never know. And don't worry…I won't be around if you meet up again with your Doc Crane. I'll keep well out of sight. But it might be good to have someone to report back to. And I s'pose I can doss at your place?"

"Sure, no problemo. It's not a palace, like, but…"

"Okay, so that's settled then. I'll book the tickets."

That was when Sandra leaned across the table and kissed her old friend.

"You're a star, Lucy Lomax," she said.

"Yeah, yeah, but enough of the kissing, right? People will say we're in love. *Lezzies* in love."

So it was that two days later, Sandra Normington and Lucy Lomax were sitting next to each other on a train heading for Euston. A few short weeks later, when the buffoon in 10 Downing Street finally accepted Covid-19 had landed on home turf and could kill people (including him), there would no longer *be* any trains to sit on, let alone ones on which folk could sit next to each other without face masks, but all Sandra and Lucy had been breathing in the last of those blind and blissful BC days were no more than draughts up the Mersey Tunnel.

Eleven

Given the prolonged silence between them after recent events, Quentin's phone call to his mother might have been expected to be a little fraught but in fact it turned out pretty well, as both struggled to distance themselves from the bad dream that had followed their last conversation by focusing on how they were both doing *now* rather than when they'd last spoken. What Quentin knew of Doc Frederick's *faux* murder charade, Doc Antoinette did not ask, and for his part Quentin made no reference to his mother's possible prior knowledge of the plan. Instead there was a tacit agreement to ignore the whole messy episode, draw lines underneath it, let water pass under bridges, and concentrate on a present marked for both of them by greater degrees of self-awareness.

It was in this context, after his mother had outlined the manner in which she was beginning to see some brighter horizons ahead, especially where Doc Frederick was concerned, and Quentin had fully approved them that he ascribed *his* altered view on the world largely to his relationship with a fairy. Which unsurprisingly resulted in Doc Antoinette's end of the line going dead for a bit. It wasn't as though she held any prejudices against homosexuality in general, far from it.

She was, in fact, very much in favour of gay rights. But that her own child should have...

"Mum? *Mum*? You still there?"

"Yes, yes," said Antoinette pulling herself together. "And I wish the two of you every happiness. Handsome chap is he? What's his name?"

"Fion."

"Pardon?"

"Fion. It's a pretty unusual name, even in the fairy world."

"*I've* certainly never heard it before, but then I have little direct experience of the gay community, so..."

Which was when Quentin twigged to the crossed wires and laughed.

"Fion isn't *gay*, Mum. Nor am I. He—or sometimes she—is a *proper* fairy, like the ones you used you tell me stories about when I was little, like the ones in my famous library. Remember that?"

Silence down the line while Antoinette wondered if her son had lost his mind as the result of the terrible experience his father had engineered and was now living a cloud cuckoo land fantasy existence, in which case she would need to seek professional help. Meanwhile she reckoned it best to play along.

"Yes, darling, of *course* I do. And what *lovely* little fellows they were."

"Mine's an elf," said Quentin. "There are all sorts you know, boggarts and goblins and suchlike, but Fion's an elf."

"Of course he is, darling. And I suppose he lives with his little friends in a grassy glade."

"Actually, yes. I've been there a couple of times. What fun they have with their singing and dancing and telling tall tales."

"I'm sure they *do*."

"And, a bit like me now, they're not afraid of anything."

"Gosh."

"So no more of the old hypochondriac worries *I* used to have, the ones that got me chucked out of the practice on gardening leave."

"Jolly good for you. I'm glad to hear it."

"Yes, it's all very refreshing. Bottle always at least half full and everything on the credit side of the balance sheet these days, even including the gardening leave, because that's how I first met Fion. He was living in my shed."

"A case of all's for the best in the best of all worlds, eh?" said Antoinette.

"Quite. Never mind the bad times, always look on the bright side of life," said Quentin with an assurance Antoinette had never heard from her son at any time in *his* life. If the boy had gone bonkers, at least it was making him happy. But what if was the result of some drug he was using?

"Darling?" she therefore said. "You're *quite* sure you're all right?"

"Never better."

"You're not on, you know, medicines of any kind?"

Which was when Quentin became a tad defensive, sensing his mother had only been humouring him on the fairy issue.

"You don't believe in my fairy, do you? Think it's just a fairy *story*, in other words a lie."

"Don't hang up on me, son. *Please* don't hang up on me... remember what happened the last time."

Quentin softened his tone. "How could I forget? But look, Mum, I tell you what. How about if I were to introduce you to Fion? Would that help? I'm sure he'd be only too pleased to meet you."

Relieved the hostility had vanished as quickly as it had arisen, Antoinette smiled, recalled her teenage love of literature, and paraphrasing Hamlet said, "There are more things in heaven and Earth than are dreamt of in *my* philosophy, eh?"

"Quite," said Quentin, who had no clear idea what she was talking about but liked the line, which as coincidence would have it, had been suggested to Willie Shakespeare by his old pal Fion the elf (see above). "Sooo, you want me to arrange a meet-up?"

"It would certainly be a novel experience."

"Can I take that for a yes?"

"You can indeed. Just give me a ring when it's convenient for the two of you."

"Great, fantastic, I'll get right on it," said Quentin ending the call with "love you."

It was the last two words that brought tears to Antoinette's eyes. Okay, she'd heard people in the street ending their mobile phone conversations that way, so maybe it was just a modern fad. But Quentin had sounded as though it came from the heart and, after the humiliation he'd been subjected to by Doc Frederick, the words meant the whole world to Doc Antoinette. Hope for the future there *had* to be.

~ * ~

It would be nice to tell a uniformly heartwarming story, but you know how it is with us humans, how we keep on digging holes for ourselves to jump into. And so it is with this tale, as sadly the encouraging developments in the lives of Quentin and Antoinette Trimble were not echoed in the case of Doc Andy Crane who, once discharged from hospital with his face sufficiently recovered, returned to Hank Orlando's office with a shotgun, coshed Sabrina over the head before she had a chance to karate chop him, locked her in a cupboard, then took revenge on his erstwhile abuser by peppering his testicles with tiny pellets.

"Take that, and that, and *that*, you bastard!" he screamed, continuing to squeeze the trigger as Robert Redford Jnr rolled himself into a wailing ball, thereby receiving a number of wounds to his bottom.

It was only when Andy was satisfied Hank wasn't dead by checking for a pulse and suchlike—he was a doctor after all—that he abandoned the Batman mask he'd been wearing for the occasion, hightailed it back onto the street, and jumped into the pre-booked taxi that would take him to Heathrow and thenceforth Sydney Eastern Australia, from where he hoped to find Wollongong and take refuge with his wayward father. Wollongong he found, albeit with some difficulty, but not the father, because he had decamped to Kalgoorlie *Western* Australia where he had yet another new "wife," although this story need not further concern us.

Of greater significance was the magnitude of the problem facing DI Derek Wilde and his Battersea cop team to whom the case had been assigned when it came to tracing the location of Andy, who they believed to have been the perpetrator of the outrage because he been identified as such in the testimonies of both the head-bandaged Sabrina and her now castrato-voiced boss, Hank Orlando. It was then an easy enough further assumption that Andy was the author of the super-encrypted tweets addressed to Miriam Proudfoot and Finian O'Toole with copies to Sandra Normington that followed some days after Andy vanished. "Watch out, next time it'll be *you*!" they said.

"Why *those* people?" Wilde asked Orlando and Sabrina at the hospital still mercifully free of Covid patients.

"Only guessing," squeaked Hank, "but O'Toole and Proudfoot were the guys who sent him to me for treatment. He must've figured that. And then Sandra dame found out too and the rest is history."

"Wanna know the way I read it," said Sabrina, who'd escaped from the cupboard and been the one to call the ambulance despite the part of her that wouldn't have minded all that much if her randy boss/lover had bled out and died. If Andy Crane hadn't shot him, she might have done the job herself—and better. But then there was history between her and Hank, so...

"Yes please," said Wilde.

"The reason Sandra is copied in may be to make Andy look like the hero paying back the bad guy who'd been gonna do the business with his lady love.

"Even if the 'lady love' looked a whole lot to me like the only reason *she*'d come around was to get the business done," Sabrina continued with a scowl at Hank, who was suddenly afflicted with a genitalia spasm and obliged to turn over out of her scowl line.

Sensing inter-partner discord of the kind he had no experience, Wilde kept his head down, jotted a random line of dots and dashes on his iPad, and said, "And you have no idea where he might have gone?"

"None," squeaked Hank. "Now, *if* you'd excuse me, I got some recovering to do?"

"Sure, no problemo, hope you get better soon," said Wilde, happy to leave Hank and Sabrina to work through their relationship issues.

Some days later, he asked the same questions of the two people on whom the hate tweets appeared to focus; the Normington woman he'd leave till later.

But O'Toole and Proudfoot were of no more help than Orlando and Sabrina, although Finian did confirm it was he who had insisted on Crane's treatment by Orlando while leaving the actual message delivery to Miriam. How Sandra Normington had found out, he had no idea. And as to where Doc Crane might have escaped to, neither of them had the faintest. Obviously enough. It wasn't as if Andy had gone around the surgery advertising the whereabouts of his philandering father, let alone it was to him he would run if ever he found himself in trouble. A big time dead end DI Wilde was facing, therefore, as well as tracing a rogue bot to its source was nobody's business, otherwise, the madman in the Kremlin would have been outed for his influence on the election of the madman in the White House years ago, wouldn't he? No, no, Wilde faced an uphill battle, that was for sure.

While he dillied and dallied, Miriam and Finian—understandably with a genitalia pepperer on the loose seeking their blood—quaked in their shoes, hid in their homes, and severed their Internet connections. Which worked well enough until the methodology changed, and they began receiving what they at first thought were the usual scam phone calls from bogus policepersons, bankers, and lawyers telling them they were in danger of losing their livelihoods unless they disclosed their credit card details. Only this time around, it wasn't their livelihoods they were about to lose, it was their *lives*. No wonder they needed a change of shoes into which to quake. No wonder, either, they should have lost much faith in the local police department. And when they called to register the shift in M.O., DI Wilde was forced to admit he had no idea *what* was going on.

"But you for sure recognized Crane's voice as the caller's?" he said in a last desperate attempt at *one* solid fact.

Which caused O'Toole to toss the question to Miriam, seeing as he had never met the bloke and it was she who'd been his boss.

Miriam folded her hands in her lap and frowned. "Good question, Mister Wilde."

"Detective In*spector*."

"Detective Inspector."

"And your answer?"

"Is no, I'm *not* sure."

Wilde sighed and fiddled with his left earlobe. "But it *was* a man's voice."

"Yes, but the accent wasn't, you know, *Brit*ish. It sounded, I don't know, more…I'm not terribly good at accents, Inspector."

"But if you were to make an educated guess? Was it American, for example?"

"No. I know American," said Miriam. "What would *you* say it was, Finian?"

"Australian," said O'Toole.

Which left DI Derek Wilde even further from a resolution to his various conundrums where Andy Crane was concerned. Talk about finding needles in haystacks. "Aust*ral*ian?" he said.

"Yes, I'm pretty certain of it," O'Toole the cricket fan confirmed. "Sounded a lot like an Ozzie to me. Mind you, he could have been a New Zealander."

That was when, none the wiser about anything regarding Andy Crane, Wilde thanked the pair for their time and wished them a safe journey home, particularly now the Chinese bug had apparently taken in interest in killing people outside China.

Not that it was going to help Wilde much, but O'Toole had been right about the Australian because the voice on the phone messages belonged to Art Scrivenger, who was one of the pals Andy had made in Wollongong. The other was Bazza Johnson, the pair of them having offered him accommodation until he got back on his feet again, and listened with sympathy to his sad story back in the UK. For which Andy was grateful. But what he couldn't have known was that Art and Bazza were computer and mobile phone freaks who made a decent, if illegal, living from bots and scam phone calls righting what they saw as wrongs. Neither was what you might think of as educated, but they knew all there was to know about the nefarious uses to which computers and smartphones could be put, having stolen a number of them, spent serious time learning how they worked, then—using the sobriquets Barry and Arthur Montgomery—selling their services to a wide array of technophobe customers who paid well for the Internet retribution they felt they deserved.

To their new pal Andy, however, they'd given a freebie.

~ * ~

In the grassy glade, Fion the elf and his best friend Bertie, shook their heads as they tuned into a replay of this whole bizarre series of events on the constantly updated ElfVision monitor that sourced information beyond the reach of any human device, including the current whereabouts of Doc Andy Crane.

Fion sighed. "When will they *ever* learn?"

"Maybe only when *all* their flowers have gone," Bertie replied.

"While we just sit and watch?"

"I guess not."

"So we tell Wilde where Crane is and let him put a stop to all this madness?"

"No, that would be giving away too much. As you well know, the less we elves are *seen* to be involved in human affairs, the more chance we have of success. No, this is a job for us, methinks, or most likely you."

Fion nodded and smiled. "As usual. I thought it might come to that."

"Well, better you than the Wilde chappie who looks to me little better equipped to trace Crane than an elephant would be to ice dance. *Now*, what say to a puff or two at a shared pipe?"

An offer Fion was unable to refuse.

Twelve

To the ears of most English speakers, Wollongong would sound a pretty weird name for a city, but not to Australians who are used to such weirdness. The name originates from the Aboriginal word "woolyungah" (five islands) where Aboriginals had lived for going on thirty thousand years. Not that those guys would recognize the place now with its fine architecture, university, Buddhist temple, wild life park, white-sand beaches and population of three hundred thousand (mainly white) inhabitants. So much for the benefits of colonization by the same masters of the universe whose disregard for the world's climate had contributed so significantly to the devastation recently caused all along the New South Wales coastline, including Wollongong, in the 2019/2020 bushfires. So many houses reduced to ashes and wild animals burnt to horrific deaths they could never have expected and didn't deserve.

Andy Crane survived all that, though, by temporarily moving out of town with his new pals in their Winnebago. Whenever the fires threatened to come closer, they just drove farther inland. And when the flames finally abated, they drove back to the Kemblawarra suburb where Art and Bazza shared their basement apartment with Andy after his several weeks of homelessness following the discovery from his father's ex-wife of Crane Snr's flight to Kalgoorlie.

"Sorry, Sport, but your dad's done a runner so can't help you there," Abegail Crane (now Knightley) had told Andy as she shooed behind her infants and children ranging from two to twelve, to any one of whom Andy might have been related.

So that was the end of the story on the father front, and Andy hadn't come equipped with much spare cash after the expense of the flight to Oz, hence the street sleeping from which he was rescued by Art and Bazza taking pity on him after a bibulous evening at a pub called the Parrot and Rabbit during which a tired and emotional Andy had vented his fury at having been so ill-treated back in Pomland *and* disclosed the names of those he blamed for having sent him to Hank Orlando for treatment in the first place.

"Nasty business," said Bazza. "I'd have shot the bastard in the goolies, too, no question about it. Bleeding Yanks."

"Me too," chorused Art. "And then cut them *off*. Mind you, I'd've given the shiela what for, too."

At the reference to Sandra Normington, Andy had calmed a little and shaken his head. "Probably not *really* her fault," he said. "It turned out she was only there to see how *I* was getting on. That was when he doped and jumped her."

Art nodded knowingly. "Had a thing going with her, did you?"

Andy shrugged. "Not really. I'd wanted to, only..."

"Same old story," said Bazza. "Been there myself."

It was such empathy that inspired Art and Bazza to hit their keyboards in vicarious revenge for the way their new pal had been treated, and produce the threatening bots and phone calls to Finian O'Toole and Miriam Proudfoot as the original causes of Andy's angst and—Sabrina had been right about this—copy in Sandra Normington to signal to her his noble reading of her role in the situation.

Often enough in those early days, Andy thanked them for the support they were affording him.

"Always glad to help out a Pom on the skids," Bazza would reply on these occasions.

"And you being a vet you can tell us what's wrong with us if we get sick," Art would add.

"Okay, great, thanks," Andy would say, thinking the reciprocal benefits Art and Bazza were talking about referred only to his recent homeless experiences in Wollongong and their offer of food and a bed. It wasn't until too late, when they proudly showed him one of their hate bots he discovered what *they* believed *him* to have been thanking them for, which was when he got furious and told them to stop it.

Such, sadly, is the nature of human discourse, misinterpretation only too often being the name of the game. As George Bernard Shaw put it: "The single biggest problem in communication is the illusion that it has taken place."

~ * ~

Watching these developments on another of their devices, the SEGPS (Super Elf Global Positioning System), which could not only locate the whereabouts of any human at any time but also provide further details of his current state of affairs, Fion and Bertie continued shaking their heads.

"Hard to see how the coppers are going to unpick *that* little can of worms, Bertie," said Fion, taking the FairyBac pipe that had just been passed him and puffing luxuriantly.

"Like I said, we could always *tell* them, Fifie."

"Yeah, but like *you* said, that would be passing the buck, wouldn't it? Not what we elves were made for, and I'm the guy whose job this probably is, and between them, the Brit and Ozzie coppers would be sure to make a pig's ear of it."

"Any other ideas?"

"Actually yes."

"Which are?"

"As we said, I go over there and sort it out."

"By?"

"Persuading young Crane it would be in his best interests to keep well away from *any* further association with Scrivenger's and Johnson's bot threats because they're only making his case worse. And to come back home."

"And if he refuses?"

Fion smiled. "Then I use some of our *other* techniques."

Bertie nodded. "Which would in my view be the more likely solution."

"Very probably. But be that as it may, I have a further proposal, just in case I need backup. How about I also take along a newly made young friend of mine who was a colleague of Crane's? Nothing like a familiar face to help matters along, eh?"

Bertie frowned. "A human?"

"Yes, but one who has suffered greatly and would benefit from the adventure. Who will, in any case, have been given a few extra skills by the time I've finished with him. Just by any remote chance things should turn nasty, you understand."

"A *him*?"

"Yes, my young protégé Doc Quentin Trimble, the one we helped out during those few days as a fairy. There's nothing would serve him better just now than a crusade to far fling climes. Okay, he's a little better after our help, but he's a case I'd really like to pursue and see finishing on a high."

Bertie nodded. "A noble aspiration, indeed."

"I hoped you'd see it that way," said Fion, passing back the pipe. "As you know, he's got his job back and indeed his patients seem to love him, but something tells me there's more than mere normality to the lad."

"A *new* normal?" said Bertie who, like Fion, was already experiencing subliminal visions of the human world in lockdown during the Covid-19 pandemic.

Fion nodded. "You could put it that way, but that's not yet their new reality. So until it is, how about a final adventure to make the boy stronger and better able to beat off the bug?"

Bertie toked at the pipe and smiled. "I'd like to be a fly on the wall when you tell him."

"Which you and I know well enough you *could* be, Bertie. Might be fun for you, too. It's been a long time since you've posed as an insect, as I recall."

"Indeed Fifie. Although you may remember my appearance as a wasp in the filmic version of *A Passage to India*, when I was the symbol of all living things and introduced Mrs Moore to Hinduism."

"Wow, I never knew that. Next you'll be telling me you were the dung beetle in Kafka's *Metamorphosis*."

"Well, now you mention it..."

"Okay, oo*kay*, enough with insects already," said Fion in his New York Bronx voice. "I'll be away to find our friend Quentin."

"Give him my best and keep in touch."

"Will do."

And with that, Fion was gone from the grassy glade, leaving Bertie to finish off the FairyBac and join a cluster of fairy folk to re-tell his long suppressed tale of twice having been a literary insect and once, as the result of a terrible acronymic mistake, a White Anglo-Saxon Protestant.

~ * ~

When she arrived back from Birkenhead at the little flat in Battersea with Lucy Lomax, Sandra Normington obviously enough knew nothing of Andy Crane having peppered Hank Orlando's genitalia or his subsequent disappearance without trace. How could she? It wasn't as if the story had hit any national, let alone Merseyside, media headlines given how many were increasingly being devoted to worries over the "Chinese bug." The last Sandra had seen of Andy, he was getting ten kinds of shit kicked out of him by the Robert Redford lookalike, about which she was beginning to feel something approaching guilt. After all, it was *she* who'd given Orlando the glad eye and *she* who Andy had bravely tried to protect from apparent rape, while all she had done was the cowardly runner back home to Mum and Dad about which she was now feeling far from proud. It was perhaps just as well she didn't know about the shotgun incident...otherwise, she might have felt even guiltier.

Given this state of ignorance, it was hardly surprising she hadn't the faintest idea either as to what the spooky "Watch out, next time it'll be *you*" text messages to Finian O'Toole and Miriam Proudfoot referred. Something pretty nasty, by the sound of it, some localized medical matter concerning her boss and her boss's boss, she assumed. Why *she* should have been copied in she had no idea. In any case, it was not something of immediate concern to her, simply an irritant. After the last of these messages, she just stowed the phone in her handbag and, with a much more pressing concerns on her mind, forgot all about them.

Of *far* greater importance was the regret she was starting to feel about the hair-washing excuse she'd used each time Andy asked her out. Perhaps if she'd accepted his advances in the first place, and gone for a coffee or to the pub or whatever, none of the awfulness would have happened. Andy might never have groped patients and been referred for psychiatric treatment, in which case, Sandra would have had no reason to visit Orlando on the excuse of asking how he was getting on and, who knew, she might even have grown to like or even love him. Although, on the other hand, if she *hadn't* gone to Orlando's, Andy would never have had the opportunity to show his bravery in trying to defend her and getting ten kinds of shit kicked out of him in the process.

Such is the perfidy of the conditional past tense, which leaves those who suffer from its usage at a complete loss to decide *any*thing reasonable about the relationship between the past and the present. Logically enough, seeing as whatever might/should/could or possibly *would* have happened as the result of a different set of circumstances is always already past and thus beyond resolution, leaving only irresolvable what ifs in its wake. What if Hitler hadn't been born, for example? Or what if he'd been so happy being a house painter he wouldn't have bothered about going on to become a dictator, exterminating millions of Jews, invading Poland, and causing WW2? In Sandra Normington's case, it was the "what if there had been no hair-washing excuse?" she'd battled with all the way on the train from Liverpool Lime Street to London Euston in a futile attempt to come to some, *any*, resolution to her feelings for Andy Crane. And which continued to plague her on the Tube to Battersea station, on the short walk with Lucy Lomax to her flat, *and* for several days thereafter.

Central to her perplexity, although she couldn't see it, was the question: Do I love Andy Crane or am I just fantasizing? Even beyond the hair-washing excuse, it was this conundrum that was driving her crazy and thus far good listener Lucy Lomax slowly even crazier. You know how it is when, with the best will in the world, you listen, and listen, and *listen* to a person trying to make up his or her mind on some tricky—normally emotional—subject and they keep on, and on, and *on* refusing to do so. How you go slightly batshit yourself in the process. No wonder rational shrinks just zone out and look at their computer screens and the clock while such mental meanderings are happening before them. After all, what use would there be in a batty shrink, although there are those who argue to be a shrink you *have* to be batty...but that's a different problem.

*Any*way, batty was pretty much how Lucy was feeling after being on the receiving end of Sandra's mental vicissitudes in the little flat with only occasional excursions for refreshments to the nearby Starbucks, where Sandra anyway continued her hapless blethering about the way forward. In Lucy's well-read book, by comparison, poor old "to be or not to be" Hamlet was the epitome of sanity. It was on the fifth of such 24/7s that Lucy could take it no more and resorted back to her Merseyside heritage.

"Look, for *fuck's* sake, Sandie, get a sodding *grip*, will you?" she told her old school friend, taking her by the shoulders and shaking her about. "Either you fucking love the bloke or you fucking don't. Make up your bleedin' mind or I'm on the next train back home." Which wasn't the subtlest of approaches, or one to be recommended to trainee mental health counsellors, or the good cop in the good cop/bad cop scenario—but it worked a treat on Sandra.

"No, no, don't go. Don't *leave* me, Luce," she wailed while being shaken about.

"On one condition, and one condition only."

"Wuh-wuh-which i-i-is?"

"That you phone the bloke and ask if he'd fancy a chat."

"Uh-uh-uh-*okay*."

"Promise? Girl scouts honour?" said Lucy, not leaving off the shaking even though her arms were starting to hurt.

"Kuh-kuh-cross muh-my huh-heart and huh-hope to duh-die."

"Okay then," said Lucy, releasing her grip with the result that Sandra collapsed on the lounge floor like a rag doll.

"Got his number, have you? Shout it out, and I'll dial," Lucy added, going for the no-time-like-the-present, strike-while-the-iron's-hot approach. But therein lay the problem. Sandra didn't have the number, never had.

"Nuh-nuh, no," she spluttered taking the hand Lucy offered in order to get her back on her feet.

"So who does?"

"Dunno. Puh-people at the suh-surgery I s'pose," said Sandra, clutching at a wall because her balance still wasn't good.

"You have *their* numbers?"

"Guh-give me a minute," said Sandra tottering to a desk by the window and yanking at a drawer that opened too far and spilled its contents over the floor. "Fuck," she added while Lucy sighed and lit a cigarette to calm her nerves. "In your own time," she said, exhaling exasperatedly.

"Ookay, here're the numbers," Sandra eventually said, staggering back to her feet and thrusting a tatty red-leather diary into Lucy's hands.

"For whom?"

"Luh-look under Tuh-T for Tuh-Trimble, Kuh-Quentin Trimble. Or Puh-P for Proudfoot, Muh-Miriam Proudfoot, she's the buh-boss," said Sandra before collapsing onto a couch.

Miriam's number didn't work, of course, because, in order to block calls from the various numbers employed by the Wollongong crew with their throwdown phones, she had programmed hers only to answer numbers from known and trusted acquaintances and friends. Even then, it was only after a specified number of rings calls were answered. And Lucy failed this test.

Quentin, however, answered on only the second ring. "Yes? Hello?" he said.

Which was how it came to pass, after announcing herself as a close friend of currently indisposed Sandra Normington, and outlining her concern for a colleague called Andy Crane, that Lucy Lomax learnt of Andy's brutal testicular attack on Hank Orlando and subsequent disappearance to heaven knew where.

"Blimey," said Lucy, turning to tell Sandra the story, but Sandra was already asleep and snoring and Lucy reckoned she was best left that way at least for the moment.

Thirteen

Understandably, after the delicate testicular, penile, and rectal surgery performed by a specialist team in New York City because he didn't trust Brit doctors with his "jewels," to say Hank Orlando was pretty pissed off would be an understatement, so let's go for the truth, shall we? Which was he was PFF (permanently fucking furious) and, as soon as he was able, took to leaping from his bed and stomping up and down his private room spitting vile oaths, all of them citing Andy Crane as enemy *numero uno*. Which worried his doctors and nurses in case he should tear out any of the clever little stitches holding together his nether regions beneath the incontinence pants.

"You gotta stop *doin'* that, Hank," lead surgeon Mike Zabludo told him when his patient had been wrestled back to his bed for the fifth time, and on this occasion strapped down. "You pay good money to get this done when you ain't even got insurance, then look what you do."

Hank shrugged huffily.

"You wanna lose your dick and balls along with your money?" Zabludo continued unfazed. "Not to mention your ass."

Hank looked surly and grunted.

"And who *is* this Crone dude you keep babbling about anyhow? I never did find out the backstory for you being with us."

"Crane, Andy fuckin' *Crane*," Hank spat. "The fucking fucker who fucking shot me."

Zabludo nodded sagely. "Right, I gotcha. And his reason for shooting you, like, *where* he shot you?"

"He was a client of mine."

Zabludo checked his American notes, which included an outline of Hank's career as a disgraced LA psychotherapist masquerading as Robert Redford Jnr.

"Who objected to his treatment and so shot you in the balls and ass? Wanna pull the other one, bozo?"

Which was when Hank attempted to punch Zabludo on the nose but couldn't because of the straps clamping his arms to the bed, so Mike continued checking his notes, this time the statement from Miss Playboy 2017 Sabrina who had recovered sufficiently from her concussion to accompany her boss/lover back to the US.

"Like you *weren't* about to ball the Crane guy's gal, her naked on the couch and you with pants around your knees when he comes into the room, goes apeshit, and comes back later to get his revenge? That I could kinda unnerstand."

"Bullshit, crap, fake fuckin' news," spluttered Hank, writhing under his restraints.

The neologism "fake news" had become very popular in America since being coined by the madman in the White House. Everyone was saying it as a defence against *any* insult or accusation, including pussy grabbing and worse.

"Not the way I read it," said Zabludo. "*Any*ways, none of my biz, that's for the Brit cops to work out. Meanwhile, you make one more attempt to git outta that bed and I ain't gonna take no responsibility for your ass, dick, or balls. I could charge you some more dollars for wasting my time."

Hank was still protesting his innocence at full volume and berating Brit cops for having no goddam idea where Andy Crane had escaped to so he would need to get pals of his stateside on board, when

Zabludo was closing the door behind him and, his nerves all a-jangle, going for a furtive cigarette break in the hospital car park.

~ * ~

Fion decided the most amusing way to contact Quentin Trimble would be to materialize into his lounge first thing in the morning. Despite this witty plan, however, the elvish voice calling, "Hello, hello-oo, anybody ho-oome?" was met first with an eerie silence and then, alarmingly, by Quentin storming in from the bedroom in his pyjamas wafting a hair dryer above his head like a weapon. Mind you, he lowered it quickly once he recognized his little friend.

"Oh, thank God, it's *you*," he said, not questioning Fion's modus operandi when it came from flitting from place to place and passing through brick walls, because he was familiar with that. "I thought it was the swine come back to murder me."

"No, no, it's just me. Happened to be passing, so I thought I'd drop in. You seem a little on edge, old chap. Swine come to murder you? What's all that about?"

"A dream, a terrible *dream*."

"And the swine come to murder you was?"

"Andy Crane."

Fion checked through his intuition indices. "You've been talking to Miriam Proudfoot, am I right?"

"Once. Before she started fiddling with her phone so's nobody could get through."

"And that was when she told you about the 'Watch out next time it'll be you' messages she thought were coming from Crane?"

'Yuh-yes."

Fion nodded. "A sad case indeed, but not one for you to worry about because clearly it won't be you on the receiving end. It's just your wrongly guilty matricidal subconscious playing up again. One dearly wishes you humans could finally understand your dreams. I did my best to advise poor old Sigmund, but would he listen? Fancy a squirt of the vermilion potion to calm the old nerves and return you to the equilibrium we'd been aiming for?"

"With pleasure, but you *do* know what's been going on, how Andy Crane escaped after shooting Orlando and started sending the death threats Proudfoot told me about."

"Sadly I do, old chap," said Fion, dispensing the soothing liquid. "Chin chin," he added when the tiny cup was safely in Quentin's still shaky hand and raising his in the toast.

Quentin downed the brew in one. "Ah, that's better," he said as it took immediate effect. "The tangled web a woman can cause, eh?"

Fion raised an eyebrow and cocked his old head to one side. "That would be Sandra Normington you're referring to?"

"Yes. I heard the story about how she went round to Orlando's, and Crane found her there, and…"

Fion reached out a hand and soothed Quentin with special elf cranium rub. "What goes around comes around," he said elliptically.

"I s'pose so, but women do seem to get under blokes' skins and cause all manner of trouble, don't they? Turn their heads, so to speak."

"And the same vice versa. Such is the tragic nature of human gender issues."

Quentin nodded. "From which, as you told me, you fairies don't suffer."

"Mercifully, no. How can we when we're both sexes at the same time and intercourse is merely a pleasant activity performed from time to time to propagate the species?"

"Not that I'm any kind of an expert on the subject. Me, a virgin at thirty-two."

"Just saving yourself for Miss Right," said Fion, refilling the vermilion potion cups. "As it should be."

"But how will I know she *is* Miss Right? What if she's Miss Wrong?"

"You'll know. Trust me."

"And then there's all that stuff that happens in, you know…bed. Taking your clothes off and kissing, and…then what?"

Fion laughed. "Don't worry, old son. I'll give you a few lessons when the time comes. At least, being a doctor and all, you'll know which bits are which and where they should go."

"Theoretically, but *any*way enough of that. I'm sure you didn't pop in to talk about my non-sex life."

"Actually no."

"So what…?"

"I thought you might be interested on an update on what happened to Andy Crane after his escape from shooting Hank Orlando."

Quentin frowned. "You *know* that?"

Fion shrugged. "We elves make it our business to know as much as we can, including the knowledge you humans know you can't know. It's just the way we are."

"So I'm learning. Anyway, please do tell, I'm all ears."

"Me too," said Fion, repeating his waggly ears dancing trick before going on to tell as requested.

"In Willygone?" said Quentin when Fion had given him the facts of the matter.

"Wollongong," Fion corrected. "As I said, it's in Australia."

"Ah-hah," said Quentin. "Wasn't big on geography at school. Knew Ozzieland existed, of course, but never sure where it *was*. Anyway, what's old Andy doing there?"

Which was when Fion explained the provenance of the algorithmically produced hate e-mails and phone calls currently being received by Miriam Proudfoot, Finian O'Toole and, as an apparent afterthought, Sandra Normington. Even Fion the elf wasn't entirely sure why she should have been included, although, like Sabrina, he had his suspicions.

"But Andy can barely *use* a computer, so how…?"

"Through new friends he has made out there, friends we will need to challenge and defeat to free him from their influence and bring him back to the UK for further questioning. Their names are Art Scrivenger and Bazza Johnson, for what it matters," said Fion. "Which brings me to the real purpose of my visit today."

Quentin Trimble was to require a further three re-fills of the vermilion tincture cup after hearing what Fion's real purpose was.

"Muh-*me*?" he managed to splutter when the explanation was over.

"You'll need a little training in certain unusual arts before we teleport ourselves over there," said Fion. "But in answer to your question, yes *you*. It seems to both me and my pal Bertie it would do you the world of good, a bit of a challenge to bolster the self-confidence and so on. What d'you say?"

Rolling his eyes, clasping his temples, and almost falling off his chair, pro tem Quentin wasn't able to say anything.

~ * ~

Where astonishment and nervous anxiety were concerned, Doc Antoinette wasn't *quite* as discombobulated as her son, but she hadn't just been told by an elf she was about to be whisked off to Australia on a major crime mission. Nonetheless, she was coming to the end of her rope with the husband she was attempting 24/7 to re-focus in matters of gender equality. So poor were her concentration levels these days, she had even been obliged, for the first time ever to take compassionate leave from ensuring babies were safely delivered into the world and begun to wonder, especially since news of some deadly disease called coronavirus had begun to filter westward, if they might not be better off staying in the womb. *That* was how close to the end of her tether dedicated gynaecologist Doc Antoinette was coming as she sat in the lounge of her grand home watching Doc Frederick marching up and down gurning at her.

"Why don't you sit down and stop pulling those stupid faces at me, Freddie?" she said. "And go off and play golf or bowls or something."

"Grrrrrr," said Doc Frederick, which was a difficult trick to pull while sticking his tongue in his left cheek, wrinkling his nose, *and* scratching both armpits like a baboon.

"Oh for God's *sake*, grow up, will you? You're behaving like a spoilt child."

"Grrrrrrr."

"And speaking of children, you'll be interested to hear our son Quentin is doing rather better these days."

"Harlot," spat Doc Frederick, ignoring the Quentin information. "Vixen," he added.

"Obviously you're not interested…more's the pity," said Antoinette as Doc Frederick took to jamming his thumbs against his temples, waggling all his fingers, and poking his tongue out. "You don't even know what day it is, do you?"

Doc Frederick wrinkled his brow. "*Vendredi,*" he eventually exclaimed proudly, employing one of the seven words he knew in French. The other six were *lundi, mardi, mercredi, jeudi, samedi,* and *dimanche.* How relieved he had been when Brexit was confirmed, and the UK finally dropped out of the EU, thus rendering the idea of knowing foreign languages obsolete and redundant.

"Sorry darling *mais c'est jeudi,*" said his wife, whose mastery of French—and German—amounted to practical fluency.

"Bah, boof, baloney and boppycocks," said Doc Frederick, falling to his knees, frowning at the carpet and sticking index fingers in both ears.

It was around then that Doc Antoinette was finally obliged to admit her husband had become a full-on basket case. Until recently, she had nurtured the belief he might be on his way to becoming the new man she'd hoped for after his meek agreement to participate in domestic lessons including egg shelling, lowering the toilet lid after peeing, operating the oven and dishwasher, making tea…and so on and so forth. All this in exchange for her promise she would be happy for him to stay in the house and, so long as he behaved himself, she wouldn't move out. But that was yesterday's news. Evidently, today's was a different matter. Possibly some sort of brain seizure overnight when Doc Antoinette wouldn't have known *what* was going on, given the bedroom distance between the two of them.

"Oh, for God's *sake,* Freddie," she therefore said. "Just when you were doing so *well.*"

In response, Doc Frederick sprang to his feet, dropped his trousers, and stuck his finger up his bottom much in the manner of Bertie's advice to Fion when he'd been looking glum only without the humorous Willie Rushton aspect.

Clearly, this wasn't the *most* opportune moment for Doc Antoinette's phone to start demanding her attention, but that's what it did.

"Quentin, *Quentin* darling, how *are* you?" she said in the calmest voice available to her as Doc Frederick removed the finger from his bottom and instead used it to fiddle interestedly with his willy.

These were difficult times for Doc Antoinette, difficult indeed.

Fourteen

The fledgling relationship between Doc Miriam Proudfoot and Prof Finian O'Toole is the one heart-warming feature in the story so far. By comparison with the difficult times being experienced by Doc Antoinette (crazy husband), Sandra Normington (infatuation/guilt issues), Quentin Trimble (new role as teleportation crime traveller), Hank Orlando (sore balls and vindictive ambitions), and DI Derek Wilde (job under threat unless he found Andy Crane), and despite the threats from Wollongong to shoot them, Miriam and Finian were, if not happy, at least coping. Which in the circs was pretty good going.

As mentioned (see above), neither Miriam nor Finian had friends or family upon whom they could rely for sympathy or support in the face of Andy's continuing telephonic threats to shoot them, but at least they were to have each other. Not that this discovery came easily to a lifelong spinster and a similarly placed bachelor both hovering just above or just below the age of 47.2 years when, according to research by some sociologist or another, humans are at their most pressurized and thus at their least cheerful. For some time during the early days of the "Crane Crisis" therefore, as advised by DI Wilde, they remained bunkered in and wary in an uncanny way preparing themselves for the advent of Covid-19 when the neologism "self-isolation" would become common parlance across a terrified world.

It was Finian who took the initiative to investigate the other person of interest on Andy's hit list to see how *she* was getting along. Sandra Normington he ignored because she was merely copied into the threats like some kind of casual observer. So that left Miriam Proudfoot, not that he expected much of a response from the surgery head honcho whose authority he had overridden when demanding Crane be checked out by Orlando and thereby effectively becoming the instigator of the troubles that followed. She would probably not be the person *most* prepared to offer him a cup of tea and a fireside chat, therefore but, bored to within an inch of his life with hiding in his house, Finian screwed up his courage and gave it a go anyway.

"What the hell?" he muttered, picking up the phone.

Mind you, he thanked the luck of the Irish when Miriam responded with, "How nice to hear from you, Professor O'Toole. A cuppa and a chat would indeed be lovely. I've been somewhat lonely after recent events. Home alone and so on."

"Me too, Doctor Proudfoot. Sequestered in one's own house just because of some probably phony threats."

Being from Dublin, Finian pronounced 'threats' as 'tretts', which produced the first smile on Miriam Proudfoot's face for weeks. Finian couldn't have known it, but Miriam's grandfather had been a horse breeder in County Kerry.

"So," he continued. "Would you care to come over to mine? I do a decent tea. Otherwise, I could come to yours."

"You to mine, Professor O'Toole. These days I'm a tad nervous of the streets all alone. You know, just in case there's some lunatic out there with a gun."

"Understandable, my dear. And by the way, it's Finian."

"And I am Miriam."

Which was the significant first step towards the shucking off of formalities, and Finian took advantage. "No fan of the streets myself," he said. "But for the sake of our meet-up, I'll brave them."

Which Miriam found romantic—heroic almost. "I'll give you the address then."

"That would be helpful...otherwise I wouldn't know where to go," said Finian, which was the line that transmuted Miriam's smile into the chuckle that paved the way to the very special cup of tea that led to the meeting of minds, and eventually bodies, which would lead much further down the line to the exchange of rings and taking of vows.

Not that the process was initially as straightforward as it sounds, for neither Finian nor Miriam was exactly a spring chicken, but on the other hand, it was precisely this maturity that played to their advantage because there was no expectation of glamour or sex on either side, merely the hope of a little friendship. Yes, Miriam liked the way Finian wore his greying hair at shoulder length and Finian appreciated the trim physique Miriam had maintained through many years of quasi-religious attendance at the local yoga parlour, but physicality was pretty much the furthest thing from their minds. Of much greater importance was the content of those minds. Beguiling indeed it was for each of them to agree with the other on the non-existence of gods of any flavour, the tragic mendacity of the Brexit process, and the desirability of shooting the noxious madmen in the White House and Downing Street then, like Mussolini, hanging their bodies by their feet for public ridicule. It was all very refreshing.

But perhaps the clincher was their shared love of Irish literature, particularly James Joyce, Flann O'Brien, and W.B.Yeats. In the early days of their blossoming relationship, Miriam couldn't get enough of Finian's readings from their works in his roguish Dublin accent. She particularly liked the way he did Molly Bloom's soliloquy in *Ulysses* and mimicked the half-man, half-bicycle character in *The Third Policeman*, but most of all, she liked his version of *The Lake Isle of Innisfree*, the one he'd set to music and sang to the accompaniment of a beaten up old Gibson guitar. That she could hear over and over again, particularly the last bit when Yeats hears the lake waters lapping in "the deep heart's core," after which Finian would do a couple of twiddly bits up and down the neck with his D-chord. Like the poet, how she too longed to get away from the evils of the city and have her own little cabin with "nine bean rows" and "a hive for the honey bee," where she could have some peace, for peace in recent days was dropping so slow as to have gone into reverse and become its precise opposite. Pie in the sky at this stage in her life, obviously, but a girl could always dream. And dream Miriam did every time Finian had gone back home—mainly of him, as he did of her.

It was all very moving and makes a nice contrast with the various travails (see above) facing Sandra Normington, Doc Antoinette Trimble, her son Quentin, and Hank Orlando *And* of course, DI Wilde and his police pals who, despite intense pressure from Chief Superintendent Imogen "The Bitch" Isaacs at Scotland Yard to make progress with the Crane case, had so far made none at all and were worrying about the sorts of pensions they'd be able to draw when The Bitch sacked them. To these folk, life was looking pretty "nasty, brutish, and short," as Thomas Hobbes had it. Yet it is to them—and, of course Andy Crane and his nefarious pals Art Scrivenger and Bazza Johnson—that, with a heavy heart after this brief interlude of uplifting human behaviour, we shall now be obliged to return, otherwise our story would become a flimsy romance fantasy devoid of reliably factual reportage, and heaven knows there's enough fake news out there these days.

Let's begin with Hank Orlando, shall we? Okay, he's a random choice, but we have to start *some*where.

~ * ~

Hank was sore in both the British and American meanings of that word. Sore because, despite release from hospital, his genitals and bottom were still hurting, and sore because he was still furious with Andy Crane. Up and down the rented two-roomed Bronx apartment he stalked, swearing revenge of the nastiest kind on the sumbitch who'd shot him. Not that he was in any fit condition to achieve this goal unaided. For crissakes, he couldn't even stalk up and down a room for more than a few minutes before needing to sit down, which hurt like hell, so he had to get up again and do some more stalking. No, no, as he'd promised Mike Zabludo, even when he'd already left the room for a sneaky cigarette, it was to his pals stateside he would need to turn for help. These were Brooklyn mob bosses Luca and Alberto Gambonio, who Hank reckoned owed him a favour for not having shopped them to the police over an infraction he'd witnessed in Times Square where two Thai tourists had been shot dead having been mistaken for members of the Vaccaro crime family in a turf war. At least that's how Hank remembered it. Equally possible as an exlanation was him owing the Gambonios a favour for not having murdered *him* for screwing the insane niece of one of their lesser members in his Robert Redford Jnr shrink days in LA. Either which way, it had been a long time since he'd been in touch, so maybe like him they'd forgotten the precise circumstances of the favour allocation. So Hank dialled the number and, after some minutes of silence while he figured his ID was being checked, got through to Luca.

"Yeah, dude, what you doin' back in town?" said the Mafioso. "Thought you was still out there in Britland doin' your Redford's kid brother number."

"Son, Redford's *son*," Hank corrected, but that cut no ice with Luca Gambonio.

"Kid brother, son, what's the difference?"

Hank didn't see a whole lot of point in explaining the genetics of the situation and instead said, "Yeah, yeah. Anyways, that's over."

"Uh-huh," said Luca, who was short on time because of a billion-dollar bullion truck heist on the Brooklyn Bridge scheduled for the next half hour. "So what's ya beef? And make it fast."

Hank explained his situation as expeditiously as he could and, hating Brits almost as much as Art Scrivenger and Bazza Johnson hated Yanks, Luca sympathized.

"Some asshole this Andy Crane, huh?" he said. "And the dame sure as shit weren't no lady. Naked on your couch, you tell me."

"Near as, and all set to rock 'n' roll."

"Until the asshole turns up wid the shotgun."

"That was a later part of the story, but you get the picture."

"And now you ain't got no dick or balls?"

Hank had over-egged that part of his current situation in the hope of a little extra leverage, hence the castrato tones he'd employed for the call, even though his normal voice was returning to something resembling masculine.

"Not a man anymore. And all because of the Brit asshole with the shotgun," he squeaked emotively.

"*Mi dispiace*," said Luca. Like he meant it.

"Okay," said Hank, who didn't speak any other languages apart from American and was going only on the apparent sympathy in Luca's voice.

"Sooo, just gimme the dude's name and address, and I'll get a guy to hunt him down and shoot *his* dick and balls off. I got guys in London. How'd that be?"

"Terrific, fantastic, thanks so much. Only there's my problem, he ain't *in* London. He escaped, and I don't know where the *fuck* to. He could be *any* fucking place."

"Oookay, no problemo."

"Wowee. No prob*lemo*, huh?"

"Like I said. We got the ways an' means in the organisation, *capice*? We're, like, innernational?"

Hank was relieved, assuming the famous Gambonios had Mafia connections around the world they could plug into whenever they wanted someone found. Which had once been true, but these days had been somewhat curtailed. In any case, as Luca made clear, a search would need more than just a name, because names could be changed. It would also require a detailed history of past crimes, favourite haunts, aliases, a photograph...and so on.

On receipt of this information, Hank was less relieved. "Which...I... ain't...*got*," he said.

"Okay, oo*kay*, don't get your boxers in a knot," said Luca.

Which wasn't the most apposite choice of ripostes, given Hank's problems in the nether regions, but Luca ignored the whines down the line and went on to explain how he and Alberto had access to a very special agency able to operate beyond all normal requirements and whom he would be happy to contact on this case.

"And thuh-they are?"

That was when Luca explained the fruitful relationship going back centuries the Sicilian Mafia had enjoyed with boggarts.

"Bog...? said Hank.

"Arts. They're like fairies, only not the funny little white hats like the ones in Disney. Always getting the *bad* press, my guys. Dontcha just love it?"

"Holy shit. And they would help me out here?"

"I only gotta ask. The couple I got in mind owe me big time. They go by Grimble and Grumble Boggart and they got systems can find guys anyplace in the universe and, for only a small extra fee, eliminate them. All I gotta do is call. You want I should?"

"Go for it," said Hank. "Only let's be clear. *I'm* the guy gonna be doing the eliminating. All I need to know is where the cocksucker *is*."

"Understood and noted. Just gimme a minute while I check my other line," said Luca, booting up his BOTD (Boggart Only Transmission Device) and punching in the ever-changing, super-encrypted digits.

"Wowee," repeated a newly energized Hank.

It was Grumble who answered the call as if he were the most pissed off boggart in the whole of Boggartville. Which he *was* and was *why* he was called Grumble.

"What d'you want?" he said grumpily.

Luca gave a brief résumé of the circumstances of Hank Orlando's painful testicular situation and added Andy Crane's name as its perp.

"What we need is to know where the guy *is*."

"All right then. Only don't hurry me, right?" said grouchy Grumble. "You think I ain't got other stuff to do?"

"In your own time," said Luca, while Hank held the line and took to pacing about painfully.

But then within femtoseconds, back came the answer.

"Wollongong," said Grumble moodily.

"You wanna say that again?" said Luca.

"Woll...on...*gong*. Australia, for fuck's sake. You don't spikka da English? I also got an address, you want that, too?" said Grumble.

"Gimme," said Luca scribbling sinistrally on the inside flap of a pack of red Marlboros.

"You want the scumbag rubbed out no extra charge?"

"Mebbe, mebbe not. I'll get back to you. And thanks."

"You're welcome," said Grumble, sounding about as welcoming as Charon the Styx ferryman.

Which was when Luca got Hank back on the other line.

"Ookay, we got him."

"You *do*?"

"Like I said, bozo."

"Where the fuck *is* he?"

"Wollongong."

"*What*?"

"Wollongong, Australia. You don't spikka da English? So now you got the info you wanted. Only question is you want him rubbed out or dontcha? It's a service I can offer free of charge."

"No way, José. Like I said, that's *my* job, and I'm looking forward to it. You have an address in this Willygong dump?"

"Like I said," said Luca, picking up the pack of red Marlboros and giving Hank the Kemblawarra suburb house number. "Our bidness done now, is it?" he added. "I am kinda busy. I got this heist I gotta see to."

"Done. What I owe you?"

"Zilch, nada. You just called in a favour, right?"

"Right," Hank agreed, *very* happy he'd remembered the favour deal the right way around. "Soo, Wallybang here I come. Watch out asshole, I'm on your tail."

Much of the unpleasantness that ensued as the result of this conversation could have been avoided had Fion been aware of it and able to tap in, but given the eon-long fire wall between news of upcoming elf and boggart activities for good on the one hand, and ill on the other, he couldn't. Even magic has its limits.

Fifteen

On the evening of her brief telephone conversation with Quentin Trimble, Lucy Lomax had left Sandra Normington asleep and snoring on the couch and headed off to her own bed. It wasn't until the following morning that a bleary eyed Sandra was given the news of her potential inamorato's dastardly crime followed by his disappearance to heaven knew where.

"Omi*god*," she said unsurprisingly. "Yuh-you muh-mean?"

Lucy shrugged. "That's the way I heard it."

"From?"

"Quentin Trimble."

"The hypochondriac."

"I wouldn't know about that, love, but he seems to know about those tweets you got copied to you."

"The 'watch out next time it'll be you' ones to Proudfoot and O'Toole?"

Sandra had wondered about those, but they had caused her less mental aggravation than the visceral machinations of her on/off besottedness with Andy Crane.

"Yeah. And, you're not going to like this, babe, but what he reckoned was they came from..."

"No-oooooooo."

"Yeah, 'fraid so. Got his fingerprints all over them. Takes his revenge on the one bloke he can get his hands on, does a runner, then spends his saddo time threatening the ones he reckons were to blame for the mess he's in."

"Including muh-*me*?"

"You were all part of the same surgery, right? And you must have found out somehow who his shrink was, or you wouldn't have gone sucking up to Orlando."

Sandra held her head in her hands and joogled it about.

"And from what you tell me, you were playing hard to get with Crane. The old hair washing line ring any bells?"

"It's just thu-that back thu-then I didn't nuh-*know*...oh *fuck*, Luce."

"Yeah, it's a tangled web all right. *Any*way," said Lucy Lomax the Scouse realist. "It's something you've got to face up to. My advice..."

"Yuh-yeah?"

"Is the bloke's a psycho, and you're well rid of him."

Sandra took a deep breath as she struggled to compute this new and grisly twist in her love life, but then, as Lucy hoped she would, gritted her teeth, and even forced a smile.

"Paul Simon was probably right, there *must* be fifty ways to leave your lover," she said.

Lucy laughed. "Atta girl."

"Only this has to be the weirdest, 'specially as I'm not even sure I *do* love him."

"Which makes it the easiest, our Sandie. No slipping off and hiding away somewhere. Job's already done for you, by *him*."

"And nobody knows where he is?"

"Not according to the Trimble bloke."

"Not even the police."

"Especially not the police. All sucking their thumbs and wondering, they are."

"Pretty mysterious. So the chances of catching him..."

"Are zero going on minus *n*."

Sandra shook her head unreadably to hide the arcane pleasure she was taking in this outcome. After all, she'd been a fool to get near naked for Orlando and, in some ironic practically heroic way, poetic justice had been seen to be done by Andy shooting him in the goolies, almost as if he were her avenging angel. So good luck to him, wherever he was, *not* that this was a thought she intended sharing with Lucy or anybody else.

"Dear, dear," she said instead. "And how did the patient frightener seem, by the way?"

"Patient frightener?"

"Quentin Trimble, the hypochondriac who was sent on gardening leave for frightening patients with false death diagnoses. I've not heard anything of him since then."

"Oh *him*," said Lucy. "Quite chirpy."

"Wonder why?"

"I don't know, he didn't say. D'you want to give him a call, see how he's getting on? We could always invite him over for a chat, if you felt like it. A problem shared is a problem halved and all that."

Sandra shrugged. "I s'pose. Couldn't do any harm, eh? You still got the number?"

Lucy pulled out her phone and checked. "Yup, here it is."

"Okay, you dial, I'll speak."

~ * ~

Quentin hadn't known *what* to expect from the training in "certain unusual arts" Fion had promised before the trip to Wollongong could be undertaken. Initially, he had thought maybe *martial* arts, a little taekwondo, kickboxing and karate, all that type of thing. Training for the mind and body with possibly a dash of ordinary military stuff like sit-ups, squats, rope climbing, six-mile marches carrying lead weights and so on. But on the very first day in the grassy glade, he was quickly disabused of such fantasies.

"So what *are* we going to do?" he asked Fion.

"Not play silly Pokémon games, that's for sure," said the elf.

"*What* games?"

"Video nonsense of the kind you humans have swallowed like kids with candy."

Never having played a video game of any kind, Quentin remained at a loss.

"Silly nonsense made up by idiots telling fairy stories," Fion continued.

"So what *am* I going to learn?"

"Powers specifically appropriate to the situation I suspect we might meet in Wollongong. As I read it, the Scrivenger and Johnson creatures are street-fighting morons, and Crane can't fight at all, so if we play our cards the way I'm about to suggest, it should be an easy peasy quick in and out."

"Oh," said Quentin, who as well as never having played a video game had never been involved in a fight of any kind or "accidentally" broken anyone's nose playing rugby, because he'd never played that game or any other contact sport. To him a street-fighting moron sounded pretty bloody frightening. What kind of a moron was it who fought streets? "So you'll lead the way while I..."

"No, Quentin, *you* will be the leader."

"*Me?*"

"Yes. Anyhow, enough of this chit-chat, let us get down to business, shall we?"

And so it was that, after a little psychic and medicinal meddling by Fion, Quentin Trimble became the first man on Earth to learn how to vanish one second, and the next to re-materialize behind his enemy as a woman armed with a frying pan destined for his opponent's head. All it needed was the magic word "xeroflud," then its sudden reversal to "dulforex," and bingo, job done and bemused enemy out cold. And, surprisingly, Quentin took to it like a duck to a mill pond, also testing out experimental versions suggested by Fion such as first shrinking to a two-foot three fairy type of man—Quentin's true height was five-foot ten—before the vanishing then reappearing as a six-foot woman with bloody teeth just in case his antagonist were to sense someone behind him, turn to look, and freeze in fear before being walloped with the frying pan.

"This is such *fun*," he chuckled as Fion watched on and clapped at his pupil's progress. "And I'm the first human you ever taught it to?"

Fion cocked his old head over a shoulder and semi-shrugged. "I guess I must have taught others, but you know how it is with the past, how we elves must've lived it but don't remember much about it."

Quentin nodded. "I've never read of any such thing, though. Never mind fiction, I might have missed it there, anyway. But you would have expected some reference in a proper history book."

Fion finished off the semi-shrug with another semi, making it a fully fledged shrug. "History mystery," he said. "You don't still believe your human histories are *true*, do you? But this is no time for *that* debate. This is a time for celebration and demonstration. Walk with me, Quentin Trimble."

And so it was that from all corners of the grassy glade there emerged grinning elves, pixies and various other good fairy types who'd been watching on as Quentin performed, and were keen to offer their congratulations by:

a) Jumping on him and kissing him a lot,

And,

b) Suggesting a party with whooping, cavorting, and general jolliness.

Quentin was overwhelmed by their enthusiasm and, testing out "exeroflud" for the purposes of size shrinkage only, reduced himself to a two-foot three person the better to conform to average fairy proportions and swap hugs with his new friends on their own level. Thereafter, it was a night that would go down in fairy lore as one of the most riotously successful ever, not that any of them would remember it the following sun-up.

If you're wondering how fairy lore ever got passed down at *all* seeing as fairies don't have memories, the answer is Oberon(a), who was *not* some god figure like the myriads of human ones down the millennia but merely a freak of fairyhood with peculiar powers. If they referred to him/her at all—which they rarely did—s/he was simply "The Mysterious Chronicler." Had they bothered to invent printing, his/her chronicles might have been actually *written*, widely distributed, and read the way humans cherished Bibles, but they didn't. Instead Oberon(a)'s reports of incidents of heroic fairy glory remained solely in the oral tradition, and were thus appropriately embellished with each telling, although those availing themselves of new media such as Elfie/Skype/Zoom were getting little glimpsed visuals to enhance previously only imagined aspects of the past.

*Any*way, just let's say everybody had a good time and, when it was over, Quentin Trimble was feeling a yet more confident person than ever. First, the positive thinking lessons Fion had inspired in him, now the belief in the powers of his body. No wonder patients at the surgery always asked for Doc Trimble when they made their next appointment. Preferable indeed he was to sixty-four-year-old Doc Patrick Sewell, whom many suspected of early onset Alzheimer's, and the newly qualified part-timer Milly McDougal, who could barely tell one end of a syringe from the other. No, no, Doc Trimble was their man, all right. Above all, it was the holistic approach he took to their various ailments that impressed them, the way they managed to leave the surgery feeling better, even though they hadn't been prescribed a single pill, let alone ordered a biopsy. Some sort of magic power he must have, they surmised. And so it was that Quentin's reputation grew and grew. By the time coronavirus hit and the surgery began operating only through telephone or on-line consultations and locums working from home had to be dragooned in to help, it was *still* Doc Trimble with whom folk craved audience, even though by then Doc Sandra Normington would be back on duty.

Sixteen

In Wollongong, Andy Crane was getting restless. Okay, Art Scrivenger and Bazza Johnson were fun guys to be around, but there was still something missing—his father. After all, the bloke was in the same bloody country, albeit two thousand five hundred miles away, so why not go looking for him? Maybe if he found Angus—that was his dad's first name—he would finally get an explanation as to why he'd run away from not only Andy's mum, but so many other wives in so many other places, leaving so many other children in his wake. Maybe he'd even *remember* Andy and tell him the reasons for the things he done. He put this idea to Art, who rubbished it.

"Nah, mate, wasting your time. The bloke's a wrong un, from what you tell me. And I speak as someone who knows. My dad left me in a basket on the road for the roos to look after when I was a babe."

"Shit. And your mother?"

Art shrugged. "No bleedin' idea. She'd just left the old man holding the baby, I guess. But I got rescued, as you can see."

"Who by?"

"Aunt Mimi, bleedin' angel *she* was. But she was old and couldn't cope, so after that I got fostered and moved around all over the place.

Old man never knew or never cared or both. And, if he had come around, I'd've shot him. Which is what I reckon your dad deserves *if* you could find him in Kal-fuckin'-goorlie. Got his address, have you?"

"No."

"Phone number?"

"Also no. I checked on the computer for Cranes but there weren't any."

"Surprise, surprise. Probably changed his name, or he's using a new cheapo throwdown every day."

Andy nodded. Art probably was right.

"And Kalgoorlie is like a billion miles from here, and you've got no money for planes or trains, so…"

"True enough."

"And even if you *did* find him, what then? He says sorry, weeps on your shoulder, and everyone lives happily ever after?"

Andy recognized this was a pretty unlikely scenario. "I could shoot him, though, like you'd have shot your dad."

"And get even more cops on your tail? Must be plenty of those looking for you back in Pomland. You want them to join forces with our boys? C'mon fella, get real. You've already shot one bloke…that should do you for the moment."

Andy nodded. Art was probably right again. "But what am I going to do *here*? Can't hang around Wallongong all my life?"

"Why not? Everyone's got to be *some*where. Maybe you'll get yourself an Ozzie doc licence and start over."

"Maybe," said Andy dubiously.

"Only, don't tell me, you still fancy the sheila back home, right? The one who was set to screw the Americano shrink whose knackers you nobbled."

Andy rubbed at his stubbly chin and half nodded. "Maybe it wasn't her fault. Maybe as well as the dope, the bastard made her some offer she couldn't refuse. Maybe when this is all over, she'll thank me for saving her, I dunno. Sometimes, I think I don't know anything anymore. It's like I've been taken over by circumstances, like they're in control, and I'm just their puppet."

"Jesus wept," said Art, extending the thumb and pinkie of his left hand and waggling them about over his right shoulder. "It wasn't *circ*umstances that screwed you over, pal, it was a *wo*man, and if you want to keep your balls out of a vise, you'll for*get* her. Wipe the slate clean and start over. No woman, no cry, right? Old Bob Marley was spot on with that one. You might not have noticed, but me and Bazza have kept well away from any long-term trouble of that kind. Both of us still have our moments with the ladies when the old hormones get twitchy, right? But that's about the size of it. No marriage vows, no Women's Lib, no PMT, no ankle biters following us around, freedom from all of that to get on with our lives, which is my advice to you. Now *if* you'll excuse me, I got work to do."

"Work?"

"You know, the stuff that makes the cash to stay alive? Tidy new contract just come in from some Sydney politico who needs a coupla rivals smeared with sex predator allegations. Should be a whole lot of fun."

And with that he was gone, leaving Andy Crane to chew over his personal relationships and come to no conclusion about either of them.

~ * ~

Where getting shot was concerned, Hank Orlando was on a run of bad luck. This time the culprit was Miss Playboy 2017 Sabrina (real name Marjory) Mackey, his secretary, occasional lover, and most recently, in his tiny rented Bronx apartment, live-in nurse. But then, in a sudden rush of accumulated righteous pique, she just couldn't stand it anymore and shot Hank through his left Achilles tendon.

"Stand *what* anymore?" I hear you ask.

Orlando's retrospective philandering, that was what, specifically the dalliance with a near naked Sandra Normington on his psych couch which Sabrina had been secretly observing only moments before Andy Crane came storming into the office and got the shit beaten out of him. Had Andy arrived only moments later, Sabrina would have done the job herself. And not with some Brit toy shotgun like Andy's, either. With the little 9mm lady pistol she'd been carrying around since way back when in her hometown of Topeka Kansas. First, like every sensible gal, she'd kept it in the glove compartment of her little Volvo, just in case of emergency. But then came her victory in the Miss Playboy 2017 contest, after which there were cat calls and dog whistles everyplace she went, *and* scam calls on her phone and faked photos of her naked all over her computer. That's when the little 9mm got promoted to her purse. Coincidentally, it was also when she met and fell in love with Hank Orlando, aka Robert Redford Jnr in a Kansas City bar, and agreed to flee Topeka to hook up with him in LA as his secretary, and then, when he was debarred from shrinkage, head with him to the UK, where nobody knew either of them.

And for a while it had been blissful. Okay, there was no dumb piece of paper saying they had to be mahogamous, or whatever the word was, so both of them had a little fun here and there. But they always fessed up to it. "No secrets" was the rule, before and after the event. Until that awful day with the dame on his couch ready to suck his goddam dick and more! Had he told her *any*thing about her? The hell he had. Which was why Sabrina/Marjory was fumbling in her purse for the little 9mm at the very moment Doc Crane turned up.

"Ookay, sad story," I hear you say. "But why should she have waited so *long* to take further revenge? You'd think enough damage had already been done. So what was the trigger for shooting him through the left Achilles tendon all this time later?"

True enough, and I appreciate your use of polysemy on the word "trigger."

Well, put it this way: Hank Orlando was a statistics freak, and the ones he liked most were those that portrayed him in the glitziest of lights. The number of followers he had on Twitter—two thousand four hundred and eighty three, he boasted—that claimed he was even prettier than Robert Redford even when Robert was at his prettiest, the faux high school yearbook records that showed him having hit more home runs than Babe Ruth and scored more touchdowns than Tom Brady. And, most false of all, there was the self-posted message claiming he'd had sex with almost as many women as Mick Jagger.

It was to the latter he'd been referring when ruing his failure with Sandra Normington because she was the one who might finally have tipped the balance in his favour. His key mistake, of course, was to repeat this lamentable tale to Sabrina/Marjory Mackey for maybe the hundredth time at the very moment she was least ready to feel any sympathy i.e. when she could stand it no more.

"Man, I've been trying to overtake Mick for soo *long*," Hank was saying at this couldn't-stand-it-any-more moment, which was when Sabrina took the little 9mm from her purse, pulled the trigger and—with the sensitivity at least not to shoot him through the genitals again—shot him through the left Achilles tendon while he was leaning backwards to top up his glass of Jim Beam.

"Aaaaaagggghhhh,' he said. Understandably.

~ * ~

On a happier note, Quentin Trimble had been only too pleased to hear Sandra Normington's voice down the telephone line.

"Sure, I'd love the come over for a chat. Unless, of course, you'd fancy a trip over to my place. It's not far from you and the change of scene might do you good," he said, intuiting the anxiety in his old colleague's voice. "Either way, it would be great to catch up. We haven't had the chance of a good old chinwag since I got packed off on gardening leave, have we?"

"That wasn't my fault, Quentin," said Sandra who, in her confused state, had taken to blaming herself for practically anything.

"Of course it wasn't. I was simply the victim of my own foolishness, although I did wonder if Andy Crane might have said something to old Proudfoot about it. Anyway, Crane is now at the centre of a whole new can of worms, so let's let sleeping worms lie, shall we? Sandra? You still there?"

"Yuh-yes," said Sandra after a moment or two of sniffling. That name again.

Overhearing because the phone was on speaker, Lucy Lomax patted her on the arm, nodded encouragingly and whispered, "He's right, a change of scene would be smashing."

"That still you?" said Quentin. "Same accent but different voice."

"It's Lucy. She's my old school friend from up in Birkenhead. She's been helping me out a bit."

"Berken where?"

"Head, on Merseyside. Where the big ships used to get built?"

"Oh, right. Well, she'd be welcome, too. Any friend of yours and so on."

And so it was, the following sunny afternoon that Sandra and Lucy took the bus over to Quentin's flat, where he greeted them at the door dressed in the white T bearing in red letters the logo *Sunshine Superman* over knee-length Levis cutoffs, the outfit recommended by Fion.

"Wear what you feel," he'd advised after turning down the invitation Quentin had extended for him to attend the meet-up, too, on the grounds that:

a) It was time Quentin took charge of situations rather than relying on fairies to do it for him,

b) Even if he were to morph into a human for the occasion, there would be the danger of Quentin introducing him as a fairy anyway,

And,

c) Having checked out Sandra's and Lucy's provenance as Birkenhead, he preferred not yet again to hear that tired old Merseysiders' joke about folk having "ferries" at the bottom of their gardens.

All of which Quentin accepted without demur. "Fair enough—or should I say fairy enough," he'd said.

Not that Fion had been entirely absent from the occasion, of course. Happily, he watched on from his shed at the bottom of the garden as Quentin hosted his guests with the sort of laid-back aplomb Fion had proposed. Gesturing them to their seats around the carefully laid garden table, suggesting which pastries were the tastiest, decorking a bottle of iced *Veuve Clicquot* with the savoir faire of a master sommelier...and so on. You get the picture. Some short weeks later, when Covid-19 began sucking the life out of people and economies, and everybody was in socially distanced lockdown such a halcyon scene would have been unthinkable, but that was for later.

When everyone was seated and sipping, Quentin conducted a conversation based entirely on the welfare of his guests, thereby enabling him to say nothing at all about himself, let alone what he might soon be doing in Wollongong. A couple of times Sandra tried asking him how things had been during his temporary dismissal from the surgery, including the horrible leaked accusations of matricide. But these Quentin batted off into the long grass by saying non-committal things like, "Oh, you know, life has its little ups and downs," and "You live and learn, eh?"

Clearly there had to be some discussion of Andy Crane's evil doings, but even those Quentin managed to divert to safer ground, particularly when it came to Sandra's part in them. All in all, it was a pleasant occasion, inspiring Sandra, on Quentin's advice, to stop worrying about being copied in to the scam phone calls and emails and get back to the surgery to take her mind off things. Little did he know it wasn't the scams that were her mind needed taking off, but her feelings (or not) for Andy Crane. Still, she promised to give it a go.

The only person not to contribute much to the conversation apart from general pleasantries was Lucy Lomax. Why? Because, as Fion had rather hoped she might, she had fallen in love with Quentin Trimble, an emotion explored at some length by Sandra on the bus home.

"Fancied him, didn't you?" she giggled, nudging her old friend with an elbow.

Silence, as Lucy stared out of the window.

"*Didn't* you?" Sandra persisted. "Mind you, he's changed a bit since the old hypochondriac days. I told you about them, didn't I?"

"Mmm."

"S'pose that's why you didn't say much. Just kept giving him those heartthrob looks."

"*Heartthrob*?" said Lucy, turning from her observation of passing tower blocks and suchlike.

"C'mon girl, you can't fool me. We've known each other long enough, and I've never seen one of those looks on your face before. Not one to suck up to some bloke at first glance, our Luce, eh?"

"No."

"So?"

Lucy squirmed in her seat. "Well, there *was* something a bit special about him, I thought."

Sandra cocked her head on one side and raised an eyebrow. "Special?"

"I dunno, something other*worldly*," said Lucy, her eyes going misty.

In the garden shed, Fion smiled. How right she was.

"It's called love. And I hope it works out for you better than it has for me," said Sandra, pressing the bus's Stop button. "Anyhow, this is where we get off."

Seventeen

Anybody intent on hanging him- or herself effectively will be aware that proper equipment is required: a trusty rope with a slip knot securing the noose at just the right angle, a secure place to which to tie it (a tree, for example) giving adequate space for the fall, and something solid beneath the feet before the final kick that will end it all forever, a discarded beer crate, for example. Even in the darkest of hours, sufficient sanity remains to ensure there are no unforeseen hiccups in the project.

It was a measure of Doc Frederick's galloping dementia therefore that he paid no heed whatsoever to those simple necessities and consequently screwed up royally. What, after all, are the chances of successfully hanging yourself by knotting together five pyjama trouser cords, tying one end to your central bedroom light fitting and the other on a loop around your throat, then jumping naked sideways off the bed onto the floor? Ruling out such flukes as landing headfirst on a six-inch up-turned exposed nail poking through the carpet, they are minus nil. At best, such a performance can only be considered a cry for help, if only to remove the pyjama cord from between your teeth, and for someone to deal with the mess caused by the light fitting shattering all over your duvet. And of course, the popping noises made by bulbs in the en suite bathroom, and then the blowing of other fuses that enveloped much of the house in darkness.

And in Doc Frederick's case, who was the person to answer this spectacular desire for attention? Doc Antoinette, of course. Who'd been watched TV downstairs until she heard the thump on the upstairs floor and the screen went blank. Understandably, it was with some trepidation she made her way upstairs in the gloom to find her husband lying supine with his eyes wide open staring at the ceiling.

"For fuck's *sake*, Freddie, what next?" she said.

Reckoning he was dead, Doc Frederick didn't reply. When Doc Antoinette prodded him with a toe, he did twitch a bit, which rather gave the game away, but still not a word passed his lips. After all, corpses' hair, finger- and toenails continued to grow, didn't they? So there was every chance post mortem that the odd nerve-end might continue to twitch. What *was* funny, though, was that he could still think these things even when deceased. Perhaps there was an afterlife after all, a paradise in which a person could look down on the living, thumb his nose, and go, "Yah boo sucks." Mind you, he didn't see any angels floating about, and St Peter must have been off-duty polishing his pearly gates or something, so perhaps he was in some kind of a dead person's queue. What was that place called again? Poogatery, some name of the sort.

What finally roused Doc Frederick from these pointless mental meanderings was Doc Antoinette losing all patience, grabbing her husband by the balls, squeezing, and hissing, "Wake the fuck up. Who d'you think you're fooling, you godforsaken dickhead?"

Perhaps not exactly textbook medical practice of the kind recommended to newbie junior doctors on A&E when faced with suicide cases, but it worked for Doc Antoinette.

"Aaaaaaggghhh," said Doc Frederick, both unsurprisingly and, from Doc Antoinette's perspective at least, encouragingly.

Then, all squinty-eyed and chewing on a soggy pyjama cord, he sat bolt upright, burst into the self-pitying tears and tugs at his sparse hair that inspired Doc Antoinette to turn on her heels and head for the stairs humming extracts from Bill Haley's "See You Later Alligator."

The line she called over her shoulder as she left the room was the one about seeing a crocodile in a while.

Leaving her husband to his self-inflicted non-injuries, she returned to the magically re-lit lounge—a Fion electronic intervention—picked up her phone, hit the Favourites app and, needing someone on whom to offload her angst, tapped at Quentin's entry. After all, the lad had seemed so much better in recent days, plus he was aware of Doc Frederick's situation, so who better to have a good moan at?

"Hi, Mum. How's it going?" said Quentin, answering on only the second ring.

So Doc Antoinette told him.

"With pyjama strings?" said Quentin.

"Py-bloody-jama strings, silly old sod," said Antoinette.

"Cry for help then."

"On the face of it. But I don't reckon he's got enough functioning neurons left for such subtlety. What we're looking at here, Quentie, is *some* kind of dementia, but there are so many varieties of it, and I'm no expert. I've heard self-harm is common enough in many of them, though."

Quentin nodded. "And nobody is sure why. Maybe sufferers just get pissed off with being demented and reckon they're the ones to blame."

"You mean he thinks everything is *his* fault?"

"Could be. Look, Mum, I'm no expert either, but I could pop round for a chat if that would help. I haven't talked to the old bastard since..."

"I *know* since when. And you were perfectly right to stay away after what he did to you. But yes, I *would* be grateful. It's all getting a bit end-of-tetherish around here."

"Okay. And listen, we never did set up that meeting with my fairy friend, did we? Crossed wires and suchlike. How would it be if I brought him along with me? There may be stuff he knows we humans don't."

"With pleasure, Quentie. With *pleasure*," Doc Antoinette was saying as there came another thump from the room upstairs. "Sorry, sweetheart, got to go, he's at it again," were the last words Quentin heard before the call was cut.

This time, Doc Frederick had tried hanging himself with the shower attachment in the en suite bathroom, but that hadn't worked either, just flooded the floor on which he was left to flounder not unlike the fish of the same name.

~ * ~

Obviously enough, Hank Orlando wasn't best pleased at having been shot through the Achilles tendon by Sabrina/Marjory Mackey, which was why, despite her tears of regret and pleas for forgiveness, he managed to muster sufficient balance to hop over to her and deliver the right hook that knocked her senseless. After that, he called the cops to report an assault against his person, the American equivalent of the Brits' grievous bodily harm.

"Yeah, that's right, and quit it with the snickering," he told Officer Jim McNulty, who didn't seem to Hank to be taking the matter nearly seriously enough. "It *was* a she who shot me through the freakin' ankle. What about it?"

"Nudn, just checkin'. Feisty dame, huh?" said McNulty, sucking in his cheeks to quell the mirth. "Ookay, so name."

"Hers?"

"Hers and yours, and the address."

So Hank told him.

"And this Sabrina? She ran away, she still with you, she gonna shoot you another time? I need the scenario here."

"She's knocked out on the floor."

"Knocked *out*, huh?"

"Yeah, after she shot me, she got kinda freaky antsy, walked into a wall and knocked herself out. You gotta get a squad car over here before she wakes up."

"Walked into a wall, you say?"

"Man, you wanna stop repeating every damn thing I say? I am in some agony here. I am gonna need an ambulance, so quit shitting me, okay?"

"Only doin' my duty, sir. Sorry about the pain but that ain't no reason to be rude to a police officer. I could book *you* for that."

That was when Hank shrieked, "Oh...for...*FUCK*" at which McNulty said "Take it easy, dude. I'll send a car. Be with you in five to fifteen," before hanging up.

"Goddam cops," Hank muttered as Sabrina took to whimpering a bit.

But mercifully, from Hank's perspective, McNulty's time frame worked reasonably well in so far as it was only ten minutes later that the downstairs bell rang and through the intercom Hank admitted rookie Officers Dorkins and Tremaine to first, the building then, his tiny apartment, both of them with Glock 17 Gen4 pistols in their hands.

"So what seems to be the trouble?" said Officer (Dickie) Dorkins, peering at the bloodstained floor and the woman with the swollen face struggling to her knees.

"Bitch shot me," Hank told him while Officer (Tommy) Tremaine squatted and, with neither sympathy nor sarcasm, asked Sabrina if she was okay.

"That true, lady?" said Dickie, raising the Glock in case she shot him, too.

Sabrina couldn't deny it. Nor could she nod her head in confirmation because it hurt too much. "Sssss," was all she could manage, which Dickie took for a yes.

"With this?" said Tommy, pointing at the little 9mm still dangling from her fingers.

"Man, Sherlock Holmes got nothing on you guys," said Hank, earning him scowls from both Dickie and Tommy. "So just read her her rights, get her the fuck outta here to the station, and leave me in peace to call the medicos."

Dickie and Tommy exchanged interrogatory looks, figured they didn't want either the guy or the dame to go dying on them and wrecking their chances of promotion, and so did as requested, thereby impacting significantly on later events in Wollongong. You know how it is when a butterfly flaps its wings in New Mexico and, sometime later, hurricanes wipe out whole cities in China. Or, to update the idea, how folk suddenly start dying in Wuhan and soon after, for no understood reason, practically the entire planet follows suit. Well, in this tiny tale, such was the knock-on effect of Sabrina/Marjory Mackey's bean spilling after her arrest.

If she *hadn't* filled in the NYPD with the backstory details to the whole Hank Orlando/Doc Andy Crane affair during her arraignment, for example, the New York cops might never have had reason to contact DI Wilde and his failing crew in Battersea South West London and propose a joint team to locate the missing genitalia shooter. Might merely thought of the current shooting of Hank as just one more domestic gone south. Corvid-19 alone knew there would be enough of *those* once NYC was locked down.

Equally had it not been for the wrecked Achilles tendon, which on Mike Zabludo's prognosis would leave him a "limpy Larry" for many months to come, thereby delaying revenge on Andy Crane unconscionably, Hank Orlando might never have reconnected with Luca Gambonio to enquire if the freebie "rubbing out" offer of Andy Crane from Grimble and Grumble Boggart was still available, seeing as in unforeseen circs he might have to stay in NYC after all. To which Gambonio acceded without demur, always having reckoned Orlando for an over-egged dork who couldn't kill a worm with a hammer, and who would have upset the whole project anyway.

"Yeah sure, I'll get back to you," he yawned into his phone before cutting the call.

Such is the nature of those little, apparently unconnected, things that come together without any prior warning to cause other, normally nasty, things to happen. If only we could know of them in advance, life would be a lot more straightforward. As US Defense Secretary Donald Rumsfeld concluded re the Iraq war in 2002, after running briefly through some aspects of the trickiness of human knowledge, "There are also unknown unknowns—the ones we don't know we don't know."

Thanks for that, Donald. And no irony intended.

Eighteen

Quentin Trimble was finding himself prey to uninvited and troubling thoughts…well not so much *thoughts* as visceral sensations, the sorts of thing others might have deemed emotions. Apart from the more cheerful sense of self-respect he'd garnered from Fion's recent teachings, the only other "emotion" he was familiar with was fear, which he had assumed to be nothing out of the ordinary, just the normal state of affairs. From early childhood through his teenage years, such fear—mainly of Doc Frederick—had served as fertile ground for the dread of disease and death leading to the blossoming of the hypochondria that had been his downfall at the surgery. Otherwise, where emotions were concerned, he was a tabula rasa. No hollering support for his favourite soccer team, no getting in the groove to the music of rock bands, no lusting after girls either imaginary or real—zilch, nada in all those respects and many others. In these circumstances, the sudden bouts of wooziness, warmth, and yearning while both awake and asleep he had recently been experiencing, came as a major surprise to his system, leading him to wonder if the *maladie imaginaire* syndrome had returned, and he were sickening for some awful illness. Worried, he put the situation to Fion who, irritatingly, winked and grinned.

"Why're you laughing at me?" he said.

"Not *at* you, *with* you."

"What? When I could be incubating the Chinese bug or something worse."

Fion waggled a forefinger in front of his nose. "Tch, tch, old chap, don't let *those* silly old ideas back into your head."

Fion already knew there was nothing much worse than Covid-19 and the global chaos it would cause, but this wasn't the time to alert an already worried Quentin to it.

Instead, he said, "You're not sick, old chap, at least not in the usual meaning of that term."

"What then?"

"From the symptoms you describe, I would diagnose love sickness, hence my winking and grinning. A jolly nice emotion, as I understand it. Not one we fairies share in exactly the same manner, but one through intuitive imagination we can understand."

"*Love*?"

"You're showing all the signs."

"And it's making me *sick*?"

"Not medically, but I assume you are behaving somewhat abnormally. Having distracting thoughts when you should be concentrating, inexplicably humming little ditties to yourself, smiling at nothing in particular, all that sort of thing. Had any of that?"

Quentin frowned and nodded. "Mmm."

"Dreaming of some other human, normally one of the opposite gender, although same sex is okay?"

More nods.

"And who *is* it, one wonders, with *whom* you are in love?" said Fion, although he already knew the answer.

"Dunno."

Which was when Fion took from his satchel his ElfVision smartphone and showed Quentin a video recording of the wine and cakes party attended by Sandra Normington and Lucy Lomax. It was on Lucy's face he froze the tiny screen three times; Lucy as she stared at Quentin and silently smiled.

"Ring any bells?" he said. "Any little ding a lings?"

It was Quentin's eyes glazing over that gave him the answer he expected.

"Well?"

"It's huh-*her*," said Quentin, through a sigh he couldn't repress. "The one I've seen in my dreams. When I wuh-woke up, she'd gone and I didn't remember but..."

"Well then, jolly good, problem solved. The only question that remains is what you're going to *do* about it."

Never having dated, Quentin had no idea. Hope he might meet her again somewhere, sometime perhaps? And what then, tell her he was in love with her? He didn't think so, far too abrupt and embarrassing. He wouldn't dare. And what if he *never* met her again? Maybe she'd gone back to Birkenhead, wherever that was. And even if he found out, what was he supposed to do? Just turn up out of the blue and say he wanted to kiss her or something? Maybe it was better just to forget the whole thing and carry on as normally as possible. He put these conundrums to Fion, who already had a plan in mind.

"And all I have to do is...?" said Quentin.

"Call on the number I'll give you inviting her to register with your surgery as a wise precaution if she's to stay in London for a while. She might, for example, require a flu jab."

Fion knew Lucy had been intending to do that, but kept forgetting.

"And then?"

"You ask her out for a coffee."

"And that's it?"

"The rest shall be up to you, old chap," said Fion. "Now if you'll excuse me, I have rather an urgent matter to deal with in the grassy glade. One of my old chums has gone a bit potty and started thinking he's a griffin."

~ * ~

When Luca Gambonio didn't call back with news of the situation regarding the freebie rubbing-out of Andy Crane, Hank Orlando called *him* and was almost as pissed off with his response as he had been with that of the cops when he was obliged to admit to having been shot again and by whom. Same snicker, same suppressed scorn, but Hank knew better than to get up the nose of a Mafia made man, especially the one who'd helped him get out of LA to the UK way back when all kinds of shit was hitting all kinds of fans over the Robert Redford Jnr screw-up. He'd upgraded the freebie notion in which he would merely witness the action from a safe distance to one that would allow him to attend the event and carry a hatchet. In this scenario, Hank would need a little help from Luca's friends, what with the gimpy leg and everything, but it would be he who would deliver the *coup de grâce*. Never mind what Zabludo said about taking it easy during his convalescence —no way José was Hank going to miss out on a pleasure he would regret not taking for the rest of his life.

"See where I'm coming from?" he asked Luca at the end of this spiel.

And Luca had to admit he did. He'd offed enough rival gang members and cops in his day to know only too intimately the satisfaction it brought.

"Sure I do, ballsy I can go with," he said.

"Oo*kay* then, so you buy my plan?"

"Lemme work on it, and I'll get back to you."

"Like soon?"

"Like soon," said Luca, shutting off the smartphone and taking from a wall safe the Boggart hotline Skype transmitter.

As he had half-expected, neither Grimble nor Grumble was much impressed by the job offer with Hank Orlando on board. Without him, they might just about have been persuaded, even though they didn't like Australia and held in particular disdain two-bit hick towns like Wollongong. But the idea of some dork limping along behind, them *plus* wanting the *coup de grâce* action was a clear no-no.

"We got our reputations to think of," said Grimble. "Foul ups we don't do, am I right, Grumble?"

"Would make us a laughing stock," Grumble muttered gloomily. "Tell the doofus he can go suck his dick."

"A guy who already got hisself shot twice recently, one time by a *dame*? Sheesh," said Grimble. "With dorks like him, we do not work. It's in the code of the boggarts. Hey, try a little respect here, Gambonio. One of your key mafia-type words, right?"

Luca couldn't deny it and didn't try. Instead, he made Grimble and Grumble an offer he figured they would find hard to refuse: namely he would *not* tell the boggart high command of the steamy dalliance some years ago Grimble had enjoyed with an elf called Veron(ica) when it was clearly stated in the same code that on fear of death *no* boggart should *ever* demean himself by indulging in sex acts with elves. Nor would he divulge Grumble's unusual interest in pixies, naked pictures of which Luca had once witnessed on his boggart transmitter, having inadvertently pressed the wrong button.

And, unsurprisingly, this tactic worked, albeit with considerable grumbling—especially from Grumble—and bad-mouthing. Grimble accused Luca of being a "scheming asshole typical of the human species, especially Eyetalians," for example. But if the pair of them valued their continuing connection with one of the biggest crime families in America, which they both did, there was little else they could do but obey. The obedience came with conditions attached, however. Top of the list came a blanket refusal to wet-nurse the Orlando bozo. If he got sick in the teleportation process, he *stayed* sick. If he fell over at any time in the Crane operation, he *stayed* fallen over. If he fucked up the hatchet *coup de grâce*, which Grumble reckoned he would, they'd do it for him...and so on. No *way* were they prepared to carry a useless, stumbling, self-glorifying passenger with them and thereby screw up an easy peasy in-and-out mission of the kind they'd performed a thousand times.

"Geddit, Gambonio?" said Grimble, after maybe fifteen minutes of such caveats and qualifications.

"Got it, no problemo," said Luca, who fully sympathized with the boggarts' stance. Orlando was a dork, no question, and deserved all he got. Only reason he was dealing with the guy at all was a Mafioso's honour when it came to reciprocating favours if they were called in. And so it was that the disproportionately gifted team of Grimble, Grumble and Orlando was assembled in the hunt for Doc Andy Crane.

Mind you, when Luca called Hank back with the news, the latter was on cloud nine.

"Jeez, woweee, fan*tast*ic, thanks like two million, Gambonio. You are one cool dude," he said.

"Yeah, yeah, talk soon," said Luca, cutting the call and pouring himself five fingers of Jack Daniels to take away the shame and pain.

Nineteen

For the purpose of their visit to offer assistance to Doc Antoinette in her travails with Doc Frederick, Fion had proposed morphing into a middle-aged human male, but Quentin wasn't having any of it.

"She knows you're a fairy, Fifie. Little hiccup on the gay issue to begin with as I told you, but then she got used to the idea, or better the *reality*."

"And her old man, your father? Wouldn't want to upset any apple carts with him."

"He's already several sandwiches short of a picnic, so I wouldn't worry on *that* front. No, no, old chap, you come as you are and let any devils take their hindmosts."

"Okay then," said Fion, secretly pleased to see his erstwhile tutee now evincing such assurance. The boy had come a long way.

Mind you, Quentin's assessment of the situation proved accurate when the pair knocked on the front door to be greeted with hugs and kisses from Doc Antoinette.

"Thanks soo much for coming," she said, embracing Quentin then leaning down to shake the hand Fion proffered. "And how *wonderful,* finally, to meet Quentin's best fairy friend. I am so grateful for all you've done for him."

"It was nothing ma'am. Your son is a quick learner."

"I always thought so, *always*. But still there were the little problems and…"

"Mum, might we come in?" said Quentin.

"Of course, of *course*," said Doc Antoinette, extending an inviting arm across the threshold. "Cups of tea with Hobnobs, how would that be?"

"Excellent, Mum. And Dad? How's he doing?"

"He's upstairs in bed with a childhood teddy bear of mine I found in the attic. It's called Teddy."

"Excellent choice," said Fion without irony.

"Indeed," Quentin muttered, ushering Fion ahead of him as they followed Doc Antoinette into the parlour.

"Do take a pew," she called over her shoulder while she fussed about with cups, a teapot, and the biscuits.

So Fion and Quentin did and, when the three of them were seated together around a small square table with a red cloth, Quentin asked how they might best be of assistance.

"Well, seeing your sweet faces has already been a pleasure," said Antoinette. "And it might be of help for me to talk through some of my fears, but my *real* problem is poor old Freddie, who's clearly off his trolley. Whether it's truly dementia he's suffering from, or some peculiar mixture of fury and guilt, I couldn't say."

"And you've not had him examined by anyone in the business?" asked Quentin, sipping at his Earl Grey.

"Too embarrassed," said Antoinette, leaning forward to nibble at a Hobnob. "You know the rep he has in the medico world."

Fion nodded. "And the fury and guilt idea?"

Antoinette finished her nibble. "Fury because he is no longer getting his own way in the manner to which he was accustomed, and guilt because he might *just* be beginning to understand he never deserved it in the first place."

"A toxic mix if you're right," said Quentin.

"Indeed. And one for which *I* am almost entirely responsible, having pointed out this nasty little aporia to him."

"Don't blame yourself, Mum. Truth will out, and it's always better that way, however painful."

"Even when the silly old sausage tries to hang himself?"

"Just as well he was no expert," said Fion, whose little mouth was having some trouble getting around his Hobnob.

"You're both right on both counts," said Antoinette. "But what are we to *do* about it? Any answer to that question would be welcome, although I know it's asking an awful lot of you both."

Quentin leaned forward across the table, took one of his mother's shaking hands, winked, and said, "Fancy trying a little elf magic? It worked wonders for me. I'm sure Fion here would be happy to oblige, wouldn't you, Fifie?"

Fion crunched down his last bit of Hobnob, nodded and smiled. "I do have a few options up my sleeve, if you'd fancy giving them a go."

Antoinette raised an interested eyebrow. "Such as?"

"Oh, you know, the odd tincture."

"Not antipsychotics, I hope. Such things can do far more damage than they correct."

"Tch, tch, wouldn't go near them, ma'am. Let us just say we elves have our own ways and medications, none of which tamper with brain cells or anything so silly. Besides, they taste nice. Not so, Quentin?"

"They *do*. And I can testify to the results, which are always positive, never negative. Such is the code of the elves for all aspects of life, Mum."

Antoinette raised her teacup in a toast to that. "Pity the same cannot be said of humans. So by all means, let's give it a go. Can I assume you came prepared for such a treatment, Mister Fion? Brought along with you the apposite tinctures and so on?"

"Indeed so, ma'am. And please no need for the mister...I'm just Fion."

"Of course, pardon me...*Fion*. Sooo, once we've finished our tea and bikkies, may I suggest a trip upstairs to Freddie's room for the ministrations? Can *you* face that, too, Quentie? Let bygones *be* bygones and so on?"

"No problemo, Mum."

And so it was five minutes later that Antoinette, Fion and Quentin found themselves in Doc Frederick's bedchamber where the twice-failed hangee was leaning back on two pillows deep in a diatribe with Teddy about the futility of existence.

"Crock of shit it is, doodly do, just one setback after another, prickly poo, ungrateful swine everywhere, dingly ding, better off never born, bongally bong," he was saying.

Not that Teddy looked much impressed, or in truth much of anything. You know how it is with teddies, how they smile gormlessly *all* the time. Even so, this Teddy wore a wan look on his face. So wan he was almost two, as the old joke has it.

"Freddie, look who's come to *see* you," said Antoinette. "Quentie and his new best friend, Fion"

Doc Frederick looked up, tossed a relieved looking Teddy to one side, and scowled. "Fucking fuckwit of a fucking son, plinkety plonk," he said.

At which Quentin shrugged and said, "Hi to you too, Dad."

Not that there was much to recognize of the father he had once known in the shriveled, unshaven, bleary-eyed non-entity growling curses at him from what he appeared to hope would be his deathbed.

What astonished Quentin and Antoinette was the moment Doc Frederick averted the *mal occhi* from his wife and son and took cognisance of Fion emerging from behind them. Never would they have expected such vitriol to morph so swiftly to beneficence as Doc Frederick sat up straight, waved cheerily, and said, "Welcome, *mon ami*, so nice to see you again."

~ * ~

The last we saw of Andy Crane, he was chewing over his darkest personal relationships, those with his father and Sandra Normington, and coming to no conclusion. And, sad to report, he had since made no progress at all. If anything, he'd regressed to something of a jabbering wreck as the relationship mastication began to fill all his waking hours and translated itself into horror show dreams at night, never mind how many bottles of Moosehead Lager he consumed in advance of bedtime, hopefully to achieve oblivion. And it wasn't as though he had anyone with whom to discuss his problems, Art Scrivenger and Bazza Johnson having told him he'd need to find a new place to stay if he went on bellyaching at them all day long. They were regular blokes, right? And they didn't need some wimp spilling his guts around the place when they had better things to do. Which left no willing ears at all, because Andy hadn't met any other Wollongongians apart from the corner-shop guy called Barney, who fed him his Moosehead Lagers on a tick account Andy could never hope to repay, and all Barney ever did was grunt. So around his head all day and night swam images of Sandra—and his father Angus, of whom he'd kept an ancient photo given to him by his mother. Sometimes these images laughed and opened their arms to him; other times they scowled and spat at him.

It was all very discombobulating, so much so that Andy had taken to spending his days wandering the streets of Wollongong muttering to himself and jabbing his index finger in the air, thereby causing other pedestrians to take a wide berth. Had he accidentally wound up in the Nan Tien temple in the Berkeley district, he might have found relief from these worldly worries by chumming up with the monks, chanting Pancasilas and other praises of Buddha all night and day, and thereby never have alerted DI Wilde and the NYPD to his presence in Wollongong at all—but he didn't. Such are life's little near misses.

It was being arrested and held overnight by the Wollongong cops for punching on the nose the "concerned citizen"—Billy Smith—who had challenged him for pissing up the trunk of a cabbage palm in Crown Street Mall that gave away his whereabouts.

"Oi there, cobber, what d'you think you're doin'? Tree don't need no more water, do it?" Billy had said politely enough.

But how could Billy have known that in Andy Crane's currently deluded eyes, the cabbage palm wasn't a tree he was pissing on at all, but instead the head of his estranged father Angus? No way, that was how. Not that it helped, mind you, when Billy added, "I know what it's like to get caught short, only at least you could have squeezed your bum cheeks till you got home."

That's when Andy zipped his flies with the hand whose index finger wasn't jabbing at the sky then, when both hands were reactivated, told Billy to mind his own fucking business. If Billy *had,* he wouldn't have got punched on the nose, but you know how it is with concerned citizens, how grinding they can be in their objections. It was the further comment that no member of the public needed to see Andy's "weenie little willie," thank you very much, that was the last straw. Hence the straight arm jab Andy didn't even know he possessed, and the phone call to the cops made on Billy's behalf by another concerned citizen called Nigel Smith, who reckoned Andy, judging by his accent, to be a "Pisshead Pom."

Anyway, *any*way, what this all led to was Andy being whisked off to the local jug, which in any other story might have had little or no significance. In this one, it did. Computers these days, eh? The way a single name written into a non-urgent crime sheet can have reverberations thousands of miles away.

Which was how it was that into the globally circulated, "persons of interest" inbox kept alive 24/7 by the NYPD and their new Battersea partners, suddenly one day pinged the name of the missing genitalia shooter, the whereabouts of whom they agreed should remain strictly confidential and top secret until they could agree on how jointly to proceed with the case.

Twenty

Sandra Normington's brother, Ronnie hadn't seen his little sister for years when, on one of the last flights out of San Francisco before Covid-19 hit, he flew in for a top level hi-tech conference at the London Business School on the Outer Circle of Regent's Park and reckoned it was time he made amends. It was to get her number he called Mum and Dad up in Birkenhead.

"Be great seeing her again, how's she doing, anyway?" he asked Mildred in a Scouse accent only faintly tinged by Silicon Valley interference.

"Hard to say, son. Seemed a bit confused last time we saw her. She's down in The Smoke, you know," said Mildred, as if that explained everything about her daughter's confusion.

"Yeah, I knew that. And she's a doctor now, right?"

"That's right. Why she couldn't have done her doctoring up here, I don't know. A sick body's a sick body, isn't it? Different accent, like, but still a sick body."

"True enough."

"Where are you, anyway? This one of them long distance calls?"

"Nah, I'm in The Smoke, too."

"Poor you. Coming up to see us, are you?"

"If I get the time. You doing OK?"

"Mustn't grumble," said Mildred, who on average per day grumbled almost as much as Grumble Boggart.

"Great, good, wanna pass me over to Dad?"

"Eh up, son, how's it going?" said Henry, taking the receiver after being whispered to by Mildred.

"All good thanks. You?"

"Same as normal."

Ronnie knew what normal meant. It was Henry's code for getting his ear bent by Mildred. Anyway, father and son chatted for a bit about vital matters like the chances of Liverpool FC winning the premier league this year, after which Ronnie got Sandra's number and repeated his hope to visit before flying back to the US. Then he cut the call before heading to the conference hall for the big debate about the pros and cons of covert algorithmic bots on consumer behaviour.

Silicon Valley computer whizz kid Ronnie might have become, but however far you took the boy from Birkenhead, you couldn't take Birkenhead from the boy. It was a *good* thing to have played his part in enabling the increased availability of information to the average Joe and Jane in the street, he reckoned, but quite the reverse to see the very same Joe and Jane shut off from the world around them by the smartphones on which the social media were able to fill their ears and minds with bogus information that sometimes led to them no longer even speaking to each other. To Ronnie's mind, this was the twenty-first century's version of the "subliminal cuts" in movies as explained in Vance Packard's classic *The Hidden Persuaders*. It was the nature and provenance of such scam interference he wanted to know more about and had gone to considerable lengths to find out. And the results were terrifying.

Top of the list, of course, came the way the neo-fascist narcissists in the White House and 10 Downing Street had been helped by Moscow to win their elections, but further down it lurked other horrors. One of the worst was the manner in which mere children were being hooked into online gambling such that by the time they reached late adolescence, they had become addicts, owing the thousands of dollars or pounds they would need to steal, which would nine times out of ten see them end up in jail. This, as well as many more contraventions of ethical behaviour, stacked up in Ronnie's mind as brainwashing as evil as ever imagined by George Orwell in his *1984*. But however minimal his contribution to the removal of such obscenities from global platforms might be, he was determined to do his best.

Not that Ronnie's pleas for social and ethical responsibility in the social media cut much ice to the top-level hi-tech debaters at the London Business School. Where there was political power and billions of dollars to be made from brainwashed suckers, how could it have? It soon became pretty clear to him as each of his contributions was met with either deafening silence or jeers and nose-thumbing, that he was on a hiding to nothing. Which was when he stalked out of the hall, wandered Regent's Park's Outer Circle for a bit, took a right turn towards Baker Street and ended up at a pub called The Barley Mow where he bought himself a pint of best bitter and a packet of dry roasted peanuts before sitting himself down at a table outside, pulling out his own carefully decontaminated phone, and punching in Sandra's number.

All this was in the BC, remember. A few shorts weeks later, and The Barley Mow would be under lockdown, and nobody would be allowed to sit outside sampling its delights.

~ * ~

In New York City, it was on the counsel of Sergeant Jeannie Quinn that Sabrina/Marjory Mackey was released by the NYPD with no more than a ticking off after having had her assault-against-the-person charge reduced to a minor misdemeanor/indiscretion. Initially, Officers Dickie Dorkins and Tommy Tremaine had been reluctant to accept Jeannie's reasoning behind this decision, despite both of them secretly having reckoned Hank Orlando an asshole who had it coming to him. Nonetheless, there was no way in their city they were going to condone gals going around shooting guys in their Achilles tendons, no way José. Dickie and Tommy were born-in-the-blood Republican rednecks who had clapped and cheered when the "big guy" was first elected to the White House and whooped even harder when he was acquitted by the Senate of the "fake news" impeachment charges brought against him by the "crazy dames" in the House of Representatives. Jeannie Quinn was a tough nut to crack, though, when it came to women's rights, and she was their sergeant.

"You ain't telling me poor Sabrina had no cause to shoot the Orlando creep when she'd been looking out for him most of his life, and then he starts bragging about screwing nearly as many women as Mick Jagger, are you?" was her core argument. "Well, *are* you?" she added when Dickie and Tommy could find no convincing rebuttal.

"Okay," Jeannie continued, "it wasn't abuse like the shitkicker had raped her, in which case nobody would be arguing about her right to shoot his feet off. This was abuse of the wormy hidden kind no woman—no *person*—deserves. Plus, *plus*, this was the woman who would have tried to save Orlando from being shot in the balls by the Crane creature if he hadn't already laid her out cold. This she told me, and I believed her."

Dickie and Tommy could have gone for "mere speculation" here, but they didn't. Not with Jeannie stomping up and down the room in front of them, ticking off agenda points on her fingers.

"But like I said, it *can* be construed as psychological abuse, the undercover kind America should be ashamed of only can't with a serial rapist for president. Movie directors we are finally learning to lock up, thank God, but not presidents."

Dickie opened his mouth to stick up for the "big guy" but one look from Jeannie was all it took for him to shut it again.

"And what I want from *all* officers on the streets of this city, gals *and* guys, is a an awareness of the possibly secret reasons that might lie behind an apparent crime of violence by a woman. All it takes is to think twice or maybe three times. You guys with me here? You on the same page?"

Given little choice in the matter, Dickie and Tommy hung their heads and semi-nodded.

"Well *are* you? You gone dumb on me all of a sudden or what is this? *Say* it."

"On the same page," muttered Dickie and Tommy, relieved no pal of theirs was in the room to witness this humiliation. Man, would it have ever been hard to hold their heads up in the locker room anymore if this had gone public.

"Oo*kay* then. So here're the keys, go release poor Sabrina. I'll be watching while you do it."

And so it was that Sabrina/Marjory Mackey was set free without charge or criminal record for having shot Hank Orlando in the left Achilles tendon and with every opportunity to walk from the police station a new woman and start a whole fresh chapter in her life.

"So did she?" I hear you ask, to which the answer, for better or worse is, "No, not exactly." Instead, beset by residual feelings of guilt despite Jeannie's exoneration, she jumped into a yellow cab and headed back to Hank's tiny apartment, albeit this time to set matters straight once and for all.

~ * ~

Sandra Normington was struggling with similar but far more convoluted feelings of remorse towards Andy Crane. To the theory he had been a hero in punishing Hank Orlando for his intended deflowering of her—at the time, and still Sandra was technically a virgin—she had now added the grinding guilt of her own responsibility for the affair that never was. If she hadn't fallen in love with Robert Redford in his Sundance Kid role at the movies, and if she hadn't heard of Hank as the new shrink on the block, and if he hadn't looked like Robert Redford, and if she hadn't found out Hank was the one giving Andy his treatment, and if she hadn't been stupid enough to doll herself up to the nines and, on the pretense of checking out Andy's progress, practically lay herself out before him and hold up a sign saying, "Fuck Me, Hank," Andy would simply have turned up for his session and had no reason to return some days later to shoot Hank in the genitals, and then escape to heaven knew where. That made a mere *five* ifs in total, but in Sandra's mind they amounted to about five hundred.

"If" is such a little word, isn't it? Yet it carries so much of the responsibility for many of the conditions that drive humans to the very edge, especially when linked up with the "should haves," "would haves," "might haves" and "could haves" of the always already conditional perfect tense. "If only I'd done this when I should have done *that*." "If only I *hadn't* done this and instead done that." And so on and so forth until you reach the awful conclusion it might have been better if you'd never been born at all. Well, that's where Sandra Normington was on the Andy Crane issue, over and again replaying in her head Tammy Wynette's "Stand By Your Man," but continuing to wonder if—another if—Andy Crane really *was* her man.

And this time around, Lucy Lomax was of no help because her own mind was too conflicted by thoughts of Quentin Trimble to think of anything much else, let alone the tribulations of a fellow sufferer. Let's just say now she was on the inside herself, she had lost all sense of objectivity in the matter of affairs of the heart. Of the fact she should be returning to her donnish duties on Merseyside, she was well aware, but somehow she couldn't tear herself away from the very place she had until recently derided as The Smoke because it contained *Him*. When she thought back on all the feminist crap she'd proudly "taught" at levels from BA to PhD back at the university, deconstructing texts by all the dead white males she could find from Shakespeare to D.H. Lawrence and beyond, she'd begun to feel a little queasy. What if (another if) the rival texts she'd promoted by women writers were, in their own way equally flawed by gender blindness? What if human love—hetero, gay, trans, whatever—was a subject beyond *any* understanding, especially in romance novels, and should never have been written about at all? Okay, there was religious love to take into account, but that too came with a whole set of brand names, most of which led to wars. No, no, to ask Lucy Lomax to talk Sandra Normington out of her current emotional impasse was akin to asking an Alzheimer's sufferer to remember the name of the affliction preventing him from remembering things.

It was during one of these protracted silences in Sandra's small flat that her phone rang, and when she took the call, an upbeat Scouse/Californian voice said, "Hi Sis, that you?"

Twenty-one

Antoinette and Quentin Trimble were astonished at Doc Frederick's cheery response to meeting Fion, and apparently not for the first time. Fion himself took the cheeriness in his stride, hopped up onto Doc Frederick's bed, shook his hand and said, "So nice to see you again too, old chap. Remind me, where was it we last met?"

"In the potting shed at the bottom of the garden," said Doc Frederick with perfect fluency. "Where *else* would one expect to meet a gnome?"

"Elf," Fion corrected.

"Elf, gnome, what's the difference?"

Fion didn't get pedantic about that. No good further angering a person who's only just stopped being furious with life and wanting to end it. Let sleeping gnomes lie and so on.

"And I suppose we went to the grassy glade together," he said instead.

"Indeed, in*deed* we did. And what jolly fun we had," said Doc Frederick, patting the top of Fion's head.

To any other observer, the obvious conclusion would have been Doc Frederick was off in la-la-land, but Quentin Trimble wasn't just any other observer, not when he too had met Fion in a shed at the bottom of the garden and been to the grassy glade. Antoinette hadn't done either of those things, but she'd believed her son when he told her about his new friend, the fairy. Nonetheless they stared on in wonder as Fion and Doc Frederick chatted happily, a wonder only marginally relieved by the reassuring wink Fion gave them while Doc Frederick was otherwise occupied blowing his nose.

"What the...?" Antoinette whispered to Quentin.

"Don't know, but you can bet it's some part of the cure."

"Without tinctures?"

Quentin shrugged and, for reasons he would never be able to explain seeing as he'd never read Shakespeare or seen the play, quoted Hamlet. "'There are more things in heaven and Earth, Horatio, than are dreamt of in your philosophy,'" he said, causing Antoinette to smile in memory of the time she had, with one minor change, used the same quote to her son. Perhaps he remembered the moment, but of greater importance just now was her confusion over what exactly it was Fion was doing to Freddie.

For which she had every justification, because the unusual modus operandi Fion was currently employing was that of the super-clairvoyant able to act as *both* the psychic conduit through which folk could contact the dead *and*, more pertinently in the current circs, to perceive each other's inner thoughts, feelings, and histories while they were still alive. It was on the latter category Fion was concentrating where Doc Frederick was concerned, his full attention focused on admitting to Doc Frederick's mind, in tiny fragments of mega-condensed bullets of metaphorical information, the erstwhile unseen and unfelt effects of his past behaviour on his wife and son… in other words, to see himself through their eyes. It was a rare talent even amongst fairies, and one that came with severe health warnings in case what the client saw was just too much to bear and led to self-destruction. A repeat of which was what Fion momentarily feared when Doc Frederick took to writhing against his pillows, his eyes closed but not in sleep—flickering—and his fists clenching and unclenching.

"Bloody hell, Fion, what've you *done*?" said Quentin, watching on as his father made little gurgling sounds and took to blatting himself on the brow.

"Shhh, shhhhh," said Fion, crossing his fingers and incanting a little prayer to Oberon. "All shall be well and all manner of things shall be…"

Which was when Doc Frederick suddenly stopped squirming and writhing, sat bolt upright in his bed, opened his arms to Antoinette and Quentin, and said, "Come to me if you can bear it, my dears. *Come* to me."

Antoinette and Quentin first checked with Fion, who nodded encouragement. Then holding hands, they went to the man who in way or another had made their lives a misery.

"I am *sooo* sorry," spluttered Doc Frederick, which Fion took as a genuine statement and confirmation his job was done, so this was the time to leave the humans in peace and hit the road, or in his case to dematerialize to the grassy glade for a big long puff at his FairyBac pipe and a chat with Bertie. So one minute he was still there; the next he wasn't. Not that Quentin or Antoinette noticed, preoccupied as they were in an unprecedented Trimble hugfest.

~ * ~

In his cell, Andy Crane was initially pleased at what he thought of as Art Scrivenger and Bazza Johnson taking the time to come and visit him in his hour of need. Okay, it was a little odd for both of them to have their hands behind their backs, but maybe that's where they were hiding the gift they'd brought him. Not that the copper who came with them was treating them with much respect, shoving them both ahead of him the way he was. It wasn't until Billy Flynn (the copper) took out a bunch of keys and took to unlocking the handcuffs securing Art's and Bazza's wrists before giving them a final shove at the two empty bunks, turning on his heels and locking the door behind him, that Andy managed to reinterpret the nature of his friends' presence. Not that they appeared particularly bothered about being banged up. Just said hi to Andy, teetered about chuckling for a bit, then collapsed onto their bunks and started snoring stentorianly. Pissed, Andy reckoned. Pissed or stoned or both.

It wasn't until the following morning after a night devoid of sleep that Andy discovered the true reason for their appearance in his cell, but even then, only in snatches of barely syntactical language between moans about monster headaches.

"Fuckin' Boodasist," grunted Art for example, before taking to hammering on the cell door demanding painkillers, none of which were forthcoming.

"Fuckin' sadist coppers," groaned Bazza, blinking his eyes in a vain attempt to reintroduce his brain to its normal functions. Which, in his brain's case, weren't anything to write home about at the best of times, but at least helped him distinguish between consciousness and oblivion.

"Boodasist sadist coppers?" said Andy, only to be told by Art and Bazza in unison to sod off back to his bunk if he knew what was good for him.

It seemed to Andy neither of the pair had even recognized him, so he just shrugged, lay back down, and let what was left of his mind drift off into thoughts of Sandra Normington and how she might conceivably have come to think of him as the saviour of her honour. *Was* it a possibility after all, or was this just wishful thinking? If only he could *know*, but there was no way of knowing, was there? How much he now regretted Andy's and Bazza's bots, and how they must have muddied already less than clear waters. God only knew what had inspired them. If God existed that was, which Andy had always doubted. What kind of a god was it that first created Earth then sat around twiddling his fingers while his (human) creatures devastated it with their polluted greed? He seemed to remember having read in the *Illawarra Mercury*, Wollongong's newspaper, that now there was this new virus on its way, threatening to decimate the entire population as the result of some Chinese peasants having eaten a pangolin. Another of God's oversights, or was this his—or Nature's— revenge for humans having wrecked his planet?

He awoke as the result of being shaken by Art Scrivenger and told to stop snoring if he wanted to live.

"Fuckin' snorer," grunted Bazza somewhere off in the background. "Fuckin' Andy the Pom, fuckin' snore machine."

Which was when Andy rolled off his bunk and had another go at finding out what crime the pair had committed to be sharing a cell with him. At least one of them now knew who he was. And the story that unfolded wasn't a pretty one. Andy was aware of Art's and Bazza's street-fighting days in which they had always cast themselves as the white hats beating back the black hats, but what possible justification could there have been for tying a Buddhist monk to a tree just because he'd offered them a pamphlet advertising the Nan Tien temple's wisdoms? None, Andy reckoned. Okay, he had himself shot Hank Orlando in the nuts for messing with what he was coming to believe was the love of his life, but that was a fair, even heroic, play he was starting to think. And also okay, he had severe doubts about God but it had never crossed his mind to capture a Protestant or Catholic, tie them to trees and throw eggs at them. No point, anyway, given how good they both were at torturing or killing each other in wars of (dis) belief, but a Buddhist? Andy didn't know much about Buddhists but reckoned them on the whole a fairly decent bunch preaching peace, harmony and suchlike.

"What d'you do *that* for?" he therefore asked Art, who had been the main narrator of the tale.

"Ah, ya know, bad day at the office, then some stuck-up punk in robes telling us how to be holy," said Art.

"Holy moly," said Bazza.

"Yeah," said Art.

"And you'd both had a skinful?" said Andy.

"Plus some good weed," Bazza agreed.

It was Andy shaking his head in evident disapprobation that caused the ruckus that alerted the coppers to the usual difficulties in a three-man cell. Wordlessly, they picked Andy up from the floor and removed him to safer quarters—from which he would that very same day be released after Billy Smith refused to press charges on the grounds the "poor Pom" would have suffered enough after "his lot" (England) had been thrashed by an innings and fifty-eight runs in the latest Perth test match. Ozzies take their cricket seriously *and* sportingly.

So it was that Andy Cole became a free man again and, while Art and Bazza remained in the slammer, he had the run of their apartment to himself.

~ * ~

"Just a little prick," Quentin Trimble told Lucy Lomax prior to her flu jab in those innocent days only a few short weeks BC when general practitioners could still treat patients face to face. "You'll hardly feel a thing, then it's no flu for you," he added with no suggestion at all of the wisdom of precautionary tests for breast and ovarian cancer afterwards just to be on the safe side.

"Okay," said Lucy, rolling up the sleeve of her blouse and smiling as goofily as she could ever remember herself having smiled.

"Righty-ho then," said Quentin as the needle delivered the goods and was then ever so carefully retracted. "You can roll your sleeve back down now."

"Thanks so much," said Lucy, vaguely recalling Sandra Normington's admission as to the reason for Andy Crane being sent to Hank Orlando in the first place. For touching up female patients with no cause, as Lucy remembered it. Which Andy would never have needed to do if only Sandra hadn't kept on pleading her excuse about hair washing. *Any*way, no danger of such behaviour, more was perhaps the pity, from *this* young gentleman—gentle man as Lucy thought of Quentin.

"*Pas de quoi*," said Quentin, unconsciously employing one of polyglot Fion's favourite phrases and thereby—equally unconsciously— sending shivers of pleasure up Lucy's spine. Such savoir faire she had *never* encountered from blokes on Merseyside.

So far so *very* good, although neither Quentin nor Lucy would have been able to verbalise the subtext of the pleasure they were both experiencing, especially after the restless nights of dream-soaked anticipation in both their beds. But now, the doctor/patient roles were over and the obvious question pinging around both their heads was, "What, if anything, next?"

In advance of Lucy's appointment, Quentin had cleared the rest of the afternoon so as to be able to follow Fion's advice and ask her out, but what Fion hadn't told him was *how* a person did that. "Fancy a coffee then, do you?" seemed far too abrupt a switch from the professional to the personal, and worse still was, "I know a nice little place around the corner." What if she just looked blank, smiled wanly, and said, "Oh" before putting on her coat and heading for the door?

Lucy was equally confounded. Would-be suitors up on Merseyside she'd known well enough how to handle when they made their all too obvious moves on her. Like Sandra, she always had hair washing at her disposal for the less insistent ones and "Slow down, pal" for the more persistent. And if push really came to shove, she shoved. The taekwondo black belt helped with that. But this lovely bloke either wasn't in any of those categories, or perhaps just plain didn't fancy her. *Or* maybe he batted for the other side. How ironic would *that* be? So many years of fending off all but a couple of possible boyfriends, and when Mister Right came along, there was zero interest.

It was while she was struggling with this unwelcome thought, picking up her coat, and sliding an arm into a sleeve that Quentin, going for the traditional British weather obsession as his only viable gambit, said, "Nice day today, especially after yesterday," which was both true and not, yesterday having consisted of constant rain with a cold wind and today merely of a cold wind with only showers and the odd burst of reluctant sunshine.

"Well, sort of," said Lucy, brushing at the wetness the showers had left on her coat.

"Indeed," said Quentin, enthused at Lucy's response, although in truth, he would have been enthused by *any* response. "Pretty unusual the weather these days. I put in all down to climate change."

Like Quentin when quoting from *Hamlet* in Doc Frederick's bedroom, i.e. for no reason she could think of, Lucy quoted Amiens in *As You Like It*. "'Blow, blow thou winter wind, thou art no so unkind as man's ingratitude,'" she said.

Which was the spur that led the two of them into a discussion of not only climate change *per se* but the blind greed that caused it, the irresponsibility of politicians worldwide who tried to brush it under all manner of capitalist carpets, and the vital importance of young Greta Thunberg's Extinction Rebellion. You know how it is when two people discover shared concerns, *vide* Doc Miriam Proudfoot and Prof Finian O'Toole for example, how that tiny spark can lead to greater things. And so it was with Quentin Trimble and Lucy Lomax.

After only ten or fifteen minutes of their discussion, Quentin found no difficulty at all in saying to Lucy, "Look, I tell you what, why don't we continue this over a cup of coffee? There's a Starbucks just down the road," and Lucy replied, "I thought you'd never ask."

Twenty-two

Had they known Andy Crane to have been the genitalia pepperer sought by cops on both sides of the Atlantic, the Wollongong police might not have released him with no more than a warning about never again pissing on cabbage palm trees and fisting objectors, or else he'd be in real trouble, but they didn't know. It wasn't as though the attack on Hank Orlando thousands of miles away in Battersea South West London had made headline news in Wollongong where folks were still clearing up after the fires and now beginning to get paranoid about coronavirus. When contacted separately by DI Derek Wilde in London and Sergeant Jeannie Quinn in New York City, both with extradition on their minds, the Wollongong coppers were, therefore, understandably surprised but also unrepentant when it came to explaining Andy Crane's release from custody. Even if they *had* known about the "bollock blasting" as they termed it, they argued there wouldn't have been anything they could have done about it anyway, because the crime had been committed neither on their turf nor by an Australian. They were equally unhelpful when quizzed about Andy's whereabouts *after* his release, saying they were sorry but there was nothing they could do about that either, because, so far as they knew, Crane was a PONFA (Person of No Fixed Abode).

Andy had lied about the Kemblawarra address partly in order to cover his own tracks but also to spare Art Scrivenger and Bazza Johnson the further accusation of harbouring a cabbage palm pisser and thus further complicate *their* release. He wouldn't have minded hitting the highways with them in the Winnebago for a while to let life calm down a little.

"Sorry, no idea *where* he is," Incremental Sergeant Jeff Smith told both DI Wilde and Sergeant Quinn during their separate calls.

And why, you will be wondering, weren't Wilde and Quinn acting in tandem on this matter? Why the split site activity when the interest in Andy Crane was something they had in common?

Answer: disagreements over extradition, Wilde arguing the genitalia peppering had happened on his patch, ergo *that* was whither the doer should be returned for trial, and Quinn countering with the assertion Hank Orlando was an American citizen who deserved a hearing in his country of origin. Such were the headline issues, beneath which, of course lay critical subtexts, namely prejudicial factors in both scenarios. If Crane were to be tried in the UK, Quinn argued, he would probably get off scot free as the result of home boy bias. Denying this, Wilde nonetheless came back with an almost exactly similar objection to the US extradition model, claiming even a character as lubricious as Hank Orlando aka Robert Redford Jnr—Wilde had done his homework—would win support from any US jury just for being the stand-up guy he clearly wasn't. In these exchanges, the "cousins across the pond" fiction clearly came under some scrutiny, although in their hearts both Quinn and Wilde knew the other to be right. After all, try though they might, neither could deny the madmen in charge of their countries had both been wrongly acquitted of clearly criminal activity as the result of endemic populist fervour. In the end, it was Quinn who threw in the white towel.

"Okay, Wilde, ookay you win," she eventually conceded. How in all honesty could she go on covering up for a legal system that couldn't even impeach a slimeball president whom she dearly hoped would soon receive a nemesis coronavirus handshake to settle his hubris forever? No way, that was how. If it had to be the UK for Crane's arraignment, then the UK it would be.

But surprising even Quinn, who to rise to the position of sergeant in the NYPD, had needed to be a pretty unsurprisable woman, Wilde rejected the offer. You know how it is in these days of normalized dishonesty, how rare it is to come across a person prepared to articulate the truth even if it plays to their disadvantage.

"Nice of you, Jeannie," he said. After so many Skype conversations, the pair were now on first name terms. "But in all fairness, I can't accept. You've been straight with me, so I'll return the favour. After the Brexit bollocks, Brits are cock a hoop with their escape from 'foreign domination,' and okay that mainly means by Europeans, but I wouldn't rule out Americans, especially not ones like Hank Orlando who have been caught trying to ravish one of their own."

"Nice of you, too. So where do we go from here?"

"Dunno. Some neutral country?"

"What, we run Crane's trial in Thailand? Gimme a break, Derek."

And so it was that the extradition question reached an impasse from which it would never recover, Quinn and Wilde agreeing on the imperative of joining forces to catch Crane but deferring to some later date any decision about what to do with him once he was in custody. Wilde had a hard time selling the idea to Imogen "The Bitch" Isaacs, but even she eventually relented, which, at least temporarily, removed the threat of suspension without pension rights from him and his team.

"Just make sure you and the Yank bint *do* catch him," she however insisted, pointing Wilde at the door of her office.

Quinn had no such problems with her superiors because she hadn't confided in them, given they were all good ole boys who would have happily seen Andy Crane on death row for what he'd done to a poor American innocent. If the whole thing went tits up and she lost her job, well so be it.

Pro tem, there was an interesting footnote to the Quinn/Wilde negotiations, namely the freebie weekend Jeannie offered Derek in New York City. At first, Derek demurred for fear of catching the new virus, but then he'd reconsidered and thought, "Screw it, if the bug gets me it gets me." Which was a wise decision, because the bug didn't get him, but he did get to screw Jeannie Quinn at her Brooklyn apartment—or to be more precise she to screw him or, to be even more precise, the two of them to screw each other and thoroughly enjoy the mutuality of the experience.

~ * ~

Having chosen the simultaneous timing on purpose, Sandra Normington met big brother Ronnie at an Italian restaurant called *La Cozza Infuriata* on Battersea high street at the same time Lucy Lomax was having her flu jab administered by Quentin Trimble. Only too well she remembered how infatuated Ronnie had been with Lucy when they were both teenagers back in Birkenhead, and how uninfatuated *she* had been with him. Terrible angst the rejection had caused in the Normington household, Mildred and Henry having no clue about the handling of adolescent passion, brother Alfie dismissing the whole episode as a "jerk off," and little sister Sandra rendered helpless by vying fidelities to her big brother on the one hand, and her best friend on the other. All these years later, the very *last* thing she needed was for Ronnie to meet up with Lucy again, especially when she had her Cupid's arrows pointed at Quentin Trimble. You know how it is with first loves, how they never completely go away. As it later turned out, Ronnie was now "in a relationship" with a half-caste Native American TV starlet called Betsy Begay, but Sandra didn't know that yet, hence her caution over the possibility of reignited desires.

Meeting at the portals of *La Cozza Infuriata,* Ronnie and Sandra fell into each other's arms and hugged and kissed in a manner quite unlike the old Birkenhead days when they'd barely even touched each other. And not just because they were siblings, generally speaking, falling into people's arms in public then hugging and kissing them had been regarded as emotional instability in Birkenhead when they were growing up and, for all they knew, still was. It was only from exposure to the mores of the wider world they had learnt such flagrant displays of affection, albeit Sandra was less practised than Ronnie who from his time in California had also become adept at knuckle and shoulder bumping with male pals which would still have been considered a little odd among white folks on Merseyside where a nod and an "all right there, lad?" with hands in pockets normally sufficed when friends met. Mind you, such *sang froid*—or "sang Freud" as more educated Scousers called it—-would ironically become the favoured mode for everybody on the planet once Covid-19 struck and social distancing became the order of the day.

*Any*way, it wasn't long after they'd unclasped each other that they were met by the *ristorante's* smiling owner, Carlo Caccavale, who as an Italian was an expert at public hugging and kissing, even including man-to-man, and shown to the table Ronnie had reserved.

"Such a pleasure," he told the pair, gesturing for them to sit while he hurried off to fetch the menus of the day.

"So, Poops," said Ronnie, employing the childhood name Sandra had never liked. "How's it going? You're looking a bit peaky, I've got to say."

"So, so," said Sandra. "Some little ups and downs."

"Mainly downs, huh?"

"Life has been a little complicated," Sandra was saying as Carlo returned with the menus.

Ronnie went for the *Linguine Alle Vongole* with a side salad while Sandra picked the *Spaghetti Carbonara*.

"And for the drinks?" asked Carlo. "The house white I can recommend but if the gentleman and lady would care to see the wine list..."

"White would be great for me," said Ronnie. "You, Poops?"

"White's good with me, too," said Sandra, waiting till Carlo had hurried off before telling Ronnie her name was Sandra and please to stop calling her Poops.

"Sorry, love. Soo sorry," said Ronnie, shaking his head. "Old habits..."

"Die hard. Like in the Bruce Willis films."

Ronnie laughed. "Yeah."

"Anyway, how have *you* been doing?"

So Ronnie gave his sister a brief résumé of his Silicon Valley life, how everyone rode around the compound on bicycles as if to play down the enormous influence they had on the planet around them, how he moonlighted a little with the FBI on bot traces, how he had this "thing" going with starlet Betsy Begay but didn't know where it would lead, probably nowhere, but it was fun while it lasted. Being blessed with litotes from his old Birkenhead days, the account lasted little more than a few minutes and was accompanied by modest shrugs at every stage. Not a "let's talk about me" person was Ronnie, who seemed almost relieved when Carlo returned with their wine and dishes and wished them *buon appetito*. Sandra remembered him for that and liked the memory.

"Sounds exciting," she said nonetheless, prodding at her spaghetti. "Lots of nice sunshine too, I suppose."

"There is that to it."

"How long are you here for?"

"Could be some time. You haven't heard?"

Sandra shook her head. "About what?"

She had kept news pretty much on the back burner since the self-obsessed buffoon was elected to 10 Downing Street and, in any case had more pressing things on her mind, Andy Crane, for example. She had a vague idea of the increasing threat of the bug issue but that was about the size of it.

"It looks like America's going to be in virtual lockdown over Covid-nineteen, only a few flights a day allowed in from Europe, so I dunno *how* long I'll be here," said Ronnie, forking some linguini and twirling them around in the seafood. "It was announced the day after I arrived. And once your dumb prime minister gets his arse in gear, the same will be happening here. And it's not just flights, there are all kinds of other closures, too, so this could be the last time for a long time we'll be allowed to sit within two metres of each other at a restaurant. *If* they're still open. Stateside it's going to be take-ways only and no loitering outside."

"Holy *shit*," said Sandra. "I hadn't realised it had…"

"Gone that far?"

"Yes."

"Well it has. You're the doctor...you didn't know about these things?"

Sandra nodded. "Not in so much detail. It was remiss of me not to chase it up. It's just..."

"Those little ups but mainly downs, right? Want to tell me more about those?" said Ronnie, sipping at his glass of Orvietto. "It's what big brothers are for, isn't it?"

Sandra raised her head, stared into his blue eyes, and said, "If you think you can bear it."

"Try me."

So, at somewhat greater length than Ronnie had devoted to *his* recent life story, Sandra offloaded the events of the past few weeks and, while her meal went cold, whimpered a lot.

"Jesus," said Ronnie, who hadn't allowed *his* meal to go cold. A person didn't grow up in Birkenhead and ever forget the waste-not-want-not adage. "*Some* story. And you think you love this guy?"

"That's juh-just it, I *dunno*," said Sandra, with a forlorn stab at a shriveled spaghetto.

"And you don't know where he is?"

"No."

"But you still have the phone you were using when you got copied in to the 'watch out, next time it'll be you' calls?"

"It's in my bag. I haven't used it since then, but..."

"You haven't deleted them?"

"No."

"Okay, want to hand it over? Like I said, I moonlight a bit with bots."

"You think there might be some trace?"

Ronnie shrugged. "It's a long shot from just one phone, and I don't have all my clever gizmos with me. But who knows? I may come up with something from this old brain of mine," he said, tapping at his right temple.

For the first time in a long time Sandra laughed. "You always were a clever bugger, weren't you?" she said, handing over the phone.

"At some things. Wish I'd been better at footie, though. Might have played for Liverpool. Looks like they're going to win the league this year. Fancy some dessert?" said Ronnie.

Over the *tartufo* ice creams followed by cognacs and Americano coffees, the two siblings came to know each other better than ever in the past and parted swearing to meet up again soon.

~ * ~

Which they did, at Ronnie's request only a few days later, seeing as he had some important information to share, namely the likely whereabouts of Andy Crane, always assuming it *was* he who had been sending the "next time it'll be you" messages, of course.

"You're sure, sure, *sure*?" he asked Sandra over coffees and paninis at a Caffè Nero almost emptied by urgent government advice about mingling with potentially virus-infested strangers. And this time, she *was* accompanied by Lucy Lomax, for whom she'd felt sorry after being told her best friend couldn't be left alone in the flat to "self-isolate." It wasn't as if she were an over-70 with underlying health issues, after all. Such was the category of folk the newly alarmed bumbler at 10 Downing Street had been advised by his equally alarmed "scientific advisers" to be most at risk from the bug rapidly heading their way.

And Sandra had succumbed. As for Lucy meeting Ronnie again after all these years, she'd just have to take pot luck with that.

"Sure as I can be," she replied. "Who else would have had bots focused only on the surgery crowd? How he managed to do it when he knew sweet FA about computers, I have no idea. Maybe he's fallen under the spell of some really nasty people, poor thing."

"And it was *only* on them, the surgery people?" said Ronnie, irritatingly losing eye contact with his sister to concentrate on Lucy crossing her long, lithe, black-stockinged legs as she relaxed back on the green faux-leather banquette beside him. Sandra was squatting on an equally faux-leather pouffe in front of them.

"Yes," said Sandra, arching an eyebrow at Lucy.

"Okay then, soo, my best guess is Wollongong, Australia," said Ronnie. "That seems to be the hub of the activity."

"Woll on *what*?" said Lucy, who was taking far more interest in the conversation than Sandra deemed appropriate. Lucy was supposed to be in love with Quentin Trimble, wasn't she?

"Gong," said Ronnie, addressing Lucy, his blue eyes misting over in ways Sandra didn't like the look of at all.

"Gosh, what a clever chap you've become since Birkenhead," said Lucy, re-crossing her legs the other way. "I like the new accent, too."

It was then that Sandra thanked her brother for his efforts, said she'd be back in touch soon, stood, reminded Lucy of an appointment her friend didn't have with a hairdressing outfit called *Cheveux* on the high street and practically dragged her away, leaving Ronnie to gaze in her wake while Lucy kept turning around to gaze back. "Ronnie distancing," Sandra named the activity, doing her best to keep up with the latest Covid neologisms.

Twenty-three

Doc Frederick maintained the new benevolence towards his wife and son for as long as they continued to humour his belief he was a fairy and allow him to spend hours every day in the shed at the bottom of the garden incanting arcane ditties to himself.

"He'll snap out of it soon, I'm sure," Quentin consoled Antoinette. "Probably just some leftover trace from Fion's visit."

"Hope you're right, Quentie, and your elf friend didn't screw up somehow."

"I've never known him to, more likely just another a glitch in Dad's mind. He hasn't been himself for some time, after all."

"Which 'self' d'you mean, the nasty old one, the nice new one, or some self nobody's ever seen before?"

Quentin shrugged. "Any of the above. Maybe this is the *real* one."

"As a *fairy*?"

Quentin had no answer to that.

"Get real, Quentie, he's off his trolley good and proper this time."

"But at least he's harmless. There is that to it."

Mother and son batted the issue back and forth until the day Antoinette burst into tears and said, "In all the years I've lived with your father, he's been a problem one way or the other and now *this.*

Well I'm telling you, Quentie, enough is *enough*. You cannot expect me to go on making breakfast, lunch, and dinner for a person who thinks he's a fairy and keeps asking me to knit him proper fairy clothes. He knows I can't knit, for God's sake."

Sympathizing, Quentin nodded. The situation *was* a tricky one, no question about it. "Okay, so what do we do?"

"Make him face reality for once in his sweet life."

So came the traumatic day when Antoinette and Quention ceased playing along with Doc Frederick, banned the garden shed routine, and told him to stop acting out his silly fairy games. At which he unsurprisingly blustered and wept. Wouldn't you if from one day to the next you were told you weren't who you thought you were? But Doc Frederick's pain was further exacerbated by the spread of coronavirus. And this wasn't just hand-washing and cold-shouldering strangers with temperatures and niggling coughs we're talking. This was the sudden edict (see above) that forbade elderly people, especially those with "underlying health issues" to leave their homes and instead to self-isolate. It was when fed this information by Quentin that Doc Frederick reverted to the nastiest of his selves.

"Get thee hence and multiply," the ex-neurosurgeon and now soon-to-be ex-fairy told his wife and his son in the King James's version of fuck off. "If you think you can lock me up in my own house twenty-four-seven, you've got another think coming," he added in his still elfin reedy voice.

"At least he's speaking grammatically," Quentin whispered to his mother, who shrugged off her son's optimism.

"Just because of this Connor virus, who's Connor, anyway?" Doc Frederick continued at full decibels. "Some rogue Irishman?"

That was when Quentin did his best to explain the most terrifying contagion to afflict humankind since the Black Death, and how elderly folk across the globe were being advised and/or ordered to stay in their homes for fear of either catching or spreading the disease.

"Which I haven't *got*. Fit as a fairy I am," Doc Frederick protested.

"Possibly you are, possibly you're not, that's the problem with this little beast," said Doc Antoinette, who'd been glued to the TV, radio, and social media for days doing her professional best to get to grips with all manner of different interpretations and been unable to come to any firm conclusion. "One day you're in ruddy good health, the next you're coughing a bit, the next you're dead," she added inaccurately.

"Especially if you're elderly and have any underlying health issues," Quentin re-emphasized. "This is for your own *good*, Dad."

"*Me*? Elderly and with an underlying whatsits?" Doc Frederick squeaked.

"You'll be sixty-six next birthday," Antoinette reminded him.

"And there's the hand tremors," Quentin added. "That little glitch in the neurological system?"

"*And* you've been thinking you're a fairy," said Antoinette conclusively.

All things considered, it would have been sensible of Quentin and Antoinette to pick a less easily escapable part of the house to hold this conversation than the lounge abutting the garden, especially as the French windows were open. Equally, it would have been preferable for them both not to take simultaneous temporary absences from the room—one for a pee, the other to put the kettle on—otherwise, Doc Frederick wouldn't have made his wibbly-wobbly bid for freedom and needed to be caught by Quentin just as he was grappling with the garden gate in search of the grassy glade. But you know how it is with the conditional perfect tense, we've been through that enough already.

Anyway, the upshot of all this was a severe wigging from Doc Antoinette as Quentin pinned his father to the lawn, and Doc Frederick shortly thereafter entered an indefinite period of isolation without the option of the self being involved in the decision.

"Swine, ingrates, poo-eaters," he squealed as he was frog marched up to his bedroom and dosed by Doc Antoinette with an illegal syringe of Valium.

"Such a shame when he'd been doing so well," she said to Quentin when they were back downstairs sharing an expensive but necessary bottle of Chateau d'Yquem. "On the other hand, one has one's limits."

With which Quentin couldn't disagree.

~ * ~

As is the way with males who believe they are of the alpha kind, and whose women will therefore always come crawling back, Hank Orlando wasn't surprised when Sabrina/Marjory Mackey knocked on his door, presumably begging forgiveness. Such groveling he expected from his cast offs and, nine times out of ten, on their return he would be right. In which case, he would allow them a few sex games with him before he gave them the final kiss-off. But in some arcane way, this tenth time was different. Why? Because this one had dared shoot him, which must have meant *some*thing, although quite what Hank couldn't figure. Maybe she was just ballsier than all the others. Not that she *had* balls, of course, but the word was the best Hank could come up with in the circumstances. Or maybe she was crazy. That was a headline possibility, in which case he should steer well clear for fear of getting shot again. Or perhaps she was after his money, which was just downright dumb of her, because he had practically none left. The one reason for Sabrina's behaviour Hank did not come up with was that, asshole though he was, sex games or no sex games, she still loved him. How could he, like the delusional narcissists in the White House and 10 Downing Street, have reached such an alien conclusion when "asshole" was the last word in the dictionary he would think of as a self-description, and "Platonic," particularly when concatenated with "love," was unheard of?

But this state of confusion didn't arise in Hank's mind immediately upon Sabrina appearing on his threshold. At that moment, as he opened the door, he smirked superciliously the way it is with alpha males, and said, "Hi babe, I figured you'd be back. Cops let you out on licence? Dumb of them, but hey, that's cops. What're you carrying this time, an AK forty-seven?"

What was really weird, though, was Sabrina neither rose to such a put-down nor wept hysterically the way of all Hank's other exes before falling into his arms and rubbing his crotch. She just asked coolly if she might step inside, there was something she needed to tell him.

"Like what? Lemme guess. You couldn't live without me no more, right?"

"Wrong," said Sabrina, "Could I come in?"

"You can come in, out, any which way you like, honey. I'm magic in the sack, you know that."

Which was when Sabrina told Hank—a first in his experience—to stop behaving like a dumb dork and try acting like a grown up for a change.

"All I'm asking is a few minutes of your time and a cup of coffee," she added.

At which Hank blinked slightly, then took a step back and did his Robert Redford Jnr thespian thing, spreading his palms and ushering her inside.

"Sorry about the leg, how is it?" she said on her way past.

"Gimpy and painful," said Hank, kneading his bandaged splint and going for guilt, sympathy, and tears of regret, none of which were forthcoming. What he got by way of reply was, "Yeah well, you had it coming."

"Huh?" said Hank.

It was this early in the meeting that the first seeds of difference and confusion were sown in his mind. No falling into his arms, no crotch rubbing, no regret, all *very* unusual—and ballsy. But how could Hank have known the single most important lesson Sabrina had learnt from Jeannie Quinn was never again to take shit from wannabe alpha males. No way, that was how.

"Like I said, you had it coming," said Sabrina, heading for a tatty ex-leather couch. "I take my coffee black, one sugar."

Hank closed the door and limped to the kitchen alcove. "Yeah, I remember."

"Glad to hear it."

"Whadda *fuck*?" he muttered under his breath as the kettle boiled.

"What the fuck about what?" asked Sabrina, whose hearing was off all normal scales.

"Nudn, nudn. Little problem with the kettle is all. Don't sweat it."

"I won't."

"Good, great."

It was when Hank sat himself down gingerly next to her on the tatty couch that Sabrina applied Jeannie Quinn's rule number one: eyeballing.

"Never look down, never look away, stare 'em straight in the eye," she'd said. "They hate that. Makes 'em go all queasy."

And Jeannie was right. When Hank asked her about the thing she'd come to tell him, he was looking anywhere except at her. At walls, the window, his trouser cuffs, *any*where but into the eyes that bored into what little soul he had left.

"Ookay, so this is it," said Sabrina, replaying more or less verbatim what Jeannie had told officers Dorkins and Tremaine, namely, "You ain't telling me I had no cause to shoot you when I'd been looking out for you ever since back in LA, and then you start bragging about screwing nearly as many women as Mick Jagger, are you?

Hank took an unnatural interest in his shoelaces and said nothing.

"Well, *are* you?"

"Nnnnnn, um..."

"Say it, man."

"Nuh-no."

"Good, right, okay. Plus, *plus*, I was the woman who would have tried to save you from being shot in the balls by the Crane creature if he hadn't already laid me out cold. You ever thought about that?" said Sabrina, tactfully omitting all reference to *her* plans with the little 9mm during Andy's first visit.

Even closer shoelace examination from Hank.

"Orlando you are starting to piss me *off*. Answer me."

"Nuh-no."

"Right, so you know what I figure? It's time you did," said Sabrina, her eyes drilling into the side of his head. "And while you're thinking it over, I suggest you also ask yourself *this* question."

Hank rolled his shoulders uneasily but at least looked up. "Which is?"

"Why?"

"Why whut?" said Hank, running down his mental list of ballsy, crazy, or just rapacious.

"I stood by you through thick and thin."

Hank dared briefly to look into Sabrina's eyes, then quickly averted his gaze to a spider's web on the ceiling.

"Oookay, so I'm gonna save you some thinking here, Hank, and answer my own question. Because I loved you, that was why. Sure, your whole surface behaviour said asshole, but in my head there was a better guy underneath the bullshit, and *that* was the guy I wanted to love. You anywhere near the page I'm on here?"

Hank wasn't. "Asshole surface behaviour?" "Better guy under the bullshit?" "Love" for crissakes? It was a heady mix, and all in one short sentence. Okay, so he'd taken a little advantage from looking like Robert Redford, but so the fuck what? A guy uses what he can to get ahead, right? And Robert wasn't an asshole, as least so far as Hank knew. He was one of the white hats. As for some *other* guy underneath, man that sounded like the psychobabble Hank happily regurgitated to paying customers, but had never applied to himself. It was around the time of this realization that the fragment of penny dropped.

"You're awful quiet, Orlando," said Sabrina in an appreciably less hawkish tone. "Anything you wanna say about what *I've* been saying, anything at all?"

Hank took a deep breath and dared look in her in the eye. "You mean the *other* me?"

"That's what I'm digging down to, honey. The other you."

Bizarrely in the circumstances, Hank Orlando guffawed.

"That's funny?" said Sabrina, inching an upturned hand in his direction.

When the guffawing was over, Hank rubbed at his head with one hand and with the other took Sabrina's. "Yeah, both funny ha-ha and funny peculiar."

"How come?"

"Because until two minutes ago, there *wasn't* another me. Or put it another way, there used to be but I killed him off. Dead and buried *that* loser was."

It took another hour and forty-six minutes for Hank to outline practically syllable by syllable the reasons for him to have obliterated from all records the gawky high school kid who'd failed every exam he ever took and hadn't even been able to make up for that by being good at sports. Then one day on TV there had been a re-run of *Butch Cassidy and the Sundance Kid* and...

Sabrina stopped him right there. "Ever since there was a new you and you never looked back."

"Right."

"Kiss me, gawky high school kid. Only if you want to," said Sabrina, raising both palms.

And Hank did, gently, and with no roaming hands.

"So we can put me shooting you behind us now?"

"Yup, sure, like you said, I'm the one who takes the rap for that."

"So maybe we can find a little peace here?"

"Sure we can. Only *after* I've found the real asshole in all this, the one who knocked you cold, then shot me in the balls. Found him and twisted his neck like a turkey at Christmas."

"You couldn't just let that ride?"

"No, ma'am, no I could not. A guy has his pride, and I got guys on the case already. They know where he is and I'm sure as hell is hot gonna find him."

Sabrina sighed. "Right. Same old Orlando You want me along?"

Hank laughed. "Your choice, hon, but a ballsy shooter like you, a gawky kid like me could surely use when the brown stuff starts hitting the fan."

Twenty-four

At this point in our tale, all the interested parties in London and New York City knew where Andy Crane was—Wollongong, Australia. Even the Wollongong police knew he was somewhere in town, if not precisely *where*. What the interested parties *didn't* know was they weren't the sole possessors of this nugget of information, because there were other interested parties who knew. The cops didn't know Hank Orlando, the Mafia, the Boggarts, Fion, and Quentin Trimble knew, for example, and the latter didn't know the cops knew. And none of the above knew Sandra Normington now knew, too. The whole thing was a no-shared-knowledge zone. And as for the target of all of the above, Andy Crane, he was still under the happy delusion *nobody* knew where he was. Except for Art Scrivenger and Bazza Johnson, who had been released from jail with stern warnings about ever again kidnapping Buddhists and throwing eggs at them, and been reunited with Andy during a mutual post-incarceration forgiveness fest at the basement flat in the Kemblawarra district.

Mind you, all aspects of this localized ignorance were dwarfed by the much delayed shift of coronavirus gears by the hubristic madmen in the White House and 10 Downing Street, who had initially shrugged off the whole pandemic thing as beneath their dignity in the apparent belief they and their countrymen and women were immune from such footling infections. This by comparison with other much savvier leaders from far less developed countries, like South Korea, who got to grips with the problem early and wisely with nationwide testing and tracing and tracking, meaning their citizens nearly all survived. Yet, even at this later stage, the populist Yank and Brit leaders had pooh-poohed such an overreaction, which was why their citizens started—and continued—to drop like flies.

"Ooops," was the response to the hideous mounting statistics on both sides of the Atlantic, hence the sudden, belated, and daily changing measures taken on the hoof in the US and the UK, like the lockdowns which saw folk "advised" (not forced) to stay in their homes and to wear masks and socially distance themselves if they dared venture out to buy the food that was flying off shelves and being stockpiled by other masked bandits. Besides, nobody was supposed to travel anywhere for any reason, except health emergencies, especially on planes which might carry foreign bugs, hence the shutdown, as Ronnie Normington noted, of many airports stateside. Bunkering in, as was already being practised by sensible countries across the globe, became the new normal for the Yanks and Brits, and they didn't like it one bit, especially when it failed to stop them dying, even if they weren't over seventy and had no underlying health issues. Such is the backlash of nemesis.

*Any*way, I hear you ask, what has all this to do with our story? That the Battersea and NYC cops had no more than a snowball's chance in hell of making it to Wollongong to find and arrest Andy Crane, that was what. Because they were regular Covid-vulnerable humans, and their only obvious source of transport would be the very planes that were virtually all grounded. The *only* humans, therefore, who would be able to cover cross-continental distances with impunity would be those with fairy connections, because fairies' instant teleportation services know *no* barriers, including deadly diseases. *They* could go wherever they liked *when*ever they liked and take equally immunized humans with them, which in this case meant the Boggarts could easily spirit Hank Orlando and Sabrina/Marjory Mackey with them over to

Wollongong, and Fion the elf would have no trouble providing the same service to Quentin Trimble and—as we shall see in a minute—Sandra Normington. Not, of course, that either group knew the other would be making the same journey at roughly the same time, albeit for fundamentally dissimilar reasons, Hank and the Boggarts to behead Andy, and Fion and Quentin to liberate him from the supposed clutches of malign computer experts before whisking him back to the UK. It was all a very muddled picture.

~ * ~

And how come Sandra Normington booked her fairy teleportation to Wollongong along with Quentin Trimble? Because for reasons she would never fathom, like an epiphany it entered her head at three forty-two a.m. one sleepless night of her lockdown self-isolation with Lucy Lomax to quiz Quentin the very next day to see if he knew anything, *any*thing at all, that would confirm brother Ronnie's conclusion as to Andy Crane's whereabouts. Under the new Covid-freaked government "guidelines," the surgery was closed to patients and the doctors were only present to give telephone appointments, but they always took a lunch break and that was the moment Sandra would choose to ask her question of Quentin. It seemed crazy to suppose he might have the slightest idea, as he had shown no interest in Andy since his disappearance, but who knew? Who *knew*?"

Well, Fion the elf did but Sandra had no way of knowing that. And Quentin also knew Sandra would be asking because Fion had forewarned him.

"A matter of the heart and you should know about *those* by now, old chap," he said.

"Sandra's in love with Andy *Crane*, the genitalia shooter? I thought she was in love with the Hank Orlando creep, the bloke whose genitals he shot," said Quentin.

"She was, but she's had second thoughts, you know how it is with women. How they have the prerogative to change their minds."

"Indeed," said Quentin, who was still uncertain as to if or how his passion for Lucy Lomax might develop or even be reciprocated. He had wanted to take *her* along on the Wollongong trip, but Fion hadn't granted this wish on the grounds she would be an unnecessary hindrance and anyway, wouldn't even know why she was going.

"But if Lucy can't go," Quentin nonetheless continued, "why shouldn't Sandra also be superfluous to requirements?"

"Because she would be under strict instructions to play the game according to my rules if she wants to get the guy who intuition tells me also thinks he's in love with *her*. Let us just say she would be a useful magnet to have along in case Crane gets silly ideas about running away before we can catch him. Call me Cupid."

Quentin sighed meaningfully. If Fion had so much insight into the apparently shared amatory feelings of Sandra Normington and Andy Crane, and a desire to promote them, why couldn't he divulge at least an inkling of Lucy Lomax's feelings towards *him*? Because of the Ronnie Normington factor was the answer to that, hence Fion's silence on the issue. What he needed on board for the Wollongong trip was a fully compos mentis Quentin, not one distraught by the possibility of a rival in love and if, as Fion dearly hoped, the boy were to emerge a hero on the occasion, *then* there would be every chance on their return home Lucy would forget all about Ronnie Normington and fall into Quentin's arms in thanks for helping out her best friend in her love quest.

Such were the circumstantial factors when, according to her plan, Sandra and Quentin took their lunch break at the surgery, and sat in the deserted patients' waiting room sipping their tea from plastic throwaway cups and munching their Hobnobs...no takeaway cooked food like pizzas being allowed for fear of their multi-handled boxes carrying the big bad bug.

"Any interesting calls this morning?" asked Quentin, hoping to forestall the Andy Crane question for as long as possible.

Sandra shrugged. "All Covid related. Are itchy bottoms a symptom? Are ingrown toenails a symptom? What if I self-isolate so much I go insane and kill myself? How would *that* count in the death statistics I see on TV every night? As the bug's fault, the sodding government's fault or *my* fault? And then, there's the favourite: Is being over seventy already a death sentence even if a person still runs marathons and rides a bike, or is this ageism gone mad? Et... cet...er...a.”

Quentin nodded. “Same with me. So what do you tell them?”

“To stop listening to the bullshit on social media,” said Sandra, who had savvied up fast after returning to work.

“Me, too. Mind you, the daily zoom TV advice from the polished-faced PM-acolyte boys playing politics isn’t much better. Changes from day to day like the mind of their boss. A pity we don’t live in Germany or Austria where rules are *laws* that everybody obeys because the police enforce them. Even the Italians and Spaniards are now dying less than us.”

And so the chitchat continued until Sandra could no longer restrain her need to know if Quentin might have any idea where Andy Crane was and, if so, whether it confirmed Ronnie’s hypothesis. Quentin saw it coming from the way she disguised the burning question by *faux* choking on a Hobnob fragment and using the moment to disguise the tears that sprang to her eyes.

Patting her on the back with one hand and proffering her a plastic cup with the other, he said, “Dear, dear, how about a sip of tea?”

“Thanks,” spluttered Sandra until the *faux* choking was over. But the tears weren’t; the tears continued.

“Anything at all I can help with?” said Quentin, knowing full well what *that* would entail.

Which was when Sandra collapsed onto her colleague’s right shoulder and wept fulsomely for the better part of two minutes before pulling herself together, removing herself from the right shoulder, sucking in her cheeks, taking a deep breath and saying, “I duh-don’t suh-suppose yuh-you’ve uh-any idea wuh-what’s huh-happened to uh-Andy Cuh-Crane, huh-have you? Where he might buh-*be*?”

Which was when, swearing Sandra to total secrecy on pain of severe reprimands should she *ever* tell *any*one—sadly for him including Lucy Lomax—what he was about to tell her, Quentin explained what he knew, and Sandra almost fainted but checked herself and instead hugged and kissed Quentin Trimble.

Necessarily, of course, when the hugging and kissing were over, Quentin was obliged to divulge to Sandra not only the source of his knowledge, but also the plan Fion had in mind for Andy's release from his current troubles and Sandra's role in it. Not the easiest of explanations to collapse into the few short minutes before the lunch break ended and virtual doctoring began again, especially not the part about believing in fairies, but for wont of any other straw to clutch, at Sandra Normington bought it.

Which was how she booked her teleportation passage to Wollongong.

~ * ~

Never having been gainfully employed in the sense of going out to work, Art Scrivenger and Bazza Johnson were already pretty well accustomed to self-isolation and thus took to the government's new coronavirus advice like kayaks to fast-flowing streams. To them it was just a continuation of ordinary life with a few inconveniences thrown in, like shops running out of necessities, for example. But Art and Bazza overcame those easily enough by stockpiling the Kemblawarra flat with sufficient supplies of beer, wine, spirits and marijuana to last an army platoon months. They had some food—frozen burgers and suchlike—but reckoned that of secondary importance. If they needed more, they'd go out separately one at a time and steal it. Meanwhile, high as kites while masquerading as professors of virology at non-existent universities, they had themselves a ball listening to full-blast heavy metal tracks and saturating the global social media with as much false Covid information as their woozy minds could generate. Perhaps their most imaginative piece of work was the suggestion that the best way to combat the virus was to smoke at least twenty-five cigarettes per day, because research had shown the bug to be nicotine intolerant and frightened of cancer. "Give the little bugger a deadly cough before you get the one he's trying to give *you!*" they counselled. Furthermore, the "little bugger" had been scientifically proven to be mortally vulnerable to alcohol *and* the scent of human spermatozoa, particularly if released under water. In a nutshell, the most reliable way of beating the illness and staying alive was to have regular sex in the bath while smoking and drinking—a tricky feat even for the youngest and most agile of potential sufferers.

To give him his due, Andy Crane did point out that from a medical point of view such a prescription might be somewhat tricky for the over-seventies, underlying health issues notwithstanding, but Art and Bazza brushed aside such nitpicking. "Do the old folks good," they riposted. "At least they'll be having fun before they snuff it and the young uns may not snuff it at all." And how right they were. The gleeful responses on Facebook, Twitter, Instagram et al were overwhelmingly positive after all the doom-goblin negativity folk had been enduring for weeks. Okay, there were a few near drownings and heart attacks amongst the elderly, but in the majority of cases it was fun, fun, fun all the way. Art and Bazza were delighted at the suggestibility of their clientele, proving as it did the very weakness in humans they'd always suspected, namely susceptibility to blatant lying so long as it suited their purpose. How else would the dickhead in the White House ever have got himself elected? For all they knew, he would be following their advice, too. Better than swallowing bleach as he had proposed as a vaccine.

When they weren't concocting such witty Covid posts, they would take the occasional ramble with Andy around the empty streets commenting to each other on how spooky the whole situation was.

"Bleedin' creepy," Bazza would say time and again on these peregrinations. "Wonder what folks're *doing* all day long?"

"Watching TV?" Andy would suggest.

"Nah, fucking each other's wives," Art would correct him. "Get tired of fuckin' the same sheila twenty-four-seven, wouldn't you?"

Then they would amble back home again, drink themselves some more beers, and try on a battered old guitar to work out the chords of the Statler Brothers' "Flowers on the Wall" with its central character's admission to spending all his days playing cards with a pack of fifty-one, smoking cigarettes and watching Captain Kangaroo. And, more significantly, his defensive denial such behaviour meant he had nothing to do. But even when Art Googled the chords, they still couldn't get it quite right, and they were crap singers.

"Ah, sod it," Art would say, laying aside the guitar and booting up the computers instead. "How about we tell the world some more about old Connor Virus?" he added with a chaos theory reference to exactly the same name Doc Frederick had given the bug when having it explained to him by Quentin Trimble.

At this point, as at many others when left out of Art's and Bazza's agenda, Andy Crane would leave the room, sprawl on his cot, cover his head with a pillow, and think of Sandra Normington. Did she love him, did she not? If only there had been a daisy or a four-leaf clover on hand. But there wasn't.

Twenty-five

So, such were the situations of the central protagonists in the UK and Eastern Australia as the day of the showdown in Wollongong approached. Back in the USA, gimpy leg or no gimpy leg Hank Orlando and Sabrina/Marjory Mackey had their bags packed and were all set to go. All it needed was the thumbs up from Luca Gambonio and whoosh... off they would be teleported—always assuming Grimble and Grumble Boggart could get their act together in time, or at all. Grimble, and especially Grumble, were still being sniffy about the whole exercise, reckoning it to be "poxy peanuts" beneath their dignity.

"All this hassle just for some dickbrain to get his revenge on some other dickbrain over some broad," Grimble complained, for example.

"Not our usual type of job," grumbled Grumble. "Talk robbing some bank, and we're there. Talk rubbing out some dumb politico, and we're there. But *this*, sheesh!"

"What? We gotta take the dickbrain's bimbo with us? What the fuck *for*? Quick and easy, in and out with no passengers is our game. Like I said before, the dude falls over, he *stays* fallen over."

"The dame pisses her pants, the pants *stay* pissed," grouched Grumble.

On and on they complained until Luca Gambonio was obliged to remind them of the weapon he still held up his sleeve, the one linking both Boggarts to an unnatural sexual interest in elves for which they could be punished in extremely unpleasant ways if such information were ever to fall into the hands of boggart high command. To emphasize this point/threat in their protracted Skype conference call, Luca drew a finger knife across his throat, coughed imaginary blood, and hung his head as if dead. Which was how it came to pass, albeit with much reluctance, that Grimble and Grumble finally signed up to the deal.

"Only give us time to get our heads around this, okay?" said Grimble.

"Sure," said Luca. "You got till tomorrow."

That was team one therefore: Hank Orlando, Sabrina/Marjory Mackey, and the Boggart brothers, their mission to make Andy Crane suffer big time before Hank Orlando delivered the *coup de grâce*.

On team two were Fion, Quentin Trimble and Sandra Normington, who were also making preparations, albeit for a somewhat different purpose, i.e. to rescue Andy from his computer bot pals and bring him back to the UK with his agreement or without it. In pursuance of this goal, Quentin continued practising his transmutation from different-sized blokes into a six-foot harridan with a frying pan, while Sandra took willing instruction from Fion in grunting gutturally like a lioness protecting her cubs and, if push came to shove, morphing into said beast. After all, Scrivenger and Johnson were also street-fighting yobbos, and Fion was taking no chances should they try to keep Crane in whatever grip they held over him. Many happy hours were spent this way in the grassy glade, once Quentin had explained to Sandra his relationship with the elf and she, rather in the manner of Antoinette Trimble, had accepted it without demur. There was a certain sincerity in the little fellow's eyes that was impossible to resist. One matter that needed resolution for both Quentin and Sandra, however, was how their absences from London were to be explained to family, friends, and to the surgery. But Fion had just smiled.

"Don't worry," he said. "We'll be operating in fairy time, which functions in an entirely different zone from your humans' hours, days and weeks and suchlike."

"Meaning?" said Quentin.

"That we'll in and out of Wollongong in about as much 'time' as it would take your mother to make a cup of tea, so nobody will even know you're gone."

This worried Sandra. "You mean we'll become other beings when we're away, *amorphous* beings?"

Fion nodded. "Not fairies exactly, but yes definitely 'other'."

"Andy won't *recognize* us then?" said Sandra, who was keen Andy *should* know who she was, *very* keen."

Sensing her problem, Fion put an arm around her shoulder. "Don't worry. It's only in transit you'll be different."

"So when we arrive, we'll be..." Sandra persisted.

"Back to your normal selves, my dear. Which is as important to our whole strategy as it is to you in particular. The last thing we need, after all, is for Andy to be frightened away by what he perceives as ghouls. He needs to know it's *you* who have come to fetch him."

Quentin shook his head and smiled. "Some adventure."

"For you guys, sure," said Fion. "But remember, for me it is routine. Tried and tested, you might say. Now, how about we run through our plans one last time."

So they did. But never mind the opposing purposes of the two team's proposed trips, two further differences are worth noting at this juncture:

1) Team two was one person short of team one,

And,

2) Neither team knew the other even existed, let alone it too would shortly be heading to Wollongong.

The stage was set for a showdown, all right, but one somewhat different from such classics as *High Noon* or *The Gunfight at the OK Corral*, for example.

~ * ~

In many ways it was therapeutic for Hank Orlando, Sabrina/ Marjory Mackey, Quentin Trimble and Sandra Normington to have their minds occupied by the Wollongong project, because it at least deflected their attention from the lugubrious debilitation afflicting those only able to focus on Covid-19 as its impact accelerated and folk faced the "new normal" of lockdown. In the UK and US, as in countries all across the globe, major cities turned into ghost towns with no traffic on the streets, no cafés to go to, no cinemas, no pubs, no gym clubs, no hairdressers, no beauty parlours, no art galleries, no theatres, no sports events, no non-essential shops, and, very possibly, no parks, if folk went on breaking government rules by not socially distancing themselves properly. *Any*where folk might congregate in numbers was banned, including churches and mosques, which made the faithful *very* cross. Who was to save them from this horror show if not their saviours, who were clearly better placed to do so than any human government? It was like a world war again, only exclusively on home soil with nowhere to hide except one's house, and no recognizable enemy to hate.

Amongst the worst prepared, most resentful and antsy were the Americans, because they were accustomed to being the masters of the universe who even *in* world wars had never suffered enemy planes flying overhead bombing them, and now they were being told by the White House and their state governors to self-isolate. It was like telling John Wayne to stop hunting down bad guys. Elderly Brits, on the other hand, tried reminding the nation of WW2, the Blitz, and the Dunkirk spirit, which had seen them through the worst of times by pulling together and muddling through. Hopes were even raised of the benefits that would accrue from such behaviour when the crisis was over, assuming it ever was. Great were the expectations of self-reliance, the development of new skills such as carpentry and gardening, and if folk got used to getting on their bikes instead of into their cars, significantly lower levels of pollution.

Not that the greed-is-good, me-me-mine younger millennials were much impressed by such woolly thinking. They thrived on consumption and were terrified of the looming economic crisis that might take it away from them. Mind you, for consolation they had the social media and Netflix to turn to. After all, what was *so* bad about government-subsidized furloughs watching TV, (c.f. "Flowers on the Wall") or gassing all day and night with Skyped, Face Timed, or Zoomed virtual friends? Not a lot, they reckoned.

Pity the earlier generation of thirty-something parents, though, those incarcerated with tetchy children they were meant to home educate—at worst in tower blocks— but who had no idea or wish to learn how to teach their offspring, seeing as they'd never benefited much from education themselves. Not since records began had the divorce and domestic violence statistics amongst that group soared so steeply.

All in all, it was a very testing time, particularly as none of the "expert" government advisers quoted daily in the media could agree with each other on how long the pandemic would last, some suggesting the "peak" had already been reached, so restrictions could soon be lifted, while others believed freeing things up would only lead to another Covid spike, and even more of the deaths currently at record levels. It was all a question of wealth on the one hand or health on the other. No wonder those of all ages who were no good at carpentry, gardening, or cycling but *were* of an philosophical disposition, pretty soon fell into the normless anomie vaunted by some existentialists as the perfect position from which to develop self-identity. But who has ever met a *happy* existentialist?

Mind you, in the UK at least, there *was* an upside to this generalized state of angst, namely the heroic efforts of National Health Service doctors and nurses across the country, who worked double and sometimes triple shifts to prevent as many deaths as possible, or at least ensure the deaths were comfortable. "Never," to quote wartime Winston Churchill in reference to the RAF, "was so much owed by so many to so few." And it wasn't even as though the few were working with all the equipment they needed, because previous governments hadn't had the foresight to prepare for such emergencies, meaning the practically overnight erection of extra hospitals and manufacture or importation of ventilators becoming a priority. As, tragically in some cases, did the provision of appropriate equipment for NHS staff treating Covid patients without masks, visors, gloves, or other essential personal protection items. But, extended in all directions, on they crusaded until breaking point was only avoided by the invitation to retired doctors and nurses to offer their services if they felt able, several thousands of whom did.

Which brings us to a paradoxical upside in *our* little tale, because included in those thousands of comeback kids were Docs Frederick and Antoinette Trimble, Doc Miriam Proudfoot, and her new lover Professor Finian O'Toole, all of whom either forgot or sidelined their personal situations, waved two fingers at self-isolation, and offered their differing skills to lend a hand to the national effort on the front line. What did it matter if their specialisms in neurology, gynaecology, or health administration weren't of any specific use? In the end, they were all *doctors*, weren't they?

The most surprising of these new recruits was, of course, Doc Frederick who last we heard of him reckoned he was a fairy, but in ways neither Quentin nor Antoinette would ever fully understand, the years of anger, depression, and encroaching dementia fell away from him the night he accidentally tuned into the TV news and heard the call.

"Tonie, *Tonie*," he shouted downstairs to Doc Antoinette, who was doing her futile damnedest to knit him a fairy outfit, "come and listen to *this*."

So knitting needles in hand, she did. "Bloody hell," she said as the broadcast showed knackered doctors and nurses pleading for reinforcements.

"Indeed, my dear, hell *is* the word," said Doc Frederick in his old modulated but authoritative tone. "And so it is on the coronavirus wards, in the A&E, and all over the hospitals. Our country needs us, my dear," he added with a poor imitation of Lord Kitchener's 1914 recruitment poster plea, pointing finger and all. "So let us dig out our scalpels and offer ourselves to the cause."

Doc Antoinette smiled and, for the first time in a very long time, took her husband's hand. "More likely it's swabs we'll need, not scalpels, but I'm with you every step of the way, darling. We always used to be a good team, didn't we?"

"Indeed we were, my dear, in*deed* we were. Now take out your mobile telephone, if you would be so kind, and call the number they're giving on the screen."

Which was how it came to pass that Docs Frederick and Antoinette Trimble, with the enthusiastic blessing of their son Quentin, were gratefully signed up for duty the very next day by their local hospital, St Bede's where, as coincidence would have it, they met up for the first time with Doc Miriam Proudfoot and Professor Finian O'Toole, who had also enthusiastically responded to the nation's need for their skills.

"You wouldn't be in any way related to *Quentin* Trimble, would you?" asked Doc Miriam as, socially distanced in the otherwise closed cafeteria, the quartet awaited their marching orders from Senior Registrar Donald Rawlinson.

Doc Antoinette raised a surprised eyebrow. "We're his mum and dad," she said, elbowing Doc Frederick in the ribs to get his attention.

Doc Miriam sucked in her cheeks. "Dear, dear, *so* sorry."

"For what, pray?" asked Doc Frederick, less combatively than might only recently have been expected. "For being his parents?"

"No, I think what Miriam meant was she was sorry for the measures we were obliged to take with Quentin over his hypochondria, frightening patients and all that," said Finian O'Toole. "Not so, darling?" he continued turning to Doc Miriam, who nodded.

"Poor chap. But for that fatal flaw, he had all the makings of *such* a good doctor," she said.

These were the opening remarks in a conversation that would lead to clarification of the hitherto unknown interrelationship between the Trimbles and those responsible for packing their son off on the gardening leave that would lead to his felicitous meeting with Fion the elf. Not that fairy folk were mentioned, of course, although as a Dubliner Finian O'Toole wouldn't have batted an eyelid, except possibly to express a preference for leprechauns. By the time Senior Registrar Rawlinson appeared with heartfelt thanks for their volunteering and a proposed duty roster in a number of different roles, they were pretty much the best of pals.

~ * ~

"Don't tell me you slept with him. Do...*not*...tell...me...you...slept... with...him," fumed a furious Sandra Normington at Lucy Lomax as the pair sat self-isolating in Sandra's tiny lounge only days before her departure to Wollongong.

"Okay, I won't," said Lucy, arching her neck and twisting it about.

"Only you *did*, didn't you? *Didn't* you? With my brother, of all people, the one you dumped all those years ago back home because you reckoned he was a bit of a tosser."

"You said not to tell you."

"Well, what *else* where you doing with him last night?"

"Talking."

"Yeah, yeah, pull the other one. You might at least have called."

"Sorry, it got late, and we'd had a few drinks, and..."

"You had other things on your mind. Like sex, for example. I only found out *where* you were when I called Ronnie at his hotel and he said you were sleeping like a baby."

"On the couch."

"Yeah, sure."

"Call Ronnie again, he'll tell you."

"Of course he will. That'll be the story the two of you cooked up together, right?"

Lucy eyeballed Sandra long and hard. "And you're calling your oldest friend and your brother liars?"

Sandra sucked down her upper lip and bit into it. "Nuh-no, it's just..."

"Like I said, we talked, and that's *all* we did, okay? About the world going down the toilet and not just because of coronavirus, because of crap populist oligarchs threatening to destroy democracy and doing nothing about climate change, and all sorts of things. Your brother has grown up since the boy I knew in Birkenhead, in case you didn't know. He's a man now and a good one."

"Suh-so's Quentin Trimble."

Lucy nodded. "So *that's* your beef."

"Yes."

"I thought it might be. And you're right about Quentin. He *is* a good guy, a different kind of good, but good all the same. I talked about him with Ronnie, and he told me about his girl back in the States. We 'shared,' as current parlance has it, and the sharing was useful."

"Okay, look, I'm sorry."

"Filthy minded bitch," said Lucy, which at least raised a smile from Sandra.

"It's just I saw the way you two were looking at each other in the Caffè Nero, and then out on the street. Don't tell me you didn't fancy him and he you."

"Another 'don't tell me.' And yes, sure, there was something going on. I just wanted to check out what it was, that's all. I'm a big girl now, Sandie. And why're you being so solicitous for Quentin, by the way? Something I don't know about?"

The straight answer to this was, "Yes, Quentin's head-over-heels in love with you," as Fion had confirmed to Sandra vis-à-vis the ongoing Lucy/Quentin question during a practice session in the grassy glade, but this was no time to divulge such secrets any more than it was to tell of the trip to Wollongong.

Instead, all she said was, "I think he likes you, that's all. It's a little feeling I have."

"And you're the wise one of a sudden, the one who didn't know if she loved the Andy Crane guy or not? The days and nights we spent talking that one through."

"Yeah, sorry about that."

"It's okay. What friends are for? *Now*, are you finally persuaded I did not fuck your brother, the bloke who's become just my new best friend?"

"Yeah, I believe you."

"Good, because I've got a great movie from Netflix for us to watch in these next few lockdown hours. You ever see *Butch Cassidy and the Sundance Kid*?"

Sandra went deathly pale. "Yes, and I never *ever* want to see it again."

"Ooops, sorry, bad choice evidently. Some special reason?"

Which was how Lucy came to hear for the first time of the Hank Orlando/Robert Redford Jnr backstory.

"So *that* was why," she said, when Sandra spluttered to a full stop.

"That was why."

"Oookay then, how about we go for *Pretty Woman*?" said Lucy, keen to avoid any more in-depth emotional conversations.

Twenty-six

Teleportation can be fun, the way you might imagine a toke at a properly loaded and heated opium pipe to be. One minute you're still the ordinary guy or gal brim full of the normal human contradictions and uncertainties, the next you're in la la land and liking it. Worries vanish, the impossible becomes possible, the dreary concrete world becomes multi-dimensional and tinged with drifting rainbow colours in which you float, glide, and couldn't give a monkey's where to or where from. It's not like riding a jet plane; there's none of that trundling down runways before the sudden lift off into the skies, nor once airborne, unexpected buffeting by high winds. Also you don't have to have a passport or go through all the hassle of airports, including the fear of quarantine when you arrive, you can just take off from *any*where. In fact, it's not like flying at all, it's just moving from one state to another the way a person might move from being awake to being asleep or vice versa.

Such was the way Fion tried verbally to prepare his two last-minute-nerves "passengers" for their transition from Quentin's back garden in Battersea to Wollongong. Immediately ahead of the event, there would, of course, be the ministration of a special tincture that would respond to Fion's whispered command of "moozozoomie," but first, nerves needed to be calmed in linguistically pedestrian human ways.

"I fuh-feel like I'm nuh-Neil Armstrong or someone," said Quentin.

"Only you're not going to the moon, old chap, you're only going to Australia," said Fion.

"But what if our guh-genetic muh-make up gets scrambled on the way and can't get fixed again?" Sandra wanted to know. "It all sounds well and good in theory, buh-but..."

"I can assure you in practice it works," Fion reassured her.

"You've done this with humans before?" quizzed Quentin.

"Many times, although to be truthful, they didn't always know it. Just let us say it was always in their interest. Making sure they were in the right place at the right time."

"Such as?" said Sandra.

"That would be telling, a breach of the confidentiality to which we elves are sworn. However, key victories in your history might not have been achieved had certain kings and generals and so on not been roused from their ignorance of coming events and swiftly moved to the seas or the battlefield with their troops to face down the enemy. And in many of those days, there was no appropriate transport apart from horses. Sooo..."

"And no genetic damage done as a result?" Sandra persisted. "No incurable diseases or lunacy or anything like that?"

"None whatsoever, my dear. Mind you, some of the kings were functioning on very few reactive neurons to start with, so the difference was barely noticeable. Now, *if* you don't mind, it's time to get down to business."

"Good with me," said Quentin, throwing an arm around Sandra's shoulders and whispering, "Andy Crane, Andy Crane."

And so it was, along with the variegated tincture she and Quentin were given to drink, that nerves were settled, Fion muttered the magic word moozozoomie and next you knew it, whoosh...just like that, Quentin's garden was empty.

~ * ~

In accordance with coincidence theory, it was precisely at the same moment, transatlantic time difference notwithstanding, that Hank Orlando, Sabrina/Marjory Mackey and the Boggarts vanished from Central Park's Strawberry Fields area opposite the Dakota building outside which John Lennon was shot. And why were they there? Because apart from looking a bit like Robert Redford, Hank Orlando reckoned he could sing every bit as well as John Lennon, especially on "Norwegian Wood." Not one to underplay his potentialities, ex-gawky high school kid Hank Orlando, and not one with any fear of teleportation either.

"Think of it as a good luck omen," he'd told Grimble and Grumble Boggart who couldn't have given a good fuck *where* they took off from and only agreed to Central Park after further threats from Luca Gambonio.

"He's the boss," he told the misery brothers. "He says you do the business from the roof of a Greyhound bus, that's where you do the business from."

"Fuckwit," Grimble commented.

"Asshole," Grumble grumped.

"Mebbe, but he's paying the bills," Luca reminded them. "And hey, this job goes tits up, you ain't looking at no more contracts from me or any other of my guys. So act *nice, capisce.*"

"Nice spice," said Grumble.

The gathering in Strawberry Fields wasn't therefore a happy one, despite the Boggart brothers' rudimentary attempts at politeness on this their first face-to-face meeting with Hank Orlando and his broad. For the occasion, they had morphed into humans dressed in all black and looked pretty much like funeral directors or the Mr Smiths in *The Matrix.*

"Nice meeting wid you," Grimble managed to grunt while looking like he would have preferred to meet an orangutan.

"So you should be," said Hank, blind to the surliness so hyped up was he on hubris and Andy Crane blood lust. "Gimme five, guys."

Grimble managed a quick slap, but Grumble stared off and kept his hands in his pockets.

Undeterred, Hank said, "And this here is my sweet podna Sabrina. Say hello to our new friends, Sabbie."

"Hullo," said Sabrina, all down beat as if addressing two dentists preparing her for a root canal intervention. Over recent days, Sabrina had lost a lot of her original resignation to the Wollongong trip, especially the freaky teleporting part of it.

"Sooo, we all set?" said Hank, performing a few squats, downward dogs, and press-ups. "Just say the magic words and kerz*oom*, eh?"

"Gimme a minute," mumbled Grimble, ferreting in an inside jacket pocket. "I got the words in here someplace."

Hank frowned. "You don't know 'em by *heart*?"

Grumble smirked. "Memory ain't what it used to be."

"Fuck's *sake*," said Hank, jerking himself upright. "And Gambonio told me you guys were the business."

Sensing the vaguest hint of a possibility the trip might yet get called off, Sabrina steepled her fingers, placed them over her lips and bowed her head as if in silent prayer. Meanwhile, Grimble went on fumbling.

"Gotta be here *some*place," he said, winking at Grumble as they played out their rehearsed delaying tactics in the hope Orlando would get antsy enough to lose faith and let them off the hook.

But he didn't. Instead, having been forewarned by Gambonio of such a possibility, he picked Grimble up by the lapels of his Mr Smith jacket, shook him about for a bit, then hissed in his ear, "You better find the words quick, pal. Elsewise, I get to tell Mister Chief Boggart about how you guys like to screw around with nude elves. How'd *that* be?"

Bad was how Grimble reckoned that would be, which was when he pouted, shrugged hopelessly at Grumble and said, "All right, okay, you win. I got the words."

Hank dropped him back down to earth. "So *say* 'em, asshole, and get us out of here."

Left with no choice, a scowling Grimble pulled the group into the huddle from which Sabrina twice tried to escape until Hank secured her presence with an arm clamped up her back and then, when satisfied all was in order, muttered "Traggob fly" which was a lot less imaginative than Fion's moozozoomie, but that was boggarts for you.

And so it was that Hank Orlando, Sabrina/Marjory Mackey, and the Boggart brothers finally vanished from Strawberry Fields NYC and headed off in nothing like harmony to Wollongong.

~ * ~

Unsurprisingly, bewilderment was the initial response of teams one and two to each other's presence on the street outside Art Scrivenger's and Bazza Johnson's basement apartment in the Kemblawarra suburb of Wollongong when they both dematerialized there at precisely the same moment.

"Whadda *fuck*?" said Hank Orlando, for example, as he peered in disbelief at Sandra Normington who was accompanied by some dorky looking dude (Quentin Trimble) and a very short person with a long white beard.

Quentin was equally astonished at the presence of a limpy, but furious looking Hank Orlando, the woman he took to be his secretary, and two mafioso types straight out of *The Godfather*, all four of them looking daggers in their direction.

"Blimey," he said. Having refused his counsel, he'd never met Orlando in person, but after the kerfuffle over the Andy Crane affair, he'd checked out the pseudo-shrink's web site and seen the Robert Redford lookalike photos. And this was Hank, all right, albeit appearing somewhat more bent and ragged than in his pictures. But then, that's how a bloke *would* look after being shot in the privates, wouldn't he? Obviously enough, Quentin couldn't know Hank had also been shot in the left Achilles tendon or that it was the weepy looking woman at his side who'd shot him. But never mind all that, the key question was what they and the two goons were doing on the same Wollongong street as him, Sandra, and Fion.

Such bewilderment was pretty soon replaced by the need to flex muscles as Fion read the minds of the Boggart brothers and they read his, thereby revealing both parties' fundamentally different purposes when it came to their presence in Wollongong. Plus, of course—aside from the Boggart brothers' perverse interest in naked elves, about which even Fion could not know—boggarts and elves had since the birth of time detested each other. In such circumstances, conflict was pretty much inevitable as was immediately evinced by Grimble Boggart taking to hissing in Hank's ear, which caused Fion to warn Quentin and Sandra to remember the training he'd given them in expectation of resistance from Art Scrivenger and Bazza Johnson, but which now appeared be superseded by entirely new and *un*expected foes. Already Hank Orlando was pawing at the ground with his good leg and snarling.

"You take the American," Fion hissed at Quentin. "And you the woman," he told Sandra. "Leave the boggarts to me. They're slow and won't know what's hit them." he added, turning away to face Grimble and Grumble who were huddled together debating tactics. Which was mistake number one, because it gave Fion the femtoseconds he needed to summon his super-eyeballing powers. Mistake number two was for them to turn and face Fion when he called out, "Over here, bungling boggarts, come and do your worst," which foolishly they attempted to do, only to be stopped in their tracks and be petrified by Fion's prolonged hyper stare. And this wasn't "petrified" in the looser meaning of "frightened," this was "petrified" in its original meaning, i.e. turned to stone. One moment the Boggart brothers had access to normal bodily functions such as breathing, speaking, movement and so on, the next they didn't and became rooted to the spot like statues.

"Whadda *fuck*?" said Hank Orlando, whose vocabulary was limited when it came to expressions of surprise.

"Wow, nice one," Quentin congratulated Fion. "My turn now?"

"Go for it," said the elf. "And you too, Sandra, while the woman's looking freaked."

Which was true. Sabrina/Marjory Mackey was wide-eyed, wailing, and tugging at Hank Orlando's sleeve to forget all about the *coup de grâce* idea and get the hell out of there especially now the boggarts were out of the picture. It wasn't even as if Andy Crane were anywhere around to *be* coup de grâced.

So it was that, despite feeling rather sorry for her, Sandra gave Sabrina some of the lioness-with-cubs treatment while Quentin sauntered up to Hank who was preoccupied prodding the petrified Boggarts in their chests for vital signs. Of which there were none.

"Game over, Orlando. Whatever it was you came for, you're not going to get," he said. "Best thing you can do now is take your girlfriend and get the hell out of here."

Which infuriated Hank just the way Quentin had hoped it would. Dodging the haymaker that whistled past his left ear, he shrank down to elf size, scuttled between Hank's legs, morphed into a six-foot harridan, said "Hi there, honey," and, when Hank turned around to look, whacked him over the head with his frying pan.

"Gluuurggg, oooffff," said Hank before he hit the deck face first.

Meanwhile, Sabrina was on her knees before Sandra who was feeling even sorrier for the woman and so, hadn't given her the full lioness morph, only the growling head.

"Duh-duh-duh-don't eat muh-me," Sabrina spluttered. "Uh-uh-I ain't duh-done nudn."

While leaning down to give Sabrina a hand up, Sandra returned to her normal self by clicking her fingers and using the magic word Fion had given her, "*hpromer*" (re-morph backwards). "I know you haven't and sorry for scaring you, love. I didn't mean you any harm, honest I didn't. It was just my part in the play. If your friend Hank hadn't been so..."

"Yeah, yeah, I unnerstand. Thu-thanks."

When Sabrina was vertical again, Sandra threw an arm around her shoulders. "Okay if I look after this one? She's hurting," she called over to Fion.

Pleased with the speed and precision of their victory, Fion saw no problem with the request. "Sure, you're the doc, you take care of her. Quentin and I have other business."

Which was to drag a goggle-eyed Hank Orlando to his feet and tie him with specially reinforced elf rope to the trunk of a conveniently placed cabbage palm where he hung semi-consciously mumbling, whadda *fuck*? Fion would decide what to do with him and, indeed his lady friend later when the central part of the operation was over. Meanwhile, from behind him on the street, he sensed interest, and sure enough, turning around he saw Art Scrivenger and Bazza Johnson emerge from their basement, stare bemusedly at the petrified Boggart brothers, walk over to them, and occasionally prod them for signs of life, of which there were none.

"Whadda fucking *hell*?" said Art, whose lexical stretch on such occasions was about as limited as Hank Orlando's.

Bazza looked bamboozled, too. "Buggered if *I* know. Weren't no statues here last time I looked. Funny staring eyes they've got," he said, poking at Grumble's left one and arousing not even a blink.

It was Quentin who took command of the situation.

"Gentlemen," he said, relieved there might be no need for further fighting if, given Andy Crane was still nowhere to be seen, his two potential protectors could at least be otherwise distracted. To this end, he adopted what he thought of as an Italian accent.

"Lette me introduce-uh myself. I am Quentino Trimbletino, the sculptor. You like-uh my pieces?"

Joining the group, Fion laughed. "Nice one, Quentie."

It was while these folk were thus distracted and Sandra was still soothing Sabrina, that Andy Crane finally emerged from the basement flat rubbing his eyes after several hours of self-isolating sleep during which he had dreamt uninterruptedly of Sandra Normington and wondered briefly if he were *still* asleep given what he was seeing or if…

But his wonderings were pretty soon over because it was only moments later, having left Sabrina in something resembling peace, that Sandra was in his arms for real and both were swearing eternal love for each other.

It was all very sudden, but nonetheless *very* romantic.

Twenty-seven

DI Derek Wilde was both astonished and furious when, accompanied by Sandra Normington, Doc Andy Crane walked into Lavender Hill cop shop and gave himself up for questioning over the Hank Orlando genitalia peppering incident, as advised by Fion, Quentin, and Sandra on their return to the UK.

"Probably best to come clean and get the whole messy business out of the way," Fion had advised when the quartet rematerialized in Quentin's garden after the showdown in Wollongong was over.

"But the cops'll lock me up," Andy countered, only recently having been introduced to the elf and his powers.

"Not unless Orlando presses charges."

"Which he surely will."

"I don't think so," said Fion, whose ElfVision monitor was showing images of a bemused Hank still wandering around with Sabrina in Wollongong with—so Fion's Elf Mind Reading programme (EMRP) was suggesting—no intention of returning to the UK come hell or high water. Which was precisely the scenario Fion had asked Art Scrivenger and Bazza Johnson to help negotiate by offering the pair Andy's old room before he, Quentin, Sandra and Andy took their leave. Little did he know, because he didn't check, that Art and Bazza too would soon be far away conducting lucrative bot business on another continent, but that's another story.

"How can you be *sure* of that?" said Andy, squeezing Sandra's hand and relaxing marginally when the counter-squeezing came.

It was Quentin who explained, concluding with, "Elves have these powers. Trust me, I know."

"But I *did* shoot the Orlando bastard in the goolies," Andy admitted.

"In the worthy course of true love," said Fion. "And the 'bastard,' as you call him, isn't dead or anything serious, so..."

"Listen to the elf," said Sandra, rubbing Andy's back. "He's on your side, trust me."

And Andy did, which was how it came to pass that, with Sandra's help, he offered himself up to DI Derek Wilde for good or ill which, as noted, caused Wilde to become both astonished and furious.

"After all the trouble me and the New York coppers went through trying to *find* you," he spluttered. "Last we heard you'd been banged up in some place called Willybong, Australia for pissing up a tree and fisting a passerby. And now the testicle shooter just walks into my office?"

"He's just trying to be helpful," Sandra explained.

"And who exactly are *you*?" Wilde wanted to know.

"My girlfriend, Doctor Sandra Normington," said Andy. "She flew out to rescue me."

"Flew out all the way to Oz when all the airports were in lockdown because of the bad bug, Miss Normington?" said Wilde, frowning and waggling a suspicious finger under his nose.

"*Doctor* Normington," Andy corrected, buying time because there was no way he could reveal the true answer.

So tapping at her nose and winking it was Sandra who replied to Wilde's question. "Friends in the private jet business, Mister Wilde. Where there's a will, there's always a way."

"Detective *Inspector* Wilde!"

"Detective Inspector Wilde. But if you'd prefer not to hear our story and us to leave right now, we'd be very happy to do so, your choice. On the other hand, if you are prepared to suspend your disbelief and listen to the true story behind the person I believe to have come to be known as the genitalia shooter, then I would advise you to quit it with your footling objections."

Andy smiled. Despite all the torments, how right he had been to trust in his love for this woman from Birkenhead. Secretly, Sandra was quite pleased with her performance, too. It seemed things were returning to normal or possibly, as the pandemic obsessed media were terming it "the *new* normal."

Wilde weighed his options, which didn't take him long. After all, how would it look to Jeannie Quinn in NYC if he were to tell her he'd had the genitalia shooter in his office and not got the full story? Not good at *all,* reckoned Wilde who, after his return from the sexy weekend in NYC, was very keen to maintain far more than a working relationship with Jeannie.

"All right then, o*kay,*" he grumbled.

"Good choice," said the emboldened Sandra, who went on the tell the tale of how she had come to admire Doc Andy Crane's bravery in, first of all, enabling her escape drugged from the rampant sex fiend Orlando, even to the point of needing hospitalization as a result of his intervention and *then*, even more nobly, like some knight errant, returning to mete out fully deserved punishment. Which was why she'd flown out to Wollongong to find him and repay his courage by offering him her love. There were tears in her eyes by the time she finished and rested her head on Andy's shoulder while he drew her in close.

Derek Wilde was moved by this performance, but he was still a detective inspector after all. "Just a couple more questions, if I may."

Sandra sat up straight again. "Fire away."

"How did you know where he *was*? It was only because we saw his name on the Wallybang cops' computer that *we* found out. You couldn't have seen that, and we told no one."

"Perhaps I could answer that?" said Andy, alerting Sandra to a piece of the puzzle even she hadn't known by squeezing her hand. "Obviously, I wasn't going to hang around in London with the cops on my tail for GBH firearm offences. Back then I had no idea Sandra might have had any feelings for me, so I headed off to Wollongong on a regular flight because the lockdown hadn't happened yet."

Despite this being the response to an entirely different question, Derek Wilde, nonetheless, wanted to know why Wallybang of all places. Which Sandra was also keen to find out.

"I thought my father was there, and he would help me."

"And did he?"

"No, he'd moved to somewhere on the other side of Australia."

Sandra stared at Andy. Either he was an even better liar than she or this was the truth.

"Okay, fair enough," said Derek Wilde. "So you just stuck around pissing up trees and punching passers-by?"

"No need for sarcasm, Detective Inspector," said Sandra. "As I said, Andy's just trying to be helpful."

"Okay, but that still doesn't answer my original question."

"Which was?" said Sandra.

"How you knew he was there."

"I called her, that's how," said Andy, which was true, so long as a person believed in psychic phenomena as opposed to telephones. Every night in his sleep Andy had called out for Sandra.

"Ah hah," said Derek, jotting a note. "And yet you didn't feel the need to pass on this knowledge to anybody, Doctor Normington?"

"It only happened a few days ago and was a secret between the two of us," said Sandra. "But now, here we are in your office ready and willing to find a solution to the genitalia shooter reputation poor Andy now has. So *if* we could move on?"

"Fair enough," Wilde repeated. "But that is certain to be a problem once Mister Orlando discovers his assailant is back in town. He's sure to press charges, and I can't just ignore them, can I? Justice is justice, that's my job."

"Mister Orlando won't be pressing *any* charges, Detective Inspector," said Andy.

"How can you know that?"

"Because we have it from a reliable source he is still in Wollongong nursing a *very* sore head," said Sandra. "And he won't be coming back to press a shirt, let alone charges."

Wilde tapped at his forehead. "He was there, *too*?"

"With two American goons. Looking to get his revenge by killing me," said Andy. "I can't image any court in the land would listen to evidence from *that* kind of person."

A point Wilde had no choice but to concede. "So why are you here? What do you want from me?"

Sandra smiled. "How would best wishes for our future be, mine and Andy's?"

Cornered and out of his depth, Wilde returned the smile. "Just promise me one thing, Doctor Crane."

"Name it," said Andy.

"You won't go around shooting anybody *else* in the goolies now you've got away with it this time."

"I promise. Unless of course anybody else tries to interfere with my Sandra, in which case, all bets are off."

Wilde chuckled. "Okay. And may I add how fortunate a young man you are to have found a woman with such belief in you. Long may she continue so to do. Now, if you would excuse me, there are calls I need to make."

And so it was that, arm in arm, Andy and Sandra left Lavender Hill cop shop with the slate wiped clean and no more fears of retribution. Outside on the street, they danced a little jig.

Meanwhile, back in his office, Derek Wilde was on a secure line to Jeannie Quinn to tell her the story and was delighted with her response.

"You done good, Derek, I know it in my bones," she said. "Once this godforsaken bug has gotten its ass kicked for good, and JFK opens up again, I'm heading out to London to shake you by the hand. And mebbe not *only* the hand."

DI Wilde liked the sound of that.

~ * ~

Also liking the sound of a suggestive female voice was Doc Quentin Trimble when Lucy Lomax called to propose a socially distanced meet-up.

"Sure, yes, why not, that would be great," said Quentin, already in a warm place emotionally having just got off the phone from Doc Antoinette who had told him all about the vastly improved health of Doc Frederick *and* of their relationship after their first few days of Covid-19 hospital volunteering.

Quite why Lucy Lomax was suddenly so keen to see him, Quentin had no idea, but then he had no idea either of the way in her locked down flat the previous evening Sandra Normington had praised him to the skies when spilling to Lucy the whole story of the showdown in Wollongong, specifically the heroic part in it played by Quentin.

"Sooo *cool* he was in the face of that grisly bastard Orlando," she told a still gobsmacked Lucy. "Even taunted him a bit before doing his metamorphic number then whacking him over the bonce with his frying pan. And all *this* from a bloke who, only a few short months ago, Andy and I were reckoning to be weirdo hypochondriac with underlying mental health problems. I hope you're impressed."

And on the surface, Lucy was. "A man of many talents, I see. And it was this Fion who helped him through the 'underlying problems' and all the way to victory in Woll-on-Bong?"

"*Gong*. And yes, that was Fion all right, whom I owe almost as big a debt of gratitude as I do Quentin. No help from those two, and I would never have found my Andy."

Lucy cocked her head, smirked, and raised a pull-the-other-leg eyebrow. "And you all travelled out there by fairy teleportation, you say?"

"Yes. I know, I *know*, it sounds crazy, but it happened."

"Not a dream then?"

"Luce, how *else* could we have got there? No flights at the moment, airports shut, quarantine on arrival even if you *can* fly."

"True enough. And you were there and back before I'd even noticed?"

"It all happened in fairy time, Luce, in a different dimension. You'll see when you meet Fion, which I hope will be soon."

Lucy took a deep breath and sighed. "Okay, okay, so I need to suspend my disbelief."

"Yes, you do," said Sandra, taking her oldest friend's hand.

"Okay, oo*kay*. So back to Quentin and his heroism. What was his interest in all this? It can't just have been to rescue your love life."

"I've never had the full story but, from what I know from Fion, the underlying mental health problem was the distorted demands of a dominant father which needed to be finally put to bed by Quentin proving to himself his own worth. That's how Fion put it, anyway."

Lucy raised the other eyebrow. "Fion, Fion, *Fion*. Now, he's also the otherworldly psychiatrist."

"You *still* think I'm making all this up?"

Lucy shrugged. "I dunno, it all sounds sooo weird...like some freaked out sci-fi romance novel."

"Well, try this for size."

Which was when Sandra reminded Lucy of the tea party in Quentin's garden where, as he had later admitted, Fion had been in the shed all along and straightway intuited Lucy's feelings for Quentin.

"Deny it," Sandra challenged. "We spoke about it on the bus going home, but you were having none of it, remember? Except to say there was something 'otherworldly' about Quentin."

Lucy swallowed hard and stared off. There *was* no denying it. "You're right. That's where it all started. God knows we talked about it often enough afterwards. And this Fion was also responsible for what I was feeling?"

Sandra shrugged. "Like I said, he knew from the start you were in love with Quentin. So if you believe in *your* feelings, you will also have to believe in those of Fion the fairy because they match. Q.E.D. I think. Anyway, *any*way enough of this, why not give the man in question a call? I'm sure he'd love to hear from you."

"Fion?"

"No, *Quentin*."

And, as noted, Quentin was happy indeed to hear Lucy's voice and jumped at the suggested meet-up. It was the very next day the couple met up at the Peace Pagoda in Battersea Park where they struggled for six minutes to maintain the two metres of social distancing before throwing off their blue facemasks, waving two fingers at the daily changing "rules" made by the petulant narcissist in Downing Street, and falling into each other's arms.

It was a case of "Screw you, Covid-nineteen, infect us if you dare." And what could be more romantic than that?

Twenty-eight

Having already met Fion and been apprised of his powers, Docs Antoinette and Frederick accepted Quentin's account of the showdown in Wollongong with less suspicion than Lucy Lomax when told the tale, but remained, nonetheless, astonished at not only its derring-do but its conception.

"By God, you couldn't *make* it up, son," said a masked Doc Frederick as he and an also masked Doc Antoinette sat two metres apart on separate easy chairs in their lounge while Quentin lolled a further two metres away on a sofa. Working as hard as they still did at the St Bede's coronavirus coalface with only the minimal personal protection equipment, his parents had only, with reluctance, allowed Quentin into the house in case they were non-symptomatic carriers and infected him. God only knew they'd caused their son enough trouble in his life without adding his death to the list. To this arrangement Quentin had agreed, despite having reassured his parents Fion had rendered him immune to the disease. Still, what if even so, he too were an unwitting super-spreader? Which was why, once inside the parental home, he obeyed the rules even if such rules were currently being changed daily by what Doc Frederick described as "the Moron of Downing Street" and his brown-nosing cronies, more interested in their careers than truth, adding it was high time Fion joined the Cabinet and saved the nation with his immunity powers.

"I'm sure he'd love to, Dad," said Quentin. "But it would be a lot to ask of just one elf, especially one who believes the moron you speak of to be a glory-seeking dork who would take all the credit for himself, anyway."

Doc Frederick nodded and grinned. "I see where he's coming from. And as far as your story is concerned, I'll trust you with no further questions asked. After all, the man you're speaking to not so long ago also believed him*self* to be fairy."

Quentin laughed. This was a first in his life, a whole new father talking. One who accepted his child as a full-fledged human in whose integrity he was prepared to have faith, however apparently preposterous the story. Plus—and this was a *big* plus for Quentin— this was the first time he had ever heard his father taking the mickey out of himself.

Doc Antoinette laughed, too, an ear-to-ear job. How magical it was finally to see the possibility of a resolution between the two men in her life whose "psychological distancing" over the years had distanced *her* almost enough to leave home.

"And *you* were the one to bash the bad guy over the head with a frying pan?" she asked Quentin, who shrugged and nodded. "It was nothing. Just following the plan we'd worked out with Fion. You should have seen the stare he gave those boggarts, though, the one that petrified them. Nothing I got taught in med school comes close."

"And all this in the name of love," Doc Antoinette continued. "How *very* romantic. Let us hope Sandra and Andy appreciate the efforts put in on their behalf."

Quentin smiled. "By all reports, they're on cloud nine, they've cleared matters with the coppers so there shouldn't be any problems there."

"Even over the business of Crane shooting the American rotter in the unmentionables?" said Doc Frederick.

"Even that, at least as I understand it, Dad. Accommodations were reached, and he walked free."

"Glad to hear it. God knows I might have done the same myself if I'd found your mother prey to such a predator."

Doc Antoinette giggled, widened her eyes, rolled them back and forth, sneaked across the two-metre social distance to Doc Frederick, sat on his knee, raised her mask, planted a smackeroo on his forehead, and said, "My hero."

Never *ever* having seen his parents behave this way—or even touch each other—Quentin was understandably gobsmacked but soon got over it. After all, there was enough misery in the world at the moment, so why not greet a little pleasure with what it deserved? Which was why he broke the two-metre rule, stood behind them and ruffled their hair, although in Doc Frederick's case it was more a matter of scalp than hair.

That was when Doc Antoinette turned to face her son and said, "And a little birdie tells me that as a result of your heroism during Wollyging showdown there's a secret you haven't felt able to share with us yet. Does the name Lucy mean anything to you?"

The "little birdie" was Fion, who'd popped into a couple of Antoinette's less cheerful dreams to add a soupçon of hope for times to come.

Quentin smiled and, without the least self-consciousness, admitted to Lucy Lomax being the love of his life with whom he was preparing to share self-isolation at his Battersea flat for as long as it took for the world to go back to normal.

"Which could be a *very* long time," he concluded. "But that's okay with Lucy and me. The longer the better, even while we do a little gardening and live the simple life."

"And good luck to you, son," said Doc Frederick. "May we perhaps now hear a little of young Lucy? One *hopes* she's young for the sake of childbearing and so on. Wouldn't we just *love* to be grandparents, Tonie?"

Doc Antoinette cleared a meaningful throat and said, "Of course, Freddie, but perhaps we're getting a little ahead of ourselves?"

Doc Frederick steepled his fingers under his chin and nodded recognition of his *faux pas*. "Dearie me, apologies, son. Foot in mouth as usual."

Unfazed, Quentin said, "No probs, Dad. Everything in the fullness of time though, eh? Just for the record, however, Lucy is around the same age as me, I reckon, although I've never asked her."

Doc Antoinette blew him a kiss. "Good to hear chivalry is still alive and well in the UK. *Never* should a woman be asked her age. And Lucy's from around these parts?"

"No, she's a Scouser."

Doc Frederick frowned. "*Scouser*?"

"Liverpudlian, Dad, a person from the Liverpool area. In her case, Birkenhead across the Mersey. Sandra Normington's from there, too. She and Lucy were best friends at school."

"Gosh," said Doc Frederick, who had spent his entire life in and around London and believed Liverpool to be some sort of fantasy town populated by Beatles, footballers, comedians, fishwives and gangsters, all of whom spoke with an impenetrable accent entirely different from the received pronunciation of English, thereby rendering them incomprehensible.

Knowing this, Quentin laughed and, to stir the pot a little further, added Lucy held a doctorate from Cambridge University in English Literature, a subject she now taught at Liverpool University.

"In Scousish?" Doc Frederick wanted to know, but by now with a glint in his eye.

"No, Dad, in Gaelic."

More laughter as Doc Frederick took this one on the chin, too.

It was Doc Antoinette who wanted to know when they might have the privilege of meeting Doc Lucy even if at a distance of two metres, to which Quentin replied whenever they wished, before coming up with the idea of a garden party at his place.

"Would probably be breaking some rule or another, but who cares? Either of you ever seen an undercover government agent skulking about looking for antisocially distanced people?"

"No," said Doc Frederick, "But if you'd witnessed what your mum and I have at St Bede's you'd wish you had."

Quentin nodded. "True enough. And the party?"

"Would be a delight," said Doc Antoinette. "Would there be other guests apart from us?"

Thinking off the top of his head while counting them on his fingers, Quentin said, "Well, Lucy, naturally. Then I'm sure you'd like to meet Sandra and Andy."

"Indeed we would, given without them there would have been no excuse for your shebang in Wollybung," said Doc Frederick.

"Okay then, that's you two, Lucy and me, and Sandra and Andy. Anybody *you* would like to invite? From St Bede's, for example?"

Docs Frederick and Antoinette exchanged masked glances and then nodded simultaneously.

"Two good friends of ours, one of whom you will know, and the other you might have heard of under somewhat problematic circumstances," said Doc Frederick.

"Titillate me, why don't you?" said Quentin.

Which was how Miriam Proudfoot and Prof Finian O'Toole were added to the guest list with no objection at all from Quentin.

"Without the gardening leave," he said, "I wouldn't be the person I am today, which I hope you will agree is a marginally better person than I once was."

Wincing at this oblique reference to the past and their part in it, but quickly setting that aside, Docs Frederick and Antoinette heartily agreed and so it was that Miriam and Finian were duly invited. As obviously were Fion and any of his pals from over the fence in the grassy glade he reckoned might add pleasure to the occasion.

It was with this fun plan in place that Quentin took his leave and, as an afterthought on his way back home, wondered if Sandra's parents might also like to sneak down from Birkenhead for the occasion, but on his return, Lucy put the kibosh on that idea.

"They wouldn't come for two reasons. For one thing, they'd be terrified of breaking the lockdown and the other they'd be even more terrified of The Smoke, where they'd almost certainly catch the Covid."

"The smoke?"

"It's what London's called up there. Reckoned to be just a tad less attractive than hell."

"Blimey," said Quentin, "Hope *you* don't think the same way."

Lucy winked and tweaked Quentin's left cheek. "I used to, love. But something happened to change all that. In any case, when the bastard bug's been vanquished, Sandie, Andy, you and I could take a trip up there, couldn't we? It would be good for you to meet *my* folks, too."

"Yeah, great idea. You'd have to give me a few language lessons first, though."

"No problemo. Just be careful not to call anybody a knobhead, and you'll be fine."

"*Knob*head?"

"We'll come to that in lesson one. Also, don't say you support any football team other than Liverpool or Everton."

"I don't support any football teams at all. Never have."

"Well, that'll be all right then. *Now* then, putting the party aside, tell me how your parents were."

The elephant in the room during this invitee conversation, from Lucy's point of view at least, was of course Pete Normington, but she was guessing Quentin didn't even know he existed, and she was right. Nonetheless, later that night on the phone to Sandra she checked on her brother's whereabouts and was relieved to find he'd had a call from Betsy Begay saying she missed him and had somehow managed to smuggle himself onto one of the few Heathrow flights still allowed into JFK.

~ * ~

The party, held in Quentin's garden on an auspiciously sunny afternoon ten days later, was afterwards deemed by attendees to have been the best thing to have happened to them in many a long year, particularly *this* one plagued as it had been so far by not only the coronavirus itself, but also the mind-and-culture-bending lockdown known as the "new normal." It was with these fears at the forefront that particularly the more elderly guests turned up swathed in blue masks and prepared for some top notch social distancing while occasionally raising their masks to be introduced, smile at each other and exchange platitudes.

Which was pretty much what went on until the whole contingent had arrived and been seated two metres apart in a circle with a six metre diameter. Once that had been achieved, Fion, dressed in traditional fairy clothes, sprang into the centre, welcomed everybody and announced he would immediately be passing around the circumference with glasses of a special pink tincture that would ensure immunity from both the bad bug *and* the new normal for at least the following twenty-four hours.

From the Docs Trimble, their son Quentin, Sandra Normington, Andy Crane and Lucy Lomax, all of whom were one way or the other wise to Fion's powers, there was no objection to this plan. In fact, it was greeted with clapping and mutters of relief. But even after Quentin explained such powers to Miriam Proudfoot and Finian O'Toole, they remained suspicious.

"Jungle juice from a chappie dressed up as a fairy?" said Miriam, while even the normally leprechaun-friendly Finian O'Toole wondered if three pints of Guinness might not be the better option.

"He's not dressed *up* as a fairy, he *is* a fairy," Quentin assured them. "Ask my parents if you don't believe me."

So, across the six-metre diameter of social distance, that's what Miriam and Finian did. Not an easy conversation without loudhailers but finally they were reassured, and Fion was given the go-ahead to distribute his "jungle juice" which, as advertised, was well capable of immunity for even longer then twenty-four hours but also contained just a smidgeon or two of marijuana to add a little zing to the party.

And zing it certainly did add, particularly once Fion's fairy folk band had been invited to join the proceedings. You may remember the group playing nameless instruments unknown to human musicians, including one consisting of cymbals attached to the knees which were clapped together whenever the wearer felt like it. Unsurprisingly, the initial response to this cacophony was disapproval laced with whispered references to more polished tunesmiths ranging from Bach

(Doc Frederick) to The Beatles (Sandra Normington) but it was Finian O'Toole who, doubtless inspired by echoes of the west coast of Ireland, sprang to his feet and took to prancing about wildly, soon to be joined in the bum-slapping and whooping by Fion, Bertie, and sundry other elves.

Well, you know how it is with wallflowers at dances, how they huddle together hoping nobody asks *them* to dance, and such was the case with those at Quentin's party who watched on in astonishment as Finian leapt about like a man half his age.

"Good God," whispered Doc Frederick, for example.

"Bloody hell," echoed Andy Crane.

But watching Finian entranced, it was Miriam Proudfoot who, driven by hidden ballerina yearnings buried deep in her subconscious, suddenly sprang to her feet, lifted her skirts and matched Finian prance for prance and bum slap for bum slap. Finian kissed her between prances, and she kissed him back.

Fion was delighted and, adopting the emcee role, opened his arms in invitation to those still crouching on their fold-up picnic chairs—Docs Frederick and Antoinette, Quentin Trimble, Sandra Normington, Andy Crane, and Lucy Lomax.

"Come join the fun, ever...y...one," he hollered, much in the manner of Joel Grey in *Cabaret*.

And you know what, like people shucking off their normal personas in a moment of blessed release, they did. For Sandra and Lucy, it wasn't too hard, given the legendary video reminders of The Cavern Club they had both seen, and they were soon able to teach Andy and Quentin a few moves, too. Which left Docs Frederick and Antoinette as spectators.

That didn't last long, though. It was Doc Antoinette who first felt the pulse running faster through her legs.

"C'*mon*, Freddie, let's give it a go," she said, grabbing her husband by an initially unwilling arm.

And you would be ast*onished*—Doc Antoinette certainly was— at the *plies* and *arabesques* her husband produced once out on the dance floor. Maybe that's what a smidgeon of marijuana can do for even the most inveterate of conservative souls.

Anyway, *any*way, let's leave our story there, shall we? Suffice it to say that, as dance partners changed and re-changed, everybody had a very good time before falling exhausted onto the grass Quentin and Fion had not so long ago mowed to within an inch of its life. Since then, the grass had grown, but then so too had the people falling onto it.

Epilogue and Final Score Sheet

A) Legal outcomes.

Andy Crane was never accused in any court of law with the genitalia peppering of Hank Orlando because as predicted by Fion, the latter, humbled by his comprehensive defeat at the showdown in Wollongong, declined to press charges. Nor was any action taken against Andy for his role in the "Watch out, next time it'll be *you!*" bots, which were eventually rightly attributed to Barry and Arthur Montgomery (Art Scrivenger and Bazza Johnson) who were never charged either, because under their pseudonyms they had disappeared from Wollongong to ply their nefarious trade much more lucratively at a bot factory in St Petersburg.

B) Emotional outcomes.

1) Saved marriages (1): that of Docs Frederick and Antoinette Trimble who, thanks to their combined efforts in combatting Covid-19, renewed their love for each other, and their vows and lived happily ever after. Well not *ever* after. Eventually they would die, of course, but not yet and not from the beastly bug.

2) New marriages (1): that of ex-Doc Professor Finian O'Toole and Doc Miriam Proudfoot, who were already soul mates but whose literary and other affinities were only reinforced by the joint efforts

they contributed alongside the Trimble docs to the heroes of the NHS in fighting the fearful pandemic.

3) Continuing marriages (1): that of Henry and Mildred Normington in Birkenhead, who had been married forever and saw no reason to change the situation.

4) Hot tips for future marriages—or enduring relationships or partnerships or whatever (5):

i) Andy Crane and Sandra Normington once they'd spent sundry hours together working back through the bumpy, lumpy, possibly once fantasized history of their passion and had concluded that outcomes from the showdown in Wollongong meant Aphrodite must have been on their side all along.

ii) Quentin Trimble and Lucy Lomax, who in their shared self-isolation were learning a lot about themselves and, clichéd though it may sound, about the "meaning of life," particularly the part serendipity can play in it.

iii) Sergeant Jeannie Quinn and DI Derek Wilde who, despite the continued enforced separation caused by Covid-19 shutting down all forms of human intercourse especially across the Atlantic, had, nonetheless, maintained a regular Skype connection, which even extended to virtual sex. For them there was certainly *some* hope once the lockdown lifted.

iv) Sabrina/Marjory Mackey and Hank Orlando who, incredibly perhaps, given the trials and tribulations of outrageous fortune—or possibly because of them—were *still* together. Just as in the old days in California, Sabrina was helping out at Hank's brand new Robert Redford Jnr pseudo-shrink practice in their adopted new home of Wollongong. Fion and Sandra had offered Sabrina free teleportation to the UK after Hank's humiliation at the showdown, but she'd refused saying she needed to stand by her man.

v) Ronnie Normington and Betsy Begay. A long shot, this one, but there was no doubt in Ronnie's mind once they hooked up again back in America that she was the girl for him. Of what Betsy thought of Ronnie, apart from having missed him while he was away in the UK, there is no record, so it's just a question of fingers crossed for them.

C) Otherworldly creatures:

Grimble and Grumble Boggart remained forever petrified in the Kemblawarra suburb of Wollongong but were at least helpful to the local economy in their new, albeit unconscious, role as a major local tourist attraction drawing attention from paleontologists from across Australia. Never again, obviously enough, would they work for Luca Gambonio. Not that Luca was around to care about that, not after he had been gunned down by a rival mobster on the street outside his NYC apartment.

Which leaves Fion the elf and his pals from the grassy glade who, immune to Covid-19 and all other earthly afflictions, remain available to those of us in need at all times. If you ever come across any of them, Fion in particular, please pass on my heartfelt best wishes.

Meet Paddy Bostock

Paddy Bostock was born in Liverpool and holds a B.A. in Modern Languages and History, a PGDip TESL, and a PhD in English Literature. Down the years he has been a barman, a road worker, a songwriter, an educational researcher, a translator, a book reviewer, a university lecturer and Chair of Department, and a high school mentor. He lives in London with his wife, writer Dani Cavallaro, and likes animals and bicycles.

Other Works From The Pen Of
Paddy Bostock

Mole Smith and the Diamond Studded Pistol - Only one way for PI gofer Mole Smith to win the hand of his beloved: to solve the ancient mystery of the diamond-studded pistol...

Two Down - Worry about your cellphone! Others may have spooky designs on it...

La Joie de Vivre - "Cherchez la femme!"—words Ambler will come to wish he'd never heard...

For the Love of a Woman - Family—you can't live with them; you can't live without them...

Foot Soldiers - When will we ever learn...?

Hand in Glove - Never judge a zebra by its stripes...

Noddy in Wonderland - Will wonders never cease?

Peace on Earth - Peace on earth? Don't bet on it....

The Basque Head Case - Of heads found ... and lost!...

The Bore - Funny thing, boredom...

The Hanging - Nothing is set in stone.

Chosen - It's only rock 'n' roll but...

What Ifs - "We are such stuff as dreams are made on..."

Fubars - Serendipity works in mysterious ways...

My Kind of Guy - Even when you can't move mountains, you might still create a few shock ripples...

Letter to Our Readers

Enjoy this book?

You can make a difference

As an independent publisher, Wings ePress, Inc. does not have the financial clout of the large New York Publishers. We can't afford large magazine spreads or subway posters to tell people about our quality books.

But, we do have something much more effective and powerful than ads. We have a large base of loyal readers.

Honest Reviews help bring the attention of new readers to our books.

If you enjoyed this book, we would appreciate it if you would spend a few minutes posting a review on the site where you purchased this book or on the Wings ePress, Inc. webpages at: https://wingsepress. com/

Visit Our Website

For The Full Inventory
Of Quality Books:

Wings ePress.Inc
https://wingsepress.com/

Quality trade paperbacks and downloads
in multiple formats,
in genres ranging from light romantic comedy
to general fiction and horror.
Wings has something for every reader's taste.
Visit the website, then bookmark it.
We add new titles each month!

Wings ePress Inc.
3000 N. Rock Road
Newton, KS 67114